ELAINE LICKED HER LIPS

When she spoke, her voice was a high, thin thread of sound. "You make me dizzy."

Ruy caught his breath. "My God, I never expected—" His mouth closed over hers.

As their lips moved together a log in the fireplace fell, popping and hissing. Elaine's lashes flew up. Just for a second flaring light bathed the embracing couple, tingeing them with the soft, gilded radiance of youth. Then the brightness died. Enveloping shadows robbed Ruy's hair of its silver gleam, restoring the darkness the years had stolen. Elaine's eyes widened. She knew. Maybe she'd always known.

With both hands she shoved herself away from him. She huddled, stricken, at the far end of the couch, one hand clamped over her mouth to still her trembling. She thought she might be sick. "Antonio!" she choked out.

ABOUT THE AUTHOR

Sacramento-based writer Lynda Ward is a
mainstay of Harlequin's Superromance line. A
painstaking artist, Lynda polishes and rewrites her
books until she's satisfied. This careful attention,
along with an uncanny insight into human
behavior and a love of learning about new
cultures, guarantees great reading. Now,
Superromance is proud to present *Race the Sun*,
the first book in a trilogy about the Welles family.
Lynda has produced one other series of three in
her life: she is the devoted mother of three boys!

Books by Lynda Ward

HARLEQUIN SUPERROMANCE

HARLEQUIN TEMPTATION

Don't miss any of our special offers. Write to us at the
following address for information on our newest releases.

Harlequin Reader Service
901 Fuhrmann Blvd., P.O. Box 1397, Buffalo, NY 14240
Canadian address: P.O. Box 603,
Fort Erie, Ont. L2A 5X3

Lynda Ward

RACE THE SUN

Harlequin Books

TORONTO • NEW YORK • LONDON
AMSTERDAM • PARIS • SYDNEY • HAMBURG
STOCKHOLM • ATHENS • TOKYO • MILAN

Published July 1988

First printing May 1988

ISBN 0-373-70317-1

This is for Jennifer Campbell,
Lisa Boyes, Joan Clark and
Beverley Katz Rosenbaum,
my super Super editors.

CHAPTER ONE

"SORRY, LADY, it looks like this is going to take all night!"

"It's not your fault," Elaine said mildly to the cabdriver as she stared through the spattered windshield at the hotel's entrance canopy that writhed beneath the wet, stabbing wind. Traffic was backed up in the circular driveway while uniformed valets with umbrellas shuttled between the curb and the etched glass doors at the top of the hotel steps, trying without success to protect arriving guests from the rain. It would be several minutes before Elaine's taxi, fifth in the queue of idling vehicles, reached the unloading zone. Maybe she was being given a reprieve.

At the head of the line a silver-haired man in an overcoat emerged from a limousine and, waving aside offers of assistance, strode purposefully up the steps, briefcase in hand. After the sleek black automobile pulled away, a sedan took its place and a family with mounds of luggage emerged. The taxi driver swore as he counted the cars still ahead of his cab. In the back seat, Elaine sighed with relief.

It wasn't too late to change her mind, she reminded herself as the taxi inched forward. Nobody had spotted her yet. If she asked the driver to pull his vehicle out of line, he'd take her anywhere she requested, and she could telephone her mother and plead an emergency. She wa-

vered. The taxi pulled into position at the foot of the
steps, and the doorman's gloved fingers closed around
the outside handle. Another car honked in the driveway
behind them. It was too late.

The driver leaned over the back of the front seat.
"We're here, finally. The Benton. Didn't you say you
were in a hurry?"

Elaine shook herself impatiently. All her life she'd attended functions at the hotel—her sister Kate's wedding
reception, for one. The place was a bit gaudy and definitely overpriced, but nothing to regard with foreboding. Quickly she counted out the fare and a generous tip.
"Yes, I am in a hurry. Thank you."

The doorman, who had an umbrella in one hand,
opened the passenger door with the other, and a blast of
clammy air invaded the confines of the taxi, raising goose
bumps on Elaine's sleek legs. As she stood on the curb,
watching the cab pull away, she shivered, and hugged her
fox jacket closer about her shoulders. She should have
worn a long coat, she realized.

"A bit nippy for September, isn't it, Dr. Welles?" the
doorman noted genially as he escorted her to the entrance.

Elaine wondered how he knew who she was. She was
the one member of her family rarely featured in the me-
dia. "It does look as if Denver's in for a rough winter,"
she agreed, feeling her hair blow. "Maybe we should all
move to California."

"That's where my son and his family are now. You remember my son?" When he told her the name, Elaine
recalled the boy, a teenager whose equally immature wife
had been one of her welfare patients; the young couple's
already complicated lives had been made more so by the

girl's difficult pregnancy. For a while Elaine had been afraid she might lose both mother and child.

"Of course I remember your son. He and his wife had a beautiful little girl about two years ago. I trust they're all doing well?"

"Yes, ma'am. The baby's walking and talking up a storm now. My boy joined the Navy and they moved to San Diego. He got his high school diploma in the service, and when he gets out he'll be a qualified mechanic."

"I'm delighted to hear it," Elaine said sincerely. "The next time you talk to them, please tell them all I'm very happy things have worked out so well."

"I'll do that, ma'am. I know they always thought a lot of you—"

The etched glass doors slid shut behind her, choking off the wind, and Elaine was in the sumptuous lobby of the Benton Hotel. After the cold outside, the heated air seemed stuffy, the old-fashioned scent of lemon verbena as overstated as the fussy Victorian luxe with which the foyer had been decorated. Ornately carved mahogany love seats with red plush upholstery and tatted lace antimacassars were grouped on rich Oriental rugs, and light emanating from the marble fireplace sparkled on the prisms of blown-glass lamps. Elaine recalled that Kate's gown and those of her attendants had been patterned after engravings from *Godey's Lady's Book*, so that in the wedding photographs the bridal party would blend with the decor.

Although the hostelry was genuinely old, Elaine knew its current splendor was the product of a twentieth-century expansion and revitalization. In the late 1800s when her great-grandparents had first arrived in Denver on a pair of mules, they had roomed in Mrs. Benton's boardinghouse and their lone window had looked out over the chicken coop. While Grampa Joseph had trudged off to the goldfields to work his claim, his pregnant wife, Maggie, had helped earn her keep by sitting up nights beside that window, a shotgun loaded with rock salt in her lap as she listened for varmints—two- as well as four-legged ones—that might be invading the henhouse.

Surveying her surroundings with cool blue eyes, Elaine was conscious of the passing years. The room where Maggie Burton Welles, the matriarch of the clan, had kept her vigil was gone, its former location now falling somewhere in the middle of a four-star French restaurant. Kate and Jennie, the youngest of the three sisters, had pooled their allowances to treat Elaine to lunch there the day she received notice she'd been accepted into medical school.

She touched the gold bangle on her wrist, a replica of an engraved circlet hammered from the first nugget dug out of the Copa de Oro mine. "I cried for two days after Joe gave it to me," Maggie had reminisced when she'd slipped the original around the twelve-year-old Elaine's skinny arm. "I'd never had any real jewelry before." Her great-granddaughter thought ironically of the glittering baubles now stored in a safe-deposit box in a midtown bank. Like the Benton Hotel, the Welles family had come a long way in the past century.

As if to reinforce the thought, her gaze flitted to the announcement board in the center of the lobby. *Welcome, Guests of Corminco International. Grand Ballroom.* "International." How long had her father dreamed of appending that adjective onto the name of their family-owned corporation? Now, almost at the end of his career, he had finally succeeded. The celebration tonight would mark the crowning achievement of Burton Welles's life. He could retire happy, and because of the sinecures they held in the company, Elaine and her mother and sisters would be richer than ever. She just wished she could overcome the brooding certainty that something disastrous was about to happen....

"SORRY I'M LATE!" Elaine declared as she stepped inside the cloakroom where her mother was waiting. "I was delayed at the hospital." Slipping off her fox jacket, she handed it to the maid, who hung it alongside the damp overcoat she'd been brushing, which Elaine recognized as the one the gray-haired man had been wearing. Close up she could see that the wool was rich and silky, and water had beaded on the lustrous strands. *Vicuña*, she noted, impressed. She turned away. Through the accordion folds of the sliding wall Elaine could hear the orchestra in the ballroom playing a sedate rendition of "The Girl from Ipanema."

Carolyn Welles said, "We were beginning to be concerned about you. The guest of honor just arrived, but your father and I—and, of course, Kate and Dan and the children—have been here almost an hour. Since this is the first time in years that the entire family has been together in one place, we'd hoped to have some photographs taken before we went into the ballroom. Now it's too late. Other guests are already being seated."

"A lot of things held me up, Mom," Elaine apologized equivocally. "One of my patients had false labor. She's a week overdue, and of course she's getting very impatient, but I really believe she's going to deliver naturally before it becomes necessary to induce her. Still, by the time I was able to convince her to go home and put her feet up for the weekend, I was running late myself.

When I returned to the apartment to change, Jennie had left already. Did she get here all right?''

"Yes."

The determined neutrality in her mother's voice convinced Elaine that, as usual, the youngest of the three Welles daughters had managed to offend their parents. Of course, Jennie had made a career out of offending people. *Over the Top*, the weekly late-night television program she produced in New York, specialized in iconoclastic humor. The biting satire of its comedy sketches had made the show a cult favorite among younger viewers, but Elaine knew her mother found the program bewildering and almost threatening. Burton refused to watch it.

A couple came into the cloakroom to check their coats. They were unfamiliar to Elaine, but Carolyn greeted them with the warmth and aplomb that had made her one of the city's most popular socialites. When she called them by name, Elaine realized the man was a state senator.

While her mother talked to her guests, Elaine stepped over to the long mirror at the end of the cloakroom to comb her hair and check the hem of her slate-blue silk brocade evening suit, which she was certain she'd snagged climbing out of the taxi. The street-length skirt appeared undamaged. Elaine's relief was short-lived when she glanced at the reflection of the people standing behind her. All the other women were wearing long dresses.

She studied her mother with a twinge of envy. Elaine's suit was stylish and perfectly tailored for her petite form, fashioned for her by a local designer who appreciated the demands of Elaine's hectic life-style. But Carolyn's tall, slender body was gowned in black crepe with hand-beaded panels—a Galanos original as classically beautiful and ageless as the woman herself, a dress that probably cost more than many of Elaine's patients earned in a year. She had always admired her mother's taste in clothes, even if she could not share it, lacking both Carolyn's height and her brunette elegance. After thirty-seven years Elaine knew she could never compete with her mother. She wondered why she kept trying.

As soon as the guests left to find their seats in the ballroom, where the orchestra was now playing a samba-flavored standard from the sixties, she fluffed her blond curls away from her face and turned to Carolyn. Steeling herself, she murmured, "So what do you think of my outfit? Will it do for Father's big night?"

Carolyn surveyed her oldest daughter with the critical eye of a connoisseur. "That seamstress friend of yours made the suit?"

Elaine blinked. "Olga's a designer, Mom. She's making quite a name for herself in the regional markets."

Her mother nodded benignly. "So you've indicated before. Please don't think I'm implying the woman isn't talented. That's not what I meant at all. Your ensemble is lovely, dear, very becoming—but I really wish you'd gone shopping in New York with me last month. I could have helped you choose something a little more...special?"

At that subtle lift in her mother's mild voice, Elaine lowered her lashes to mask her hurt. Touching her bracelet for strength, she said steadily, "The suit was created specifically for tonight's banquet. To me that makes it very special. Besides, if I wore a dress like yours, there'd be no place to put my beeper."

Carolyn scowled at the black plastic receiver clipped to her daughter's belt. "You're on call tonight?"

"I always am."

"Elaine, even dedicated physicians deserve an occasional break." Carolyn sighed. "I suppose we'd better join your father before someone summons you back to the hospital. Our guest of honor is eager to meet you."

"Really? Why?"

The blunt question flustered her mother. "What do you mean, why? The man did fly all the way from South America, you know. Surely it's not asking too much of you and your sisters to show him simple courtesy? After all, the three of you are technically stockholders in Corminco even though you've never exercised any of your options—"

"We've always been content to let Father do all the work while we sit back and collect our dividends. Just like you."

Carolyn froze, her Madonnalike tranquility wavering. "I work," she said.

Watching the expression of weary pain that weighted and scored her mother's petal-smooth skin, Elaine felt ashamed. She was so used to regarding Carolyn as the epitome of timeless perfection, with a face and body that never aged or sagged, and sable hair that showed no silver, that for months on end she would forget the woman was sixty years old. Now, under the pressure of her daughter's unwarranted disdain, Carolyn's face displayed every one of those endless years and more. Elaine said remorsefully, "I'm sorry. I was shooting off my mouth. I know how much you do." Of course Carolyn worked. She might not have a job outside the home, but for almost four decades she had acted as her husband's hostess, maintained his social contacts, raised his children and cared for his dying relatives. Being Mrs. Burton Welles was a damned demanding career—and not a very rewarding one, except for the money.

"I'm sorry," Elaine said again, and slowly her mother's poise returned, bringing with it that air of calendar-defying serenity. "Look, Mom, I didn't mean to be rude. It's just that I'm very confused. I still don't understand the purpose of this command performance tonight. I realize this venture means a lot to Father, but why has he suddenly decided he wants Jen, Kate and me to meet his new business partner? You know as well as I do that up till now he's always actively discouraged us from taking any interest in the company. This sudden turnaround bothers me. Why is it so necessary all of a sudden for us to make a good impression on this Senhor Areias? Shouldn't it be the other way around? I was under the impression the man had approached Father, not vice versa."

"I don't know what's going on," Carolyn admitted frankly. "Burton rarely discusses Corminco with me, either. But he did mention that Brazilians seem to take a very personal, rather paternalistic interest in the well-being of their employees and business associates. When the man specifically asked if he might be introduced to the family, your father could hardly refuse—"

"Especially not when he stands to make millions off this deal!"

"Burton assures me the consortium will benefit all of us." For a moment the women in the cloakroom were silent, and through the wall they could hear the orchestra embarking on a tune that Elaine connected vaguely with an old movie about flying down to Rio. "Oh, dear," Carolyn murmured in dismay, "I'm going to have to speak to the conductor. When he told me his group could play Brazilian music, I should have asked him to be more specific about his repertoire. That one predates Carmen Miranda." They turned to leave the cloakroom. At the door Carolyn hesitated. "Darling," she said, "when you're introduced to our guest, you will be polite to him, won't you?"

Elaine was astonished by the question. "Is the guy some kind of creep?"

"Oh, no! In fact, quite the contrary: he's charming and attractive, and he exudes an Old World gallantry that I find almost intimidating. It's just that, well, Kate's no problem, but Jennie has that bizarre show-business sense of humor, and sometimes even you can be so outspoken—" She broke off helplessly. Gazing down at her oldest daughter, she said, "Elaine, I can't emphasize enough how important this deal is to your father. Just when he'd almost given up hope of ever fulfilling his dream before he retired, this opportunity came along. I don't want anything to spoil it."

Dear God, Elaine thought, listening with wonder and compassion to Carolyn's soft plea. She had few illusions about her parents' relationship: she knew her father had lost interest in his wife when, after Jennie's difficult birth, she had refused to "try again" for a son. How was it possible for a woman to still be in love with a man who had effectively ignored her for thirty years? If such was the kind of devotion and self-sacrifice that marriage demanded, then Elaine was almost grateful her own life had veered in a sharply different direction while she was still a girl.

"Gramma, Aunt Elaine, look—real Brazilian money!" Daniel Brock, Jr., cried, bounding into the hallway to meet the women as they approached the private room where the family was gathering prior to the banquet. The boy, chafing in a miniature dinner jacket, clutched what appeared to be a proof set of coins framed in rosewood. Behind him in the doorway, his twin sister toyed with a heart-shaped locket on a gold chain. "Lissa only got a stupid necklace," Danny dismissed.

The girl had the same honey-colored curls her brother did, but at twelve she was taller and more mature than he, her coltish body aglow with budding femininity. When Danny tried to present his treasure to Carolyn for her inspection, Melissa snorted with a faintly disgusted air. "Honestly, Danny, can't you go five minutes without showing off your present? You know everybody's waiting." Her tone reminded Elaine of the way she used to order around her own sisters at that age.

"I'll look at it later, dear," Carolyn assured her grandson, stroking his hair as she glided past. Elaine and Melissa followed. The girl caught her aunt's wrist and whispered excitedly, "Have you seen Aunt Jennie's dress? It's fantastic!"

As soon as they stepped into the room, Elaine spotted Jennie and understood the reason for Melissa's enthusiasm—and Carolyn's reticence. Jennie was the beauty of the family, the only one of the three daughters to inherit their mother's willowy height and her classic features. Her brunette coloring, combined with Burton's sapphire eyes, made Jennie stunning no matter what she wore, but tonight, instead of dressing formally as everyone else had, she was sheathed in a vividly striped African homespun, a length of fringed, hand-loomed cotton that was wrapped around her lanky body and pinned over her breast into a strapless tube. With her dark hair french-braided into a single long plait and large hoops of hammered gold in each ear, she looked sultry and exotic. Elaine guessed she'd chosen the costume deliberately to annoy their father.

Her impression was confirmed when Melissa informed her in worshipful tones, "Aunt Jennie told me she bought her outfit in Kenya!" Elaine shivered, once again stricken with trepidation. Jennie's well-publicized trip to Africa had been made in the company of the actor she'd been living with, the one who had recently left her to become Hollywood's latest hunk. *People Magazine* had done a two-page spread on their junket, and the mere mention of it caused Burton to turn purple.

"Nice dress," Elaine muttered to her sister, refusing to let her anxiety show. "Didn't I see it in the Banana Republic catalogue?"

Jennie arched a feathery brow and smiled as regally as a Russian grand duchess. Elaine regarded her assessingly. After a rocky start in New York, Jennie had enjoyed a brief flurry as a television actress—a logical progression from those long-lost days when she'd devised elaborate games of make-believe for the three girls. Despite her seven years' seniority, Elaine had never minded Jennie taking the leading role for herself; Kate was the one who had resented being eclipsed by her younger, prettier sister. Jennie's interest in acting had continued through school, but surprisingly, as an adult, her career had soon moved into production rather than performance. Still, when she was in the mood she could emote like Ethel Barrymore. Elaine prayed Jennie wasn't in the mood.

All at once Jennie grinned and hugged Elaine. "Don't worry, big sister," she whispered in her ear, "I promise not to embarrass you too much."

"How generous," Elaine drawled.

Jennie's eyes twinkled. "Of course, if you were Kate..."

Elaine's glance shot to the far side of the room, where Kate stood sandwiched between Burton and her husband. The group chatted with a third man hidden from Elaine's view by Dan's broad shoulders. Kate's light brown hair, less golden than her children's, was styled in a classic twist, and like Carolyn, she was wearing something long and chic and black—a mistake, in Elaine's opinion. Elaine knew that, at thirty-one, her sister still hoped to achieve the same elegant simplicity that distinguished their mother, and her husband encouraged her, sometimes to the point of selecting her wardrobe—conveniently ignoring the fact that Kate was only five foot two, an inch shorter than Elaine. Without Carolyn's statuesque grace to give importance to the drab color, black tended to make Kate disappear. Standing among the men in their stygian dinner suits, she almost did not exist.

Sometimes Elaine wondered cynically if Dan didn't prefer Kate to be invisible.

Carolyn tapped her husband on the shoulder and announced, "Dear, Elaine has arrived. I believe we're all here now."

Burton frowned at his firstborn. "It's about time. There are five hundred people in the next room, you know. We can't hold things up forever."

"I didn't expect you to." Crossing the room to her father, Elaine rose on tiptoe to press a ceremonial kiss on his worn cheek. Burton Welles was sixty-three years old, and he looked every day of it. Photographs of Burton as a youth showed an attractive young man of medium height, slender and athletic, with dark blue eyes and unruly blond curls ruthlessly slicked down with hair tonic. But the demanding years behind a desk had exacted their toll. The strapping body had grown thick and slack, the blond hair thin and grizzled. The penetrating eyes could still light up his seamed face when he smiled—but he rarely smiled.

Burton had had sole charge of Corminco since the days when it was still the Copa de Oro Mining Company. His older brother, Joseph III, had inherited the firm from their father—Maggie's son—a quiet, conservative man who had lived in his colorful mother's shadow his whole life. Never as interested in the business as his younger brother was, Joe had left Burton to manage the company while he marched off to the Korean war. He died at the Yalu River. Flags were still flying at half-staff outside company headquarters when Burton announced he was changing the firm's name.

In the years since, he'd taken a small but profitable family business and singlehandedly multiplied its worth many times over, diversifying into construction and development and now the international gem trade. Elaine was proud of her father's accomplishments and she frankly enjoyed the money she earned as a stockholder in the private corporation—but she often wondered what life would have been like for the Welleses if Burton had been a little less obsessed with his work, and a little more concerned about his wife and children.

"I came as soon as I could, Father," she apologized when Burton asked why she was late. "You know I can't just walk out on my patients."

He grimaced grudgingly. "I suppose not. At least you're here now. There's someone I want to introduce you to." He turned, and behind him, Dan Brock, Kate's husband, the former college football hero and now executive vice president of Corminco, stepped aside, giving Elaine her first clear view of the third man in the room.

She recognized the silver hair at once. Her father's guest was the man she'd seen stepping from the limousine. *Suave,* she thought, absorbing his impact at close range. The word was not an adjective she normally applied to people, and she suspected that, even if she hadn't spotted him leaving that luxurious automobile or wearing that almost decadently extravagant overcoat, she would have known he was a very suave man, polished and urbane, with the tremendous self-assurance that usually indicated excellent taste and the money to indulge it. If there was a Brazilian edition of *Gentleman's Quarterly*, he could have modeled for it. His evening clothes were impeccably understated, the black dinner jacket and white pleated shirt starkly elegant against his olive skin; his shining hair and carefully clipped mustache were flawlessly styled. He had strong features, an aquiline nose and pronounced cheekbones, but there was something more to him than striking good looks and obviously expensive clothes. Elaine read strength in the proud lift of his head and sharp intelligence in those fine eyes. He was two or three inches less than six feet tall, but the dignity with which he carried himself gave him added stature. Suddenly she understood her mother's peculiar remark about their guest's intimidating charm. The man had *presence.*

Burton said, "Elaine, I'd like you to meet my new business partner from São Paulo, Ruy Fonseca Areias. He's the head of Companhia Areias e Oliveira—or A&O, as I have to call it in self-defense. Areias, may I present my oldest daughter, Dr. Elaine Welles."

"Encantado, doutora," Ruy murmured, his gaze locking with hers as his forthright grasp closed firmly around the hand she extended. Close up, his eyes were very dark brown, almost black, with rays of gold radiat-

ing into the irises, giving them light and depth. *"Muito prazer em conhecê-la."*

Elaine shivered. She did not know whether it was his scrutiny that unnerved her, or perhaps the shock of hearing aloud the fluid syllables of the language that had haunted her dreams for over twenty years, but suddenly she wanted to jerk her hand away. His other hand clamped around her fingers, and he moved closer. "H-how nice to meet you at last," Elaine said, trying to swallow the thickness in her throat.

Ruy continued to stare at her, and all at once Elaine realized she had misjudged his age by decades. At first glance she had assumed he was her father's contemporary, but now, assessing his unlined face and vigorous carriage, she discerned that despite the silver sheen of his hair, he was a relatively young man, not much older than she, perhaps in his early forties. For some reason the knowledge disconcerted her.

As Elaine tried to gather her wits, the man continued talking, his deep voice articulating words that sounded peculiarly lush and romantic—probably because she could not understand them, she thought. Lamely she said, "I'm sorry, *senhor.* I don't speak Portuguese."

He released her hand, but he did not move back. His brows came together as he switched to English. His command of the language was excellent; his foreignness was revealed only by his formal diction and a tendency to faintly trill his *R*s. "It is I who must beg your pardon, Dr. Welles. I understood that in addition to being a physician, you are also a linguist."

"Not really. I'm fluent in French and Spanish, but I'm afraid I've never known more than half a dozen words of Portuguese." Besides, the liquid, luscious endearments she'd learned—*namorado*, *querido*, *meu coracão*—weren't exactly suitable for casual conversation.

"She's just being modest," Kate said, joining the conversation for the first time. "Elaine's the scholar of the family, the only one of us who ever made it all the way through college, at least so far. She even studied in Europe for a while when she was a teenager."

Burton interrupted abruptly. "Now, girls, this is no time to stand around reminiscing. Our guests won't be served until we take our places." He turned to his associate. "Areias, if you'd care to follow me—"

"A moment, please, Welles. There is something I'd like to do before we join the rest of your party. I was waiting until we were all together." The Brazilian picked up a leather briefcase that had been lying unnoticed at his feet. "I am aware that American businessmen rarely conduct their affairs in this manner, and I hope you will not consider me presumptuous, but in addition to the trinkets I gave your grandchildren, as a goodwill gesture I have also brought gifts for the women of your family."

Burton looked surprised. "That really wasn't necessary."

"I did not do it because it was necessary," Ruy corrected him as he pulled out four velvet-covered jewel boxes, "I did it because it was my pleasure. I thought the ladies might enjoy seeing what all these months of negotiation have ultimately been about." He presented the boxes to the women. "These stones came from the state of Minas Gerais, where A&O's holdings are located. Some are actually products of our Serra Brilhante mines."

"Good Lord," Carolyn gasped when she opened her gift. She stared at the glittering choker of marquise-cut diamonds, her exclamation of stunned appreciation echoed by the family. She turned pleading eyes to her husband. "Oh, Burton, may I?"

"Of course," he muttered gruffly. With uncharacteristic attentiveness he draped the necklace around his wife's slender throat and fumbled with the catch. "Areias, I don't know how to thank you."

"Seeing the diamond worn is thanks enough," the Brazilian countered smoothly, turning his attention to Kate and Jennie, who were opening their own treasures. Jennie's was an exotic gold comb set with tourmalines whose warm pink color would look stunning against her dark hair. Speechless, she stared at the ornament, then suddenly she flung her arms around Ruy and kissed him. He returned the embrace with obvious pleasure before releasing Jennie to accept Kate's stammered thanks for her emerald earrings. She, too, shyly pressed her lips against his cheek. Elaine quickly looked away.

Standing slightly apart from the crush, she felt confused by her adverse reaction to the sight of her sisters kissing Ruy. She did not understand why she should find her sisters' chaste salutes so unsettling. Puzzled, she momentarily forgot about the box in her own hand until Ruy moved silently to her side.

"Is there some problem with your gift, Dr. Welles?"

"Oh, no, of course not!" She cared very little for jewelry, but her disinterest was no excuse for bad manners. "I'm sure it's lovely," she declared dutifully as she snapped open the hinged case. On a nest of white satin rested a delicate platinum bracelet set with faceted stones the pure, pale blue color of the spring sky. Her polite smile warmed. "What a wonderful color. Are these aquamarines?"

Ruy shook his head. "Aquamarines are darker and denser. Those are blue topazes."

"I thought topazes were yellow."

"The yellow ones are the most common, but they come in all colors from wine red to white. I confess the blue stone is my favorite."

"Then I'm especially grateful," Elaine said. *"Obrigada, senhor."*

Ruy's dark gaze caught hers again. Elaine wondered if he expected her to kiss him, too. "There, you do speak Portuguese," he murmured.

His words were neutral, but something about his voice, his intonation, disturbed her, stirred dreamlike echoes of distant intimacy. Elaine tried to sound nonchalant. "No, really, that's about the extent of my vocabulary."

"Hey, Aunt Elaine, let's see your present!" Danny's voice shattered that odd moment of awareness.

"May I help you try it on?" Ruy asked. Elaine held out her arm. The family gathered around to watch. As his fingertips slid caressingly over her skin, Elaine noted with curiosity that despite his manicure, the skin on his palms and the pads of his fingers was tough, scored with the kind of deep, permanent calluses that indicated years of hard physical labor. She wondered what background the Brazilian hoped to efface with that cushy life-style of his.

When he pushed back the sleeve of her suit, baring her wrist, the bangle she always wore worked loose from the brocade and slid down her arm. Ruy's hands stilled. Elaine glanced up at him. His eyes were focused intently on the engraved gold circlet, and she could swear he was holding his breath. Kate chirped, "Oh, you're already wearing a bracelet. Couldn't you do without that old thing for once? It won't go with platinum at all."

"You know I never take off Grandma Maggie's bracelet," Elaine said curtly. To Ruy she suggested, "Just push the bangle out of the way, why don't you? Nobody will ever notice it alongside those beautiful topazes."

Ruy exhaled roughly. "Whatever you say, Dr. Welles." He snapped the glittering links around her wrist and released her hand, stepping back as the family crowded closer.

"Let me see, darling," Carolyn ordered, and obediently Elaine extended her arm. Knowing she ought to show more enthusiasm for what was, in fact, a very extravagant gift, she exclaimed, "Don't you just love the color of these stones, Mom?"

Her mother said fondly, "I always have, dear. That's the exact color of your eyes."

Elaine was discomfited by the compliment. When the children craned their necks to squint into her face, she tried not to titter with embarrassment. "Oh, Mom...."

"But it's true," Carolyn persisted. "The blue couldn't have been a more perfect match if it had been deliberate. Don't you think so, Mr. Areias?"

Ruy's lips curved inscrutably. "A most amazing coincidence, Mrs. Welles."

Burton scowled impatiently. "Yes, we all agree it's quite a fluke, but now, if you girls have thanked our guest, we really must join the rest of the party." He turned to his new business associate. "If you'll follow me...."

The Brazilian nodded. "Of course, with pleasure. Mrs. Welles, may I have the honor?" With grave courtesy he presented his arm to Carolyn. Dan and Kate followed them; Elaine, grateful attention had been diverted from her, fell into step alongside Jennie.

"Wait a second! I have to take the kids to Miss O'Brian," Kate declared suddenly. She motioned to the twins. "Come on, you two. As soon as you've eaten dinner, Miss O'Brian is going to take you to a movie."

Dan looked irritable. "You should have done that earlier."

Kate tensed. "Mother and Father wanted them here," she said steadily. She ushered the children from the room.

Elaine heard Jennie mutter, "Ah, marital bliss...."

Refusing to meet her sister's cynical smile, Elaine turned away. Her gaze drifted to the man standing between her parents. He was staring at her. Elaine lowered her eyes.

Oh, hell, why shouldn't she let herself admire him if she wanted to, she asked herself irritably. He was very nice to look at with his strong, intelligent features and the unusual and eye-catching contrast of lustrous silver hair and dark skin. It was simple aesthetics that attracted her.

Wasn't it?

CHAPTER TWO

THE ORCHESTRA BROKE OFF in midmeasure when the family filed through the double doors into the packed ballroom. A rustle of greeting rose to the crystal chandeliers as five hundred people turned in their seats.

"Good Lord," Jennie hissed out of the corner of her mouth, "they look as though they're about to bow to us." A press photographer aimed his camera in the direction of the long, linen-draped table on the dais, and the sisters twisted their lips into bright, artificial smiles. "How on earth did I let you talk me into coming to this shindig?"

"You did it for Mom," Elaine reminded her in a hoarse whisper. "Besides, what do you have to complain about? I knew this evening was going to be a disaster, but, honestly, Jen, I never felt so self-conscious in my life! I'm used to Father treating us as if we were six years old, but I thought Mom had better taste. 'That's the exact color of your eyes.' My God!"

"Don't worry about it." A waiter pulled out their chairs for them. As Jennie settled gracefully into her seat, she continued quietly, her attention apparently focused on the flower arrangement in front of her, "Even Mom is allowed an occasional gaffe, you know. She meant well. Besides, she's right about the color—the similarity is striking."

Setting her evening bag alongside her napkin, Elaine folded her hands in her lap and sighed. "Maybe so, but she sounded so…" She sighed helplessly and brushed her fingers over the topaz bracelet to stroke the inconspicuous gold bangle behind it. Odd about his hands—rough yet incredibly gentle. "Damn! What that man must think of me." When she heard Jennie's knowing chuckle, she glanced up. "What's so funny?"

Twin dimples formed in Jennie's cheeks as she grinned teasingly. "My circumspect big sister is attracted to the sexy Brazilian. Who'd have thought it?"

"Why do you say that? I may not publicize my affairs in the national press, but that doesn't mean I don't appreciate a handsome man as much as the next woman."

"Don't be bitchy, darling," Jennie countered goodnaturedly, ignoring her sister's growing tension. "I'm well aware that you've always handled your love life a lot more discreetly than I have. Good for you. But you have to remember, up till now I've never seen you involved with anyone but anemic-looking yuppie lawyers and other doctors."

"I am not involved with anyone," Elaine insisted.

Jennie shrugged her bare shoulders. "Perhaps not at the moment. Still, I'm warning you, if you are interested in our magnetic friend from the Southern Hemisphere, don't expect the same kind of vanilla-flavored relationship you've settled for in the past. I know enough about acting to recognize genuine passion when I see it. The guy hasn't been able to take his eyes off you since you walked into that room."

Elaine froze. Jennie was out of her mind, or else she was indulging the wicked sense of humor that had made her television show such a success. Elaine had no intention of falling for her sister's little joke, regardless of how appealing it would be to believe it. She was experienced enough to know that most men found her reasonably attractive, but in thirty-seven years, no one—no one—had wanted her on sight.

"You're not going to catch me this time, Jen," she said brusquely. "I know you too well. Besides, the man's probably got a wife and six or seven little Cariocas waiting for him at home."

"Paulistas, darling," Jennie drawled. "The luscious senhor comes from São Paulo. If he were married, and I understand he's not, his children would be Paulistas. Cariocas are natives of Rio. That soccer player who hosted the show a couple of seasons back explained the difference to me."

Leaning closer to Jennie as the waiter set salads of chicory and arugula in front of them, Elaine said, "All right, I bow to your superior knowledge. You'll have to excuse me, but this is the first time I've ever met a Brazilian. In fact, I don't think I've ever known anyone from South America before."

"Then take my word for it, and I promise you I'm perfectly serious: that's one South American who'd like to get to know you a *whole* lot—"

Just then Burton stood up and the audience fell silent.

"Speech time," Jennie muttered.

"Ladies and gentlemen—" Burton adjusted the microphone on the podium, and a squeal of feedback echoed off the walls of the banquet hall "—fellow employees, friends, don't let me stop you from eating. I just wanted to take a moment to thank you all for coming tonight to help us celebrate this great occasion in the history of Corminco International...."

Bemused by Jennie's comments, Elaine tuned out her father's voice. So her baby sister suspected that the dashing Brazilian with the silver hair was "interested." *That* was a novel reaction. Of the three girls, Jennie had always been the one who had drawn men's eyes—even as a child. Elaine had never particularly cared, since she was so much older than the other two and did not consider herself in competition with them. Still, she had to admit there was something gratifying about attracting attention away from the acknowledged beauty of the family. Maybe the mysterious Senhor Areias just preferred blondes.

"The consortium between Corminco and A&O will ultimately mean more jobs for Coloradans as well as our friends in South America. The Serra Brilhante mines include some of the richest pegmatite veins in the world, with diamonds, topazes, aquamarines and tourmalines, but to date they've never been exploited to their full potential. With the equipment and mining technology we provide..."

Or maybe Jennie was misreading the situation, Elaine conceded, disheartened, as she picked at the dark, bitter greens dressed with vinaigrette. She wished she could see the man and judge for herself whether he appeared to be as entranced with her as her sister seemed to think. Unfortunately, as guest of honor he'd been seated at Burton's right, several places away, and her father was standing between them—not that a clear view would necessarily prove illuminating. The Brazilian's manners were so punctilious that anyone used to less formal etiquette might easily mistake simple politeness for something more personal. It wouldn't be the first time a Welles girl had been wrong about a man's motives.

"The precious stones that will make our joint venture a major source in the world gem market..."

The waiter cleared away the salads and replaced them with the main course: filet mignon in a tantalizing sauce of shallots and red wine. Elaine suddenly realized how hungry she was.

"Please join me in welcoming Ruy Fonseca Areias."

An ovation greeted Ruy as he rose to join Burton at the podium. Elaine clapped dutifully. While he spoke, she would be free to stare at him openly, study that strong profile and draw her own conclusions—figure out why he struck her as dangerous.

"*Boa noite*, ladies and gentlemen. First of all, let me say what a pleasure it is—"

It was probably the Portuguese that bothered her the most, she decided. Even as a girl she'd found something oddly seductive about that uniquely infuriating language with its harsh consonants and maddening diphthongs. She could still recall the feel of warm fingers stroking her face, trying to shape her mouth around the unfamiliar sounds. *Pucker your lips like this, Elena, as if we were about to kiss.* Or perhaps Ruy Fonseca Areias worried her because he was too striking with his silver hair and dark skin, too Latin, too—too different from the other men in her life.

Elaine was well aware that Jennie considered her to be a coward about men. Maybe she was. The yuppie lawyers and doctors her sister disparaged were always dependable and discreet men Elaine knew she could trust. Men like that held no surprises. After the disastrous affair she'd suffered through when Jennie and Kate were still too young to understand what was happening, Elaine had decided she'd had her fill of surprises. So what if her adult relationships were a little—what was Jennie's term—vanilla flavored? Lots of people liked vanilla, she told herself. It was sweet and bland and familiar and safe.

It might not be the most exciting flavor in the world, but at least it never suddenly turned bitter as more exotic spices sometimes did.

"I look forward to the day when I may welcome you all to my country. Until then, *saúde*."

Elaine again joined in the applause as Ruy completed his remarks. As he started to sit down, she deliberately returned her attention to her meal. Except for the salad she'd nibbled at, she'd eaten nothing since breakfast. She reached for her fork.

Her beeper sounded.

The electronic summons cut piercingly into the murmur of conversation filling the room. "Damn," Elaine muttered, thinking that her overdue patient must have decided not to wait out the weekend, after all. Flicking the Off button, she glanced at her steak and quipped to Jenny, "Oh, well, I was trying to give up red meat, anyway." She started to push back her chair. Before a waiter could assist her, Ruy was at her side.

His fingers brushed Elaine's shoulder as he drew the chair away from the table and she rose. She could smell his cologne, something fresh and woodsy. She smiled weakly, flustered. "Thank you. I'm sorry to have disturbed you."

The light from the chandeliers glinted on his hair as he shook his head. "You have not disturbed me—at least, not the way you mean."

Out of the corner of her eye Elaine could see Jennie watching indulgently, and suddenly she was aware of hundreds of stares directed at the two of them. "I—I have to find a telephone," she said thickly.

"Will you be coming back?"

"I don't know. Please excuse me." She fled.

In the cool quiet of the corridor Elaine telephoned her service, who put her call through to the hospital. The patient who had just been admitted was not the one Elaine had expected, but another whose due date was still a month away. At her last examination only a few days before, Elaine had detected no evidence that the woman would deliver sooner. Frowning worriedly, she conferred with the nurse. "No signs of pre-eclampsia or fetal distress? Good. But I want you to go ahead and attach a monitor, just in case. And you'd better alert neonatal that we may be sending them a preemie...."

As soon as she hung up, Elaine dashed to the cloakroom to pick up her fox jacket, then made her way back to the ballroom to relay the news that she was leaving. Above the clink of china and cutlery the orchestra could be heard playing a subdued bossa nova. The air was warm and redolent of good wine and good food. Despite her reluctance to attend the banquet tonight, Elaine suddenly wished she didn't have to go.

With a sigh she mounted the dais. "Stork time?" Dan asked as he and Kate glanced up. Elaine nodded resignedly and leaned between her parents.

Before she could speak, Carolyn noticed the fur. "Oh, darling, don't tell me you have to go back to the hospital."

"I'm afraid so, Mom. The instant I can get a taxi—"

Burton scowled. "Where's your BMW?"

"In the shop. Two days ago, somebody stripped it while I was on duty at the clinic."

"Confound it, girl, I've warned you more than once about working in that part of—"

Elaine gritted her teeth. "Please, Father, don't start that now. I don't have time to argue. If you'll excuse me, I really must—"

At Burton's right, Ruy slid back his chair. "My limousine is at your disposal."

"Thank you, but that really won't be necessary. The doorman will fetch me a—"

Burton caught Elaine's wrist. His grip appeared casual, but his fingers crushed the jeweled bracelet into her skin. "Listen here, young lady," he growled in a forceful undertone, "when my partner offers you a ride, *accept* it."

Elaine stared at her father, too stunned by his outburst to feel anything but bewilderment. What the hell was going on? He hadn't used physical coercion on her since she was a small child, when he'd spanked her for playing with matches. "Daddy!" she yelped. The gray-haired man standing beside her stiffened.

Carolyn touched her husband's arm. "Burton, please," she warned, "remember where we are."

Elaine saw her father's dark blue eyes flicker obliquely over the crowded room. Fortunately, the guests seemed too involved with their steaks to have noticed the interplay of the people at the head table. His glance returned to his wife and his new business associate, and he dropped Elaine's hand. The pattern of platinum links were imprinted on her wrist. Flushing, Burton stared at the floor and muttered gruffly, "Forgive me, child. I didn't mean— I'm sorry."

Elaine's bewilderment was being superseded by embarrassment and anger. "Father, will you kindly explain—"

At her side Ruy suggested quietly, "Dr. Welles, perhaps explanations would be better left to another time. Have you forgotten you have a patient waiting? Even if you prefer not to use my car, you must get to the hospital."

Elaine gazed at him. Behind the trim mustache his lean dark face was somber and concerned, his eyes expectant. She wondered again what there was about Ruy Areias that worried her so. The man was kind, well-bred, generous. She had absolutely nothing against him, and yet his presence made her uncomfortable, as bashful and inept as an adolescent. Perhaps Jennie was right; perhaps she *was* emotionally stunted.

She nodded to Ruy. "Thank you for reminding me. Nothing is as important as my patient. If your offer still stands, I'd very much appreciate a ride."

His smile was dazzling. "I'll get my coat."

"I REALLY DIDN'T EXPECT you to come with me," Elaine said as the long black car began its journey through the wet streets of Denver. Through the windows she could see trees and signs being buffeted by the wind, but inside the limousine all was peaceful and silent, except for the low purr of the powerful engine. With the Plexiglas partition raised between the passenger seat and the chauffeur, she and Ruy were cut off from the rest of the world, contained in a bubble of serenity amid the storm. Nestling into her corner of the back seat, Elaine glanced at the man in the elegant overcoat and noted again, "As much as I appreciate the ride, it bothers me that you've left the banquet. After all, you are the guest of honor."

"I'll return to the hotel as soon as I know you've reached your destination safely. I would not feel right sending you out into the night unaccompanied."

She didn't know whether to be flattered or offended by his protective attitude. "Mr. Areias, perhaps it's different in Brazil, but surely you must realize I've been traveling unaccompanied most of my life. I'd be pretty ineffectual as a doctor if I had to make my rounds with a chaperon in tow."

Ruy shrugged. "You misunderstand me, Dr. Welles. I promise you, modern women in my country are as independent as in yours. The *aia*, the duenna, exists only in historical romances. I chose to come along just now because the hour is late, the weather is bad, and I know you are concerned about your patient. I thought you might find the presence of a friend . . . reassuring."

A friend. He wanted to be her friend. The idea was oddly comforting. Elaine relaxed. "You're right. No matter how many times I've done it, these drives across town can be pretty dreary. It's nice to have someone along. Thank you."

Sinking back against the seat, she flexed her wrist. It still felt tender where her father had squeezed it.

"Are you all right?" Ruy asked suddenly.

"Y-yes, of course," she stammered, stiff with embarrassment. She tugged the cuff of her jacket down over her hand. "I-I'm a little confused, that's all. My father isn't usually so—"

"Perhaps he's worried about the consortium."

Elaine peered at Ruy through slitted eyes, alerted by his honey-smooth tone. Was he pumping her? Was that the reason behind his extraordinarily solicitous attention? Although none of the Welles women had had any role in the negotiations between Corminco and A&O, Kate had confided to Elaine that Burton had bulldozed the deal through over the objections of his staff. Joining the consortium meant that Corminco had to cut back on domestic construction and development in order to fund the South American venture. Dan and the other senior executives had argued that diverting so much of the company's resources into a frankly speculative undertaking could jeopardize the entire business, but Burton had refused to be swayed. All his adult life he'd dreamed of becoming a tycoon of international stature. Now, almost at the end of his career, the prospect of at last achieving that goal was too seductive to ignore. He'd risk anything—including the family fortune.

Could knowledge of Burton's recklessness be used to A&O's advantage? Regardless of her attraction to Ruy, family loyalty demanded that Elaine keep quiet until she understood the situation better. She declared bracingly, "I'm sure my father has everything under control."

Determined to change the subject, she stroked the suede upholstery and surveyed the roomy interior of the passenger area. In a console behind the chauffeur's seat she spotted a telephone, a stereo tape deck and a small television screen. She wondered if there was a refrigerator hidden somewhere. She could use a snack, she realized. "Nice wheels," she commented dryly. "Courtesy of Corminco?"

"No. I always hire a car and driver when I plan to be in a strange city more than a day or two and I don't know how dependable the taxi service is. At home I drive myself."

Elaine nodded. "All us Welleses prefer to drive ourselves, too." She paused, her eyes soft with reminiscence. "Actually, when I was little, we did have a limousine. It was an Hispano-Suiza, I think—very old, very stately, with puckered silk on the walls. It belonged to my great-grandmother. She must have bought the car right after the First World War. I remember that to me it seemed about a block long, and whenever she'd take me out for a ride, I always pretended we were leading a parade—" Elaine broke off, suddenly embarrassed. God, she was gushing like a schoolgirl. Ruy was sure to think her an idiot. Chuckling abashedly, she added, "Of course the limo was completely impractical. I doubt it could go even five miles on a gallon of gas. After Grandma Maggie died, my father sold it to an antique-car collector."

From his side of the passenger seat Ruy watched Elaine in thoughtful silence. After a few moments he noted, "You're very fortunate to have such vivid memories of your great-grandmother. Not many people can look back over four generations."

Elaine's fingers burrowed beneath the cuff of her fur jacket, ignoring the topaz bracelet, until they closed around the thin gold bangle on her wrist. Her sensitive fingertips could just make out the engraving that the jeweler in Bern had copied so meticulously. "Grandma Maggie was quite a lady," she agreed, "the great matriarch of the clan. Her husband made the strike that started the Copa de Oro mine, but she was the one who had encouraged him to search for it and then fought single-handedly to hold on to it after a claim jumper shot him. If it wasn't for her, the Welleses would probably still be poor dirt farmers in Missouri." Elaine sighed. "I was only twelve when she died, and I've always been sorry that she didn't live a few years longer, so my little sisters could get a chance to know her." *Or so she'd be there when I needed her most...*

Elaine turned to stare out the window. The limousine was gliding along the freeway, and in the distance she could see a sign marking the off ramp that would take them to the hospital. As the driver edged the car into the right-hand lane, another vehicle with flashing lights and an ululating siren overtook and passed them, splashing water onto their windows as it sped by, headed for the same exit. Elaine shuddered. She hated the horrible up-and-down wail of the siren; it sounded like the death rattle of some prehistoric monster. All the way to the hospital, that awful day in Switzerland, she had begged the paramedics to make the dinosaur stop screaming....

"Is something wrong?" Ruy asked when she shifted away from the window. "You look pale."

Elaine started. She'd had no idea her emotions had been so transparent. Hastily she said, "I'm fine, really, just a little tired and hungry, I suppose. It's been a busy day and I keep missing meals. I'll have to see if one of the candy stripers can scrounge me a sandwich." The limousine turned off the freeway and descended the ramp to the surface street. The hospital was visible a few blocks ahead. Elaine glanced at her wristwatch. Despite the weather, they'd made good time. Pressing the button that lowered the partition, she instructed the driver, "Drop me off at the emergency entrance, please."

Moments later, the car pulled to the yellow curb behind the ambulance that had passed them. As the chauffeur opened Elaine's door, positioning an umbrella to block the rain, she held out a hand to Ruy. "Thank you again for the ride. I really appreciated it, though I do feel bad about your leaving the banquet."

"The celebration will still be going on when I return to the hotel." His fingers closed around hers. "And what about you? How long will your presence be required here?"

"I have no idea. For however long it takes." She gazed down at their joined hands. The air blowing into the car was cold, but the touch of his rough skin was warm and strangely welcoming, as if he'd held her before in some past life. The banks of lights around the entrance were reflected in his dark eyes. With an effort, Elaine looked away. As she glanced over her shoulder at the double glass doors that opened onto a corridor of cold white tile and harsh fluorescent lights—a corridor that she knew would be sharp with the nose-stinging odors of disinfectant and denatured alcohol—she realized she did not want to leave the cozy security of the limousine—or Ruy. For once she almost wished she were less committed to her patients.

Elaine shook herself. Inside that hospital was a woman who needed her—needed her *now*. "I have to go," she said hoarsely. "I'd better hustle to my locker and change before someone spots me. If I show up on the floor wearing silk and a fur coat, people are going to say I overcharge my patients!"

Ruy asked, "How secure is your locker? You might be wise to store your bracelet in the hospital vault, if one is available."

Elaine looked blank. "But I never take off my bracelet."

"I was referring to the one I just gave you."

At his grim tone, Elaine felt her face grow hot. God, if she weren't sitting down, she'd kick herself, she thought, glancing with what she hoped was proper enthusiasm at the shining white metal links and the sky-colored stones. The man had bestowed that costly little bijou on her barely an hour before, and she'd as good as told him she'd already forgotten it! Carolyn would cringe at the thought of such rudeness. Elaine said, "You're right, of course. Even though I've never heard of any problem with theft in the hospital, a piece of jewelry as expensive as this would be a powerful temptation to anyone. I'll make certain it's stored someplace secure." She hesitated, noting the chauffeur who waited impassively in the rain. "And now I really must be going. Your poor driver is getting soaked, despite his umbrella, and I have a baby to deliver."

At the word *baby*, Ruy's expression softened. "Yes, you do have important duties to perform, don't you—far more important than catering to my bruised vanity." Before Elaine could tug her fingers from his grasp, he raised her hand to his face and brushed his lips across her knuckles, the silver-gray mustache as soft as angora on her skin. "*Adeus*, my dear," he murmured. "I'll come back later to drive you home."

The courtly caress confused Elaine. The man was moving too fast, too forcefully; she felt like a leaf skittering in the wind. Trying with difficulty to regain the initiative, she swallowed hard and said huskily, "No, don't come back tonight. I have no idea how long I'll be here or what kind of mood I'll be in when I'm finished. Let me find my own way back to my apartment."

Ruy's eyes were speculative. "Apartment? I assumed you lived with your parents."

Elaine shook her head. "Not since college. Kate and Dan and the children live with Mom and Father, but I prefer my privacy."

Ruy studied her shuttered expression. After a moment he released her hand. "May I see you tomorrow night, then? Perhaps we could have dinner, to make up for the one you've missed this evening?" Elaine hesitated, and Ruy added, "I know this is short notice, but I have only another day or two left in Denver."

She licked her lips. "Tomorrow night sounds wonderful...about eight, perhaps? Presuming, of course, that no babies decide to spoil the rest of my weekend."

"We must pray for them to forbear a few days longer. Until tomorrow night, then...Elaine."

His voice toyed with her name, drawing out the second syllable and giving a Latin lilt to the soft vowels. It sounded almost like "Elena."

Gulping, Elaine said, "Till tomorrow." She paused. "Here, you'll need my address." She scrawled it on the back of one of her business cards. "I hope you can read this: you know what they say about doctors' handwriting! If you have any problems or should want to get in touch with me, my answering service can always reach me." She pressed the card into his fingers. "*Boa noite*, Ruy," she said huskily.

She slid out of the back seat and declined the chauffeur's proffered umbrella, choosing instead to sprint across the last few feet of wet asphalt to the shelter of the emergency entrance. Just inside the hospital, shaking raindrops from her tumbled curls, she confronted an orderly who surveyed her ensemble appreciatively and trilled a long, lurid wolf whistle. "Wow, doctor," he declared, "when you're not wearing your scrubs, you look as sexy as Linda Evans!"

"Flatterer!" Elaine said, laughing. And suddenly she realized her grin was the first genuine smile she'd displayed all evening.

CHAPTER THREE

"ROUGH NIGHT?" Jennie asked sympathetically when Elaine dragged herself into the breakfast room on bare feet and sat herself down at the table. The sunbeams that made the polished cherry wood table gleam bleached her features, still slack with sleep. Jennie slid the coffeepot and bread basket toward her sister. "I toasted some bagels. You're out of juice."

"In the freezer," Elaine mumbled as she brushed her hair out of her eyes. Hugging her quilted robe around her shoulders, she poured coffee into a mug of hand-painted Italian earthenware and stirred cream into the revivifying fluid. After scalding her mouth with the first swallow, she squinted at the cheery folk-art pattern of blue and yellow daisies on the mug and yawned windily. Only when her lips quit stinging did she feel capable of answering her sister's question.

"It wasn't nearly as rough a night as I'd expected it to be, thank God, although I wasn't actually sure what to expect."

"What do you mean?"

Elaine shook her head wryly. "My patient's fairly levelheaded, but for months her husband has been hounding me about everything from the proper prenatal diet to ensure a Nobel Prize winner to the importance of reading Proust aloud during labor. I told him if he wanted French spoken in the delivery room, he should move to

Montreal. I was afraid he might have done something stupid in his quest to produce the perfect little status symbol. In the end it turned out he was so busy choosing a prep school for the baby that he forgot to paint the nursery, and his wife decided to do it herself. The exertion started things going a little sooner than any of us expected."

"But mother and child are okay now?" Jennie pressed as she spread cream cheese over a split roll.

"Oh, yes. Even Daddy came through all right. When it came time to coach his wife, he forgot all about speaking French and really gave her the support and encouragement she needed. When I visited the three of them in the recovery room, he was crying and talking baby talk to his new daughter."

Elaine smiled tenderly at the thought of the beautiful, healthy infant she'd helped bring into the world. During her career she'd delivered hundreds of babies, but the exhilaration and wonder of each birth still awed her. Sometimes she thought that assisting in the miracle almost made up for having no children of her own. Almost.

For several minutes the women ate in silence. Then Elaine asked, "So what happened after I left the banquet?"

"Not a whole lot. There was a white chocolate mousse for dessert, and then dancing to work off all the calories. A reporter for the *Denver Post* got a shot of Mom and Father doing the samba; it's probably in this morning's paper somewhere. Later he asked me for an interview. I thought he wanted to discuss my show, but instead he seemed to think I knew all about Andy's new movie. When I told him I didn't, he lost interest, the jerk."

"You can't really fault the man for trying," Elaine pointed out reasonably. "Considering how much fodder you and Andrew Proctor have provided for the tabloids and fanzines in the past, I'm sure he just naturally assumed you'd have all the inside information."

"Well, he was wrong, wasn't he?" Jennie snapped.

Elaine studied her sister's tense face pensively. Until now she'd assumed that Jennie and her longtime lover had parted by mutual consent. "I'm sorry, Jen," she said quietly.

Jennie shrugged. "Don't be. It was bound to end sooner or later. In retrospect it's a wonder we lasted four months, much less four years. Neither one of us is any good at commitment. Besides, when you live with a man who's prettier than you are, you keep fighting over the bathroom mirror." She sank her teeth viciously into her bagel. After she swallowed, she asked, "Speaking of gorgeous men, what went on between you and Father's new business partner after he dashed to your rescue? I was impressed by his gallantry."

Elaine smiled into her coffee. "I wasn't aware that a lift to the hospital qualified as gallantry."

"It does among my friends. Most of the people I know wouldn't have offered a ride even if *you'd* been the one in labor."

Trying not to wince, Elaine forced a weak chuckle. "Well, then, I guess it's lucky I was only the obstetrician." She turned to gaze out the window. The clouds had blown away, at least for the moment, and the autumn-burned plains to the east shone golden beneath a freshly washed sky. She suddenly remembered she'd left the topaz bracelet in her locker at the hospital, tucked into the toe of an aerobic shoe. She'd have to pick it up later in the morning. She had rounds to make as well as an appointment she wasn't looking forward to. "Didn't Ruy return to the banquet? He said he was going to."

"Oh, yeah, he came back, but except for one duty dance with Mom, he kept a low profile, mostly talking business with the upper staff people. Are you going to see him again?"

"We have a dinner date this evening."

Jennie nodded approvingly. "Fantastic! I was pretty sure he planned to ask you out, but I was afraid that paralyzing caution of yours would make you say no. I'm glad I was wrong. He strikes me as perfect for you."

Elaine sipped her coffee. "You don't think he's a little *too* perfect?"

"I don't understand what you mean."

Lacing her hands together, Elaine propped her chin on her fingers. "I'm not sure I know what I mean, either," she admitted, "except that somehow Ruy strikes me as almost too good to be true. He's handsome, intelligent, cultured, single—"

"Straight," Jennie supplied dryly.

Elaine recalled the gleam in his black eyes as his lips brushed her skin. "Yes, I think we can definitely assume the man is not gay," she conceded. "All of which leads me to ask myself, *Why me?* Why should a man with all that going for him evidently flip over me on sight?"

"Maybe because he finds you pretty, intelligent, cultured, single and straight," Jennie said impatiently. "For God's sake, what difference does it make? Why can't you accept the fact that there seems to be a mutual attraction between the two of you, and let it develop from there? Stop thinking like a doctor! You're always dissecting things."

Elaine felt strangely vulnerable. "You really believe I'm foolish to worry?"

"I believe it would do you a world of good to take a chance for a change."

As she spoke, Jennie glanced at her wristwatch and jumped to her feet. For the first time Elaine realized her sister was dressed for travel. She frowned in dismay. "Surely you're not going already? You only flew in from New York yesterday."

"I'm booked on an 11:00 a.m. flight," Jennie said. "I came to Denver and did my duty to Father, the way you begged me to, but now that the stupid party is over, I just want to get the hell out of here."

"You're not going to take any extra time for the family?"

Jennie's expression turned mulish. "You already have plans. Who else do you suggest I spend time with? Father? Kate and her brats? *Dan?*"

Elaine was surprised by Jennie's acid tone. After all these years, she tended to forget that her younger sisters' estrangement dated back to the days when the two teenage girls had been rivals for the affection of Daniel Brock. Personally, the man's charm had always escaped her.

Refusing to be drawn into an old and pointless argument, Elaine said calmly, "How about spending some time with Mom? She told me you two missed each other in New York last month. She's going to be disappointed when she finds out you didn't stay in Denver longer."

"She didn't seem all that thrilled to see me last night."

Elaine grimaced. "What did you expect, with that costume you had on? You know what a stickler she is about 'appropriate' dress."

"*I* liked it. Besides, *my* wardrobe doesn't run to designer—"

"Bull," Elaine interrupted pithily. "I suppose you *borrowed* the little Norma Kamali number you wore to the Emmys? You know perfectly well the only reason you showed up at the banquet in that sarong, or whatever it was, was because it was guaranteed to drive the folks up the wall. Damn it, Jen, you're not a teenager anymore. Why do you deliberately keep antagonizing them?"

Jennie remained tense. "Habit, I suppose," she answered slowly, letting out her breath with a hiss. "Of course, you wouldn't understand, would you? You've never made a wrong move in your life."

Elaine stared, remembering the disasters that had shaped her life. "Do you really believe that?"

Just for a moment Jennie's dark blue eyes looked exposed, unprotected. "I don't know. I only know that our parents seem genuinely pleased that you're a doctor and that Kate's a wife and mother. Nothing I've ever done has met with Mom's approval—or made Daddy notice me...."

LONG AFTER a taxi had borne Jennie off to the Stapleton Airport, Elaine puttered around her apartment. A Julian Bream album played softly on the stereo while she laid out her rain-spattered silk suit for the dry cleaners and lovingly dusted her Wedgwood collection. As she worked, she mulled over her sister's wistful remark. She wondered bewilderedly how Jennie could be so blind as to think that she was the only member of the Welles family who had been affected by Burton's indifference.

Yes, Elaine knew, it was all too tragically true that her father had never paid much attention to his youngest daughter—but he'd never paid much attention to any of his daughters. He had wanted sons. It was ironic that the scion of a line that had in effect been founded by a woman should be so obsessed with male offspring, but Burton was as traditionally dynastic as any Tudor king.

From remarks Carolyn had made in the past, Elaine suspected the fault lay with Burton's father, Maggie's son. Even after she had turned control of the family firm over to him, the man had felt intimidated by—and resentful of—his awesome mother, and his resentment had shown in his marriage and in the way he had raised his own two sons. No woman was ever going to wield such power over a Welles man again.

Joseph, Jr., predeceased Maggie by over a decade, but his influence continued to be felt down to the present generation. Elaine's birth had been a disappointment to Burton, and when the long-awaited second child proved also to be a girl, the frustration had been even harder to endure. Jennie's arrival eleven months later had been entirely too much to bear. On that day Burton abandoned the girls emotionally, just as he abandoned his wife shortly afterward, when she refused to "try again." He turned all his energies to Corminco and left the girls to Carolyn's care, with the expectation that if she could not give him male children, she could at least raise her daughters to make good marriages and themselves bear sons to take over their grandfather's company. Now, decades later, Carolyn and even Kate, the one daughter who had actually followed that scenario, recognized that Burton's blatant chauvinism was almost laughable—except nobody was laughing.

Didn't Jennie realize that, one way or another, each of the Welles women had suffered because of Burton's attitudes? Elaine knew all about it. Her own life was a long series of *if only*s, running back to her girlhood. If only her father hadn't been so obsessed with the idea of turning his daughters into compliant wives, he would not have ignored her dreams of an academic career and bundled her off to an exclusive finishing school in Switzerland to learn the art of being a society hostess. If only Elaine had received the kind of support she needed from her parents, she would not have fallen victim in her misery and loneliness to the seductive blandishments of Antonio, a nineteen-year-old boy from Portugal, who was a waiter at her school. If only she'd found the courage to tell somebody, anybody, that she was pregnant, she would not have tried to conceal her guilty secret until it almost killed her. If only someone had loved her, she would not have been left a barren shell of a woman at the age of fifteen.

The blue jasper candlestick Elaine was dusting slipped through her hands; by sheer luck she was able to lunge and catch it before it shattered on the floor. With quaking fingers she set the ornament back on the piano and straightened the taper that had come askew. She shook herself impatiently. God, what was wrong with her, waxing maudlin now over something that had happened more than two decades before?

While she was in medical school she had written to Switzerland for her hospital records, and the words had all been there—cold, clinical terms for the pain and mindless terror she had suffered as she had tried to hide her condition from her teachers, from the other students, from herself.... Antonio had disappeared before she could tell him about the baby, and each morning in her chaste dormitory bed, she had prayed that the pregnancy was a bad dream; that if she ignored it, it would go away—just as her lover had. She could not eat; sleep was fitful. Her grades plummeted. Despite her expensive education, she had only the vaguest notion of her own bodily functions, and she was far too frightened to confide even in a doctor. She received no prenatal care at all. Unable to recognize the signs that meant something was going wrong, she pretended her increasing nausea and dizziness were due to a bad cold. She kept on pretending until one overcast February morning she collapsed in convulsions during her music-appreciation class.

Surgeons managed to save her life, but only at the cost of any future children she might have had. As a physician herself, Elaine knew they'd had no choice. Interestingly, it was her sterility that led directly to her choice of career. After her parents brought her home to Denver to recuperate, Elaine decided that if she could not have children of her own, she could at least help other women with theirs; she could prevent other girls from suffering as she had. When she announced she wanted to go to medical school, Burton and Carolyn proved surprisingly supportive. It wasn't until much, much later that Elaine realized they must have been willing to humor her request because she was no longer of use to the Welles family as a woman.

Elaine felt annoyed with herself for succumbing to her welling depression. She had no reason to be dejected, not really. She had never regretted her decision to become an obstetrician. Her career was challenging and worthwhile—most of the time. Lately she'd felt very frustrated in her work. Many of her private patients seemed to regard their babies as status symbols, an attitude she deplored, and she was being forced to limit her welfare cases on account of government restrictions and skyrocketing malpractice insurance premiums. Still, no matter what cuts she had to make in her practice, there would always be women who needed her. She was a damned good doctor.

The only problem was, being a good doctor no longer seemed enough.

In moments of self-analysis Elaine admitted she probably should have married somewhere along the line; at least then there'd be another person to share her loneliness. Finding a husband would have been easy enough. Regardless of the outwardly bland appearance of her relationships, the men in her life had almost always proposed. Even Antonio—hell, especially Antonio.

The guitar music issuing forth from the compact disk player suddenly reminded Elaine of the scratchy Segovia record that had hissed on the cheap monaural phonograph as Antonio had pleaded, *"Marry me, Elena."* In those two months after she had first timidly accompanied him to his basement room, she'd heard that album about twenty times; she'd planned to buy him a new one for Christmas. What she really would have liked was to get him a decent stereo, but she had known he would refuse such an expensive gift. Antonio was proud and ambitious, she had realized, and someday he'd be a success, but on his own terms. Since that day in early September when he'd found Elaine sobbing over a crayon picture her baby sisters had drawn for her, he had refused to accept anything from her—except her love.

Then he had repeated, *"Marry me, Elena. Why should we wait until we are older? We will move to America. I know I have nothing to offer you, but your family is rich. They can afford to set me up in business"*—and her romantic illusions had shattered as she had recognized him for what he was.

Each year, youths from all around Europe flocked to the Swiss girls' academies to prey on the wealthy students; they vied for jobs at the schools or the places where the girls congregated on holidays, and they waited,

preening themselves like hawks.... Whenever some girl
was whisked away for a discreet abortion or a hasty
marriage, the older, more sophisticated students were
scornful. Boys like that could be fun for an occasional
fling, they hinted, but nobody in her right mind would
ever think of taking one *seriously*. Elaine had, to her
lasting regret, and in what was probably the saddest
consequence of that ill-starred teenage affair, she hadn't
been able to take another man seriously since.

ELAINE GAZED SOBERLY at the couple seated opposite
her. Sylvia and Jeff Miles-Hatfield were upwardly mo-
bile professionals in their early thirties. He was a computer programmer, she a certified public accountant in
the first trimester of her first pregnancy, and on the other
occasions when Elaine had consulted with them, they'd
both been dressed in gray flannel. Today they wore ve-
lour warm-up suits—his by Pierre Cardin, hers Calvin
Klein—and at their feet lay matching cases for their racquetball equipment. Elaine noticed Jeff glance surreptitiously at his Rolex.

Clearing her throat, Elaine said, "First of all, I'd like
to thank you both for making time this weekend to see
me. I know your free time is limited—as is my own, for
that matter—but since we were unable to schedule an
appointment during the week, there seemed no other
choice. As I emphasized when I telephoned, it is vitally
important that the three of us talk."

She flipped open the manila folder in front of her.
"What I have here is the result of the ultrasound tests we
conducted on the fetus last week. As you know, I wasn't
satisfied with the outcome of the first tests and I ordered
a second series. I showed those films to one of my colleagues for his opinion." Elaine took a deep breath. "I'm

very sorry to have to tell you that his conclusion was the same as my own—"

"There's something wrong with the baby," Sylvia said.

Elaine's eyes narrowed fractionally. She was not surprised that her patient had guessed what she was about to say; both she and her husband were very intelligent, and in any case it didn't require much brain power to figure out that a doctor would not have called them in for a special consultation had everything been proceeding normally. What did surprise Elaine was the lack of feeling in the woman's voice. *"There's something wrong with the baby."* She had uttered the words so calmly, without any sign of stress or notable anxiety or indeed any particular emotion beyond mild curiosity. For all the sentiment she displayed, she could have been a housewife noting that the milk had turned sour. Elaine wondered if she was in shock.

Carefully Elaine said, "I'm afraid you're right: there does appear to be a problem. The tests confirm that the baby's heart contains a slight septal defect, a hole in the wall separating the chambers of the heart. I realize it sounds ominous, but I want to assure you, congenital malformations of this sort are not uncommon, and when the opening is a small one, as in your baby's case, the defect should be easily correctable surgically after birth."

She paused, waiting for either of the couple to speak. They stared at her in blank silence. After a moment Elaine continued in soothing tones, "I realize news like this is always a blow, but I want you both to consider how very fortunate we are to live in an age when medical technology permits us to diagnose a problem in advance. We'll be able to monitor the progress of the pregnancy extra carefully, so that we'll know at once if there is any sign of fetal distress. At the moment, the only ef-

fect this should have on your activities is that we'll have
to revise the appointment schedule we made for you, Ms.
Hatfield. You'll want to start coming in more often than
once a month, and, while it's too early to say, it may become necessary for you to begin maternity leave from
your job sooner than—''

"No." This time it was Jeff who interrupted Elaine.
"No, my wife will not be leaving her job."

Elaine smiled sympathetically. "I appreciate that an
early leave may impose some hardship if the two of you
had counted on your wife's working up until the last
moment, but I promise I won't ask it of her unless it becomes imperative, for her sake as well as that of the baby.
And probably—''

He said, "Doctor, you don't understand. There's not
going to be any baby, not this time. We intend to terminate the pregnancy."

Blinking, Elaine murmured, "I beg your pardon?"

Jeff reached for his wife's hand. "When Sylvia and I
decided to start a family," he declared, "we agreed from
the very beginning that if there was ever any problem
with the baby, we'd terminate it. We feel it would be
morally wrong to bring a handicapped child into the
world."

Elaine gulped. "I'm sorry. You'll both have to forgive
me. I must not have made myself clear. Your child will
not be handicapped. Once corrective surgery is performed, there is every reason to expect him to live a perfectly normal life."

"But you can't guarantee it," Jeff persisted.

With quiet strength Elaine said, "Mr. Hatfield, in
medicine only quacks give guarantees. However, I can tell
you that over the years several of the babies I've delivered have suffered the same defect yours has, and every

single one of them has not only survived but thrived. The oldest, a girl of ten, is a promising ballet student, and one of the boys pitched the winning game for his Little League team's divisional championship. I'm sure any of the parents involved would be more than happy to talk to you about what was involved in their child's recovery."

If she'd hoped either of the Miles-Hatfields would be swayed by her little pep talk, Elaine could see now that her efforts were doomed. The only discernible emotion she could see on either of the couple's faces was irritation.

Sylvia leaned forward. "Doctor," she said earnestly, "I appreciate your concern, but you have to understand. Jeff and I are very goal-oriented people. We have plans, ambitions. Our life-style is a good one, but it's also very demanding. We never expect less than the very best from either of us, and when we have children, we will, of course, expect the same from them. It wouldn't be fair to the baby or, frankly, to us, to produce a child who might not be able to . . . well . . . to fit in."

Elaine gazed steadily at the sleek couple in their designer sweat suits, spouting pompous platitudes and sweetly holding hands while they talked about discarding their unborn infant as if it were a bruised peach. She wondered if they had any idea how many of her patients considered their lives blessed by exactly the kind of child Sylvia and Jeff apparently considered unworthy of existence. She wondered if they ever thought of the millions of women who would sing eternal hymns of thanksgiving if they could only hold babies in their arms. . . .

Hoarsely she said, "Well, since you two have obviously made your decision, I suppose there's no point in my trying to dissuade you."

"I'm glad you see it that way, doctor," Sylvia replied briskly. "So I guess all we need to do now is set up a time."

"A time for what?"

"For the abortion, naturally. Since you're my doctor, we naturally assumed—"

"You assumed wrong," Elaine said stonily. "I do not perform abortions."

The woman opened her mouth to protest, then shut it again. At her side her husband grumbled, "I think it's time we find you a new doctor, hon."

"Perhaps it is," Elaine agreed evenly.

Reaching for his racquetball equipment, Jeff urged his wife to her feet. "Come on, Sylvie," he muttered, "we'd better get going. Our court's reserved for one o'clock."

After the Miles-Hatfields had stormed from her office, Elaine propped her elbows on the edge of her desk and covered her face with her hands. There were times when she hated her work, times when the appalling ignorance and want of her welfare patients made her sick with frustration, times—like now—when the selfish, overfed, overprivileged yuppies she treated privately made her sick, period.

She needed to get away. The ennui she'd been feeling lately was a danger signal. It was a fatal flaw for a doctor to become emotionally involved with her patients. If she didn't learn to push people like Jeff and Sylvia from her mind as easily as they apparently were pushing their unborn child from their lives, she was going to end up with a classic case of burnout. *Forget them,* she ordered herself, *they're not worth the effort of worrying. Relax. You've got a date with a gorgeous new man tonight. Enjoy it . . . enjoy him. And when he's gone back to Brazil, maybe then you can start figuring out how to enjoy life again....*

"PLEASE COME IN," Elaine said invitingly as she and Ruy stood in the entryway of her apartment. Brushing off the water droplets spotting her handbag, she dropped the purse onto the console table beside the door and tossed back the hood of her raincoat. The downpour that had threatened all evening had finally caught up with the two of them while they'd been strolling across Capitol Hill, but the limousine had pulled alongside to rescue them before either had been more than lightly spattered.

Ruy watched her unbutton her coat with quick, economical movements. "We were fortunate in our timing. I was afraid the rain was going to spoil your evening."

"Nothing could have spoiled this evening. It's been wonderful," Elaine said, meaning it. Recalling Jennie's admonition that she simply accept the attraction between herself and the handsome Brazilian, and remembering her own instructions that she forget everything but enjoying herself, Elaine had given herself up to the pleasures of the moment. The task had not been an arduous one. Ruy had seemed determined to make the evening perfect for her. After attending a guitar recital at the university, he had carried her off to late supper at a restaurant on Colfax Avenue, where the two of them had debated the merits of the cuisine and Elaine had entertained Ruy with stories about her great-grandparents' early days in Denver....

"Grandma Maggie always said she didn't really mind the mud Grampa Joseph tracked into the house whenever it rained, but she drew the line at him drying his wet dynamite in the kitchen stove!"

"At least he was able to use explosives," Ruy observed. "When I was in the Amazon goldfields, the only tools I had at my disposal were a pickax and a strong back."

Elaine glanced across the table at the manicured hands. She remembered the thick calluses on his palms. "When were you in the goldfields?" she asked curiously.

"A lifetime ago," Ruy dismissed, shrugging. He had averted further questions by summoning the wine steward.

Later, when he returned the conversation to the subject of Elaine's family history, she offered to show him the house where the Welleses had lived prior to moving to their present estate farther out of town, in Cherry Hills Village. Like many of the other Victorian mansions near the capitol building, the first home Maggie built with the Copa de Oro fortune was now a museum. It was closed for the night, but Elaine and Ruy stood outside the wrought iron gates, gazing in silence at the graceful gingerbread turrets dwarfed by the concrete-and-steel high rises that surrounded the area. She studied his strong, stern profile, his silver hair gleaming in the glow of the streetlight, and all at once she was certain it was no accident that had brought them together in this place, at this time. She and Ruy had been fated to meet. She started to speak, and the rain began....

"May I take your coat?" Elaine asked tentatively as he lingered in the entryway, his hands shoved deep into the pockets of his vicuña topcoat. "I thought I'd fix us some coffee—" She broke off, momentarily diverted. "On second thought, perhaps I'd better offer you Grand Marnier, instead. I don't know if I have the nerve to serve coffee to a Brazilian."

Beneath his mustache Ruy's lips quirked. His eyes remained obsidian, unreadable. "Anything would be fine, but it's very late. I don't want to impose."

Elaine lowered her lashes, trying not to stare at his hard, lean body. Gradually it was dawning on her that she was more attracted to this stranger from South America than she had been to any man in a very long time. "Please stay," she whispered.

Ruy unbuttoned his coat. "Whatever you want, Elaine," he said, and once again her name echoed in his mouth like a voice from the past.

At her suggestion, Ruy started a fire in the fireplace. By the time she returned from the kitchen with the drinks, he was reclining against the arm of the sofa, his legs stretched in front of him, his jacket open, his tie loosened. The flickering flames provided the only illumination in the room and the rays of light reflected off the angular planes of his face. His tanned torso was a dusky shadow beneath the white silk of his shirt. In the dark V exposed by his open collar, Elaine noticed with surprise that he was wearing some kind of charmlike object on a string around his neck.

Setting the decanter on the cocktail table alongside the box of Perugina chocolates he'd brought her, she poured the fragrant citrus-flavored liqueur into small fluted glasses and handed one to Ruy. When she kicked off her high-heeled pumps and curled on the couch alongside him, her legs tucked beneath her, she could see that his pendant—a tiny fist with the thumb protruding between two fingers—appeared to be made of cheap plastic, sharply at odds with Ruy's otherwise elegant dress.

"Is something wrong?" Ruy inquired, noting the direction of her gaze.

Elaine grinned sheepishly. "Forgive me for staring, but is that some sort of amulet you have on?"

He pulled the string away from his throat so that she could get a better view of the little ornament. "This is a *figa*, a good-luck symbol. Charms like these are quite common in Brazil. I was twenty when an old woman gave this one to me. She was an Umbanda priestess, and she said it would protect me from devils."

"Umbanda?"

"One of the principal spirit religions of my country," Ruy said matter-of-factly.

Elaine puzzled. "Oh, I see," she murmured, not certain she did. Although she was unfamiliar with Brazilian culture, she'd always been more or less aware that many people there adhered to a complex set of beliefs first brought to that country by African slaves, beliefs her own culture tended to dismiss ignorantly as "voodoo." She knew the Hollywood image of witch doctors sticking pins in dolls was unfair and demeaning to what were, in fact, several highly evolved religions, but she had never dreamed that someone as sophisticated as Ruy might practice one of those religions. "I see," she mumbled again, helplessly.

Sipping his drink, Ruy said dryly, "You're skeptical. You shouldn't be."

"Then you do believe your charm has brought you good luck?"

He shrugged. "I don't know whether it was the *figa* that brought my luck, or just hard work. I've never worried about it. The fact that my friend believed in its power was enough for me. Still, I've certainly prospered over the years, and the devils never caught up with me." He glanced at her wrist. "And what about you? You seem to regard that gold bracelet as some kind of charm. You touch it whenever you get nervous.''

Following his gaze, Elaine found her fingers wrapped around the thin engraved band. Embarrassed, she jerked her hands apart, disguising the motion by reaching for her liqueur glass. She shook her head as she insisted, ''No, you're wrong. I suppose I do have a bad habit of fidgeting with the bangle, but that's only because it reminds me of my great-grandmother, who gave it to me. Sometimes when things bother me, her memory helps me find the strength to cope. But that certainly doesn't mean I think the bracelet itself has any intrinsic power.''

Besides, Elaine admitted dispiritedly, *even if there had been any magic in Maggie's bracelet, it's all gone now. Antonio stole the magic when he stole the original.*

To forestall further questions, Elaine sipped her drink. She savored the syrupy liquid and felt it burn its way down her throat like sweet flames. The heat radiated through her arms and her breasts, and she relaxed deeper into the cushions of the sofa. She could hear rain pounding against her windows, but in front of the hearth she was cozy, sheltered, safe. Stretching luxuriously, she declared, ''I love fireplaces.''

''At the moment, I think I love fireplaces, too,'' Ruy agreed. ''This is the first time since I've been in Denver that I haven't felt cold.''

''It must be hard, facing this weather when you're used to the tropics.''

Ruy set his glass next to the decanter. ''You misunderstand me. We have cold weather in Brazil, too. São Paulo is not a tropical city. In fact, when the wind blows north from Argentina, it becomes quite chilly. But when I left home, it was spring.''

Elaine frowned thoughtfully. "I hadn't thought of that. I've never traveled across the equator, but I imagine it must be difficult to accustom yourself to the reversal of the seasons."

"I find the transition harder to cope with than jet lag, and unfortunately, in two days I must make the journey all over again."

"I wish you didn't have to go," Elaine admitted candidly.

Ruy's gaze met hers. "I'm not ready to leave, either." He sighed and looked away. When he spoke, he sounded angry. "But no matter how much I long for an opportunity for us to get to know each other better, I cannot delay my return home any longer. Now that the deal between A&O and Corminco has been finalized, I have a great many things to do. With the equipment your father is sending, as well as his financial backing, we will begin our expansion. For that we will need miners, other men to process the gem gravel and still others to sort and grade the stones we find. The town I have built for the workers and their families will mushroom. I have promised the men who sign with me that in return for their moving out into the wilderness, I will provide housing, education and entertainment—not exactly a small undertaking!"

"But don't you have subordinates who can handle the logistics?" Elaine asked, recalling her mother's comment about Brazilians taking a personal interest in their employees. Until this moment she had not realized exactly how comprehensive that interest might be. "Surely you don't expect to make all the arrangements yourself."

"My associate, João Santos Oliveira, is doing much of the work. Still, there are a number of problems that require my attention. One you will appreciate is the question of providing medical care. I've already built a clinic—a small hospital, really—in Serra Brilhante, but now I'm having difficulty finding people to staff it."

"Why is that?"

"Compared to the United States, my country has relatively few doctors for its huge population, and in general, most physicians prefer to practice in places like São Paulo or Rio. I don't blame them. Not only are the wages and conditions far better in the big cities than in the small towns, but urban Brazilians seem to have an inborn aversion to anything remotely 'rural.' The idea of moving into the wilderness strikes most of them as sheer insanity. Consequently, despite the inducements I'm offering, I have so far been unable to interest qualified medical personnel in working at Serra Brilhante. But I persist. Somewhere there must be a doctor who will help me, even if only temporarily."

Elaine listened intently. The idea forming in her mind was outlandish, and yet— "I'm a doctor," she said.

Ruy's chin jerked up. He shook his head. "No, Elaine. It is very sweet of you to suggest the idea, but . . . no. It is impossible."

"Why is it impossible? You said the miners were going to be bringing their families with them. That means women and children and, inevitably, more babies. I happen to be an excellent obstetrician and gynecologist, and I can double in pediatrics, if necessary. Of course I realize there would be a language barrier, but I couldn't leave Denver for several weeks, anyway, and in the meantime I'll bet there's someone at the university who'd give me a crash course in Portuguese. At the same time, you could be looking for somebody at the site who could translate for me, if not into English, then Spanish. I'm fluent.''

Her enthusiasm seemed to surprise Ruy. "What about your patients here in Denver?" he reminded her, scowling. "You cannot just abandon them."

"I wouldn't be abandoning anyone. I'm not giving up my practice. We're only talking about a few months at most, aren't we, until you can locate a permanent resident? I can obtain a leave of absence from the hospital for that length of time, and I know I could arrange for other doctors to take over my patients until I return to Denver. As you pointed out, there are a lot of physicians in the United States."

Ruy closed his eyes tiredly and massaged the aquiline bridge of his nose. "Elaine, my dear, as much as I appreciate what you're offering, I don't think you have any idea of what you'd be getting into. The culture shock would be phenomenal. Compared to what you're used to, working conditions would seem primitive. São Paulo may be a thoroughly modern city of fifteen million people, but in the backcountry of Minas Gerais you'd be dealing with people who *are* primitive, in the case of some of the Indians literally only a generation away from a Stone Age society."

Elaine turned to face him squarely, her fingers digging into the soft cushion on the back of the sofa. She wasn't sure why it was so important that he believe in her. "You don't think I can handle it, is that it?"

Ruy opened his eyes again. "I think that there is no reason for you to find out whether or not you can handle it," he declared flatly. He paused. Noting her tension, he laid his hand over hers and stroked it soothingly until some of the strain eased. "*Namorada,*" he whispered, his voice as caressing as his fingertips, "don't worry about it. These people are my concern, not yours."

The rhythmic glide of his skin over hers unsettled her. All at once she felt hot, dizzy, and she did not know if it was the wine and liqueur she'd drunk during the evening that was making her head spin, or if it was Ruy's voice murmuring endearments as intimate and troubling as a half-remembered dream.

The fire crackled, and glowworms of light flickered over them. Appalled by the lack of resolution in her voice, Elaine stammered, "But I-I'd like to help, if I could. Lately I've felt so frustrated here in Denver. As much as I love what I do, I doubt that many of my patients would notice if I suddenly just disappeared. I want to feel more worthwhile than that. It would mean a lot to me to work among people who really need me." She gulped nervously. "Besides, I think it would be nice if you and I were to have a little more time together."

Ruy's grip tightened around the hand he was holding. "Do you really mean that?"

Elaine hesitated. "Don't you want us to have more time together?"

"You know I do. But I didn't dare hope."

"Neither did I. It frightens me how fast it's happening. I don't think I've ever felt this way before."

Something flickered in his eyes. "Don't be afraid," he murmured. Slowly, without force, he urged her nearer.

Because she was seated with her feet tucked beneath her, the motion made her rise wobbling to her knees. Unsteadily she put out her free hand to balance herself. Her fingers burrowed beneath the lapels of Ruy's jacket, splaying across the hard muscles of his chest. Through the thin silk of his shirt she could feel the crisp hair feathering his skin; his heart was pounding. Elaine licked her lips. When she spoke, her voice was a high, thin thread of sound. "You make me dizzy."

Ruy caught his breath. "My God, Elena, I never expected—" His mouth closed over hers.

As their lips moved together, a log in the fireplace fell, popping and hissing. Elaine's lashes flew up. Just for a second, flaring light bathed the embracing couple, tingeing them with the soft, gilded radiance of youth. Then the brightness died. Enveloping shadows robbed Ruy's hair of its silver gleam, restoring the darkness the years had stolen. Elaine's eyes widened. She knew. Maybe she'd always known.

With both hands she shoved herself away from him. She huddled, stricken, at the far end of the couch, one hand clamped over her mouth to still her trembling. She thought she might be sick. "Antonio!" she choked.

CHAPTER FOUR

ANTONIO!

Strange about her voice, how little it had changed, was his first thought. Most women's voices ripened with age, but at thirty-seven she sounded much as she had at fifteen, when she had cried his name in those same light, breathy, deceptively guileless tones.

Deep in the bowels of the rusty freighter on which he had fled Europe, he'd been frightened and seasick and half-suffocated by the pervasive odors of diesel fuel and raw coffee, but it was the memory of her voice that had tormented him most. *"Oh, Antonio, we mustn't,"* the whisper sounded in the thrum of the engines. *"Oh, Antonio. Oh...."* In the Rio brothels where he had consoled himself after laboring on the docks all week, it was Elaine's voice that had moaned lying love words against his throat: *"Oh, Antonio, I never imagined it would be like this."* And in the swelter of the Amazon goldfields, where he had wallowed like a hog in the two-by-six-meter rectangle of muck that had constituted his claim, she had laughed at him in the whistle of the pickax slicing the air: *"Antonio, Antonio, what makes you think you're good enough to marry a Welles, Antonio?"*

Now she seemed bereft of speech. In the wavering firelight he studied the slim body crouched at the opposite end of the sofa, the sky-colored eyes watching in wary, bewildered silence. As her fingers dropped away from her mouth, he could see her lips quiver. Her lips, damn them, warm and moist....

Deus, it was stupid to think of wanting her. There had been too many women in his life for him to be distracted now by her moonbeam allure. The adult Elaine might be far removed from the shy, clumsy virgin who had endured his equally inept embraces, but it had not been a desire for sex that had brought him to Colorado. He told himself he ought to be savoring his moment of triumph. He should be glorying in her shock, her confusion as she tried to equate the ignorant, underfed teenager she had spurned with the sleek and accomplished man of the world who confronted her. He was glad she had not identified him on sight; he would have been affronted if recognition had come too readily. Ruy Fonseca Areias's learning and sophistication had been fabricated laboriously, with as much deliberation as his new name, which he had pieced together from a history textbook. He'd hate to think all those years of effort had been wasted.

Still, she did not speak. Ruy reached behind him to switch on the lamp so that he could get a better view of her. Elaine blinked against the light, but otherwise she seemed transfixed by some powerful emotion. Alarm, perhaps? He wanted to believe it was guilt that was making her ivory cheeks ashen. It would be very satisfying to think Elaine Welles regretted the way she had despised him.

"I wondered how long it would take you to remember me," Ruy observed with infuriating calm, hoping to jar her loose from her silence. "I find it curiously... romantic...that it required a kiss to stir your memory. I suppose I ought to be—"

At the sound of his voice, she looked away. "What are you doing here?" Despite her agitation, there was no fear, no hint of compunction in her breathy demand. Staring at the fireplace, she squared her shoulders and exhaled raspily. When the jerky movements of her breast subsided and she spoke again, there was no emotion at all. "Why are you here in Denver, Antonio? Why are you posing as a wealthy Brazilian?"

Ruy's eyes narrowed. "I *am* a wealthy Brazilian. I've lived in South America since I was nineteen, and I made my first million before I was thirty. And my name is no longer Antonio."

She shrugged. "Of course not."

Ruy watched her fingers wrap instinctively around the bangle she always wore. When he'd selected the jewelry for the Welles women, he had intended Elaine's topaz bracelet as a subtle, smugly ironic joke, a glittering replacement for the gold circlet he'd wrenched from her arm during their final, unforgivable argument all those years ago. It had been a jolt to discover the copy on her wrist. He'd never guessed she'd go to the trouble of having a duplicate made, although perhaps he should have. From the beginning, she'd cared more about that blasted trinket than she had about him.

Elaine stared at the bangle. After a long moment she sighed, slipped it off her hand and tossed it onto the cocktail table. The little hoop clinked as it landed on the polished wood surface, alongside his liqueur glass. Somehow Ruy knew she'd never wear it again.

Rubbing her naked wrist, she murmured, "You stole everything from me."

"Only a bauble that you had no difficulty replacing," Ruy countered grimly. "That's hardly 'everything.' Besides, you called me a gigolo—"

"So, like a gigolo, you demanded payment," Elaine finished. "Then you ran off to Brazil. I wondered where—and why—you had gone."

"There didn't seem much point in staying at the school waiting for you to denounce me to my employers. But in fact I didn't leave Europe right away. I hung around Bern for a few months before I . . . realized I'd have more of a future in another part of the world."

"Why? Did you think there would be more poor little rich girls for you to prey on?" Despite her scornful words, Elaine's tone was one of disinterested approval. When she turned to face Ruy, her hands were folded demurely in her lap and she was surveying him calmly. "Obviously relocating to South America was the right career decision for you," she noted. Only the vibration of her lashes as she gazed at him made him wonder if she was in quite as much control as she pretended.

Ruy decided to put her composure to the test. Leaning nearer, he laid his hand experimentally on her forearm. Her muscles were as taut as piano wire.

She recoiled, color flooding her cheeks. "Don't touch me!" she hissed.

He settled back, satisfied. "Why not? You enjoyed my touch well enough when you were a girl. And you liked it a few minutes ago."

He could see her wince. "I didn't know who you were then."

"And now that you do?" Ruy persisted. "When we were teenagers you made it very clear that I wasn't good enough for one of the mighty Welleses of Denver. Well, *meu coração*, the situation has changed. Perhaps you'll feel different when I tell you that in terms of personal assets, I may possibly be wealthier than your father."

"Money has nothing to do with it." Elaine jumped up and padded across the carpet in her stockinged feet to stand in front of the fireplace. Without her three-inch heels she looked smaller than he remembered—petite and defenseless. The fire Ruy had lit earlier was dying, and she hugged her slight shoulders against the chill air while she stared bleakly at the sputtering coals. As the ruddy light faded, her blush subsided. After a moment she knelt on the hearth and placed a fresh log atop the embers. She scooped a handful of cedar chips from a wicker basket and sprinkled them over the fire. One by one the bits of kindling took flame, popping and filling the room with their incense.

Through the thin fabric of her dress Ruy could see the curve of her spine. She looked fragile, oddly vulnerable, as she bent over her handiwork. He watched her carefully draw the safety screen shut. Every motion was graceful and mannered, as studied as the movements of the Kabuki dancers he'd seen during one of his business trips to Tokyo. Her concentration was so intense that somehow, he suspected, she was using activity as a substitute for feeling.

"Tell me what you are thinking, Elaine," he demanded softly.

She did not look at him. "I think it is time for you to go."

"There is much we must talk about."

"We have nothing to talk about."

He paused. "What about your trip to Brazil?"

Elaine jerked around, her imperturbable expression replaced at last by sheer astonishment. She gasped. "Surely you don't expect me to go through with those plans now?"

"Why not? Why should knowing who I am have any effect on your decision to work at Serra Brilhante?"

She rose to her feet. "Because I don't want to have anything to do with you, that's why," she declared bluntly, beginning to pace the room.

Ruy reached for the Grand Marnier he had set aside earlier, half-finished. As he sipped the last of the syrupy liqueur, he noted, "What about the women you claimed to be so eager to help? What about your professed need to feel 'worthwhile'? I thought you were sincere."

"I was sincere." Elaine halted her jerky strides. Brushing a lock of hair away from her forehead, she confronted her adversary. "Look, Antonio—or Ruy, or whatever you call yourself these days—I'm not going to lie. When I offered my services a few minutes ago, at least part of the reason was because it seemed an ideal opportunity to get to know you better, as well. After last night, I felt—I was so drawn—it seemed—" She grimaced. "Hell, I thought you and I might have something special going for us. Even my sister Jennie noticed the electricity. Too bad I had no idea that what I mistook for some sort of mystical attraction was in fact only déjà vu." Shaking her head, she insisted, "I really would like to help the women at your mine site, but I am not a saint. Even for the sake of others, I will not deliberately seek out pain."

Wondering why her confession did not give him more pleasure, Ruy pressed, "And working with me must inevitably cause you pain?"

Elaine smiled with weary dignity. "As a doctor I'm well aware that opening old wounds always hurts. Now, if you don't mind, it's going to take me a while to get used to the idea that you've been toying with me ever since we first laid eyes on each other last night. I've never been big on game playing, especially not sadistic little cat-and-mouse games like this one, and I need some time to work it out in my head. So I want you to leave. Please."

Ruy stood up, straightening his tie. "Very well, I'll go. But I'll be back."

"No," she said. "Don't come back. Don't ever come back."

He reached for his overcoat. "It's too late, love. I'm already here."

ELAINE DRAGGED HERSELF into the kitchen, where she filled the coffeepot with water and fished a packet of beans from the freezer. Maybe the bite of caffeine would alleviate the hollow, fuzzy feeling in her head, she thought glumly. The leaden lassitude was so intense she almost wondered if she were in shock. *Physician, heal thyself,* she thought glumly as the grinder whirred.

But how could anyone heal a wound that had festered for twenty-two years?

Why was he here? Why had he sought her out after all this time? Not for a moment did she believe simple coincidence had brought him to Denver—not all the way from another hemisphere. She put her mind to work. Kate had told her that Dan said A&O had made the first overture to Corminco. Ruy must have recognized the company name, Elaine realized. Of course he had. When they were teenagers, when he had seduced her in hopes of marrying into easy riches, he'd known all about her family fortune.

Now he appeared to have a fortune of his own. *Appeared* to. Was his name the only thing he'd lied about? Suddenly Elaine wondered whether she ought to warn her father, who was clearly unaware of Ruy's true identity—not that he'd ever really known it. In the hospital in

Switzerland, while she had recovered from surgery, Burton and the school officials had ever so gently interrogated her until at last she had revealed the name of the baby's father. But by then Antonio was long gone. After she had laughed at his proposal, he had stolen her bracelet and disappeared into the night like the common little thief that he was.

She wondered what had become of the bangle. She supposed he must have pawned it decades before. She hoped he had. She'd rather he had sold it than carried out his other threat.

"Give that back to me!" she had yelled shrilly, her wrist stinging with pain where he had scraped her, wrenching off the gold hoop. "It's mine!"

"No, it's mine now," he'd taunted, holding it just out of her reach. She could still recall how flushed his face had been, how his dark eyes had been opaque with fury as she'd flailed at him. "If I'm some kind of whore, then I've earned it! Do you think it's any fun screwing a skinny little snob like you? I'm going to find me a *real* woman—lots of women, who'll do anything I want them to. When one of them pleases me enough, maybe I'll give your precious bracelet to her!"

Had he done it? Had Maggie Burton Welles's golden bracelet eventually graced the arm of some European streetwalker? Elaine didn't want to know.

Staring at the coffee maker, Elaine admitted to herself that she did not have the courage to tell her father the truth about his new business partner. The episode with Antonio had been her most shameful failure in Burton's eyes—one he seemed to have blotted from his memory—and she could not bear to remind him of it. She vowed she wouldn't, unless it proved absolutely necessary. *Maybe, please God, it will never become necessary.*

Maybe the consortium is legitimate.... Maybe, she thought in desperation, for some obscure reason of his own her long-lost lover had decided to seek her out and then only secondarily realized the advantages of dealing with her father. Maybe. In any case, Burton Welles was an astute and formidable businessman in his own right, with a lifetime of experience behind him—definitely not an easy man to cheat.

But whether or not Elaine warned her father, she needed to confide in someone. The question was who. At the hospital there was a neurosurgeon she'd dated in the past; they'd remained friends and they still sometimes used each other as sounding boards for their problems. But Elaine felt uncomfortable asking one old lover for advice on another. Besides, his new wife probably wouldn't appreciate his receiving calls from her at two in the morning.

Her closest women friends were her sisters, but they'd both been little more than babies when Elaine had suffered through her first affair. By the time they were old enough to understand what had happened, the topic had become a non-subject in the Welles household. And the timing didn't seem right to reveal that dusty secret now. Jennie was still smarting over her breakup with Andrew, and Elaine had sensed lately that all was not blissful between Kate and Dan. When her sisters had problems of their own, she could hardly expect them to listen patiently to her sad tale of something that had happened over two decades ago.

That only left her mother—who had pretended that Elaine's near-fatal illness was a ruptured appendix followed by peritonitis; who had sighed with mute despair as she had packed up Elaine's tiny christening gown—the

gown she'd been saving for her firstborn's first child—
and donated it to the Junior League rummage sale.

The rich, dark fragrance of French-roast coffee wafted
under her nostrils as she settled on the sofa again. Noting the unopened box of candy on the cocktail table, she
wished distractedly that she could believe the folklore
that claimed chocolate contained enzymes to cure broken hearts. Not that her heart was broken, of course.
Right now she was just bewildered—and damned mad.

With a sigh she reached for the telephone, "Oh,
Mommy, please be there for me this once," she whispered as she punched her parents' number.

The call was answered on the first ring. Elaine could
hear the receiver rattle as someone fumbled to pick it up.
"Whoever this is, this had bloody well better be important," Burton grumbled sleepily.

Elaine hung up without speaking.

"THANK GOD you're here!" Kate exclaimed, pouncing
on Elaine as soon as she stepped through the arched entryway into her parents' home. "I don't know what I
would have done if you hadn't come tonight."

Neither do I, Elaine thought, her boot heels clicking on
the marble terrazzo. Tired of using taxis while she waited
for her BMW's repairs to be completed, she'd rented a
car early that morning before making her hospital
rounds. She had considered shopping or going to the art
museum in the afternoon. Instead, she'd spent most of
the day lying on her couch in a haze, exhausted by her
sleepless night, yet too agitated and confused to rest. At
one point she had tried to telephone Jennie in New York,
but there had been no answer.

"I was afraid you might have to work today," Kate
said.

"My patients have apparently decided to let me have Sunday evening off for a change, knock on wood."

"You do look a little tired," Kate agreed.

Elaine handed her coat to the maid, revealing trim wool slacks and a hand-knit sweater. Pasting a cheerful expression on her lips, she murmured her thanks and turned again to her sister. Her smile faded slightly when she noticed that Kate was wearing a silk shirtwaist of deep rose, the becoming color offset by the rather staid cut of the dress. Her hair, which was the same honey-brown color as her eyes, hung straight and shining to her shoulders, where it was clipped into an unimaginative pageboy. Kate was an attractive woman, and Elaine wondered, not for the first time, how she always managed to look as if she'd just stepped out of *Vogue*—the 1955 edition.

Squelching the catty thought, Elaine asked, "What's up? When Mom called this morning, she caught me on my way out, so all she had time to say was that she wanted me to join you for Sunday dinner. I assumed it was only the family. I didn't realize I was supposed to dress."

"You look fine," Kate said, "warm and comfortable." She grimaced. "I would have worn slacks, too, except that Dan has decided I'm getting too hippy for pants, and he's already being so bullheaded that I decided I'd better not antagonize him any more than necessary."

Elaine tensed. She'd forgotten that she wasn't the only Welles woman with problems. The bad vibes she'd sensed between her sister and brother-in-law seemed stronger than ever. "That sounds ominous."

"Not 'ominous' exactly, but..." Kate shrugged. "Oh, hell, he's mad at me because I was busy yesterday and he had to take Melissa along with him and Danny to the Broncos game."

"Why shouldn't Melissa go to the football game if she wants to?" Elaine asked. "Don't you all have season passes?"

"Yes, but if I'm not there, it means Dan might actually have to pay some attention to his daughter for a change," Kate snapped, shaking her head in exasperation. After a moment she sighed and admitted, "Of course, Dan's being a jerk today mainly because the reason I didn't go with them to the game was that I was attending a seminar at the university."

"Oh, really? What was it about?"

Kate's expression was inscrutable. "Women resuming their education after long delays."

Elaine listened with surprise. Kate had been eighteen, a college sophomore, when she'd married Dan, and after she had become pregnant on her honeymoon, both her new husband and her parents had urged her to drop out of school, which she did. Until now, Elaine hadn't guessed that Kate regretted not earning her degree. "So you've decided to go back and finish your B.A.?" she asked. "That's great!"

Kate smiled skeptically, her eyes shifting toward the interior of the house. "I wish everybody else agreed with you."

Realizing her sister needed to share her frustration with someone, Elaine suggested delicately, "Maybe we could have lunch sometime soon. No Mom, no kids, just the two of us. It's been a while since we've had time simply to talk."

"I'd like that," Kate said with relief. She turned and led Elaine through the house to the library-music room, where Burton, Carolyn and Dan were waiting.

After kissing her parents, Elaine plopped into a puffy leather armchair near the grand piano. She glanced around fondly. She loved the room with its musty perfume of paste and old paper. When she was a girl, she used to spend hours secreted in it, practicing scales or poring over the collection of books dating back four generations. As a family the Welleses all read a great deal, but by the time Elaine left home for college, she had gone through virtually every book in the house. Her mother had often chided her for spending so much time reading when she could have been at the country club perfecting her tennis game or socializing with other young people....

Elaine noticed that Melissa and Danny were missing, and asked curiously, "Where are the twins?"

Kate said, "Their nanny took them to the Oktoberfest in Golden. Today was their last chance, but I thought I'd never convince Miss O'Brian to switch one of her days off."

Dan, who was manning the bar cart that had been wheeled into the room, griped, "Considering how much we pay that woman, you'd think she'd be happy to work an occasional Sunday. Not that I understand why a couple of twelve-year-olds still need a nanny."

Kate's voice grew strained. "They don't *need* a nanny, darling. They need someone who can drive them to school and dancing lessons and computer class—"

"I thought that's what mothers were for," Burton interjected.

Kate's mouth tightened as she glanced at her father; then she turned back to her husband. "After the first of the year, when the new semester starts," she said steadily, "I'm going to be too busy to play chauffeur."

The tension in the room suddenly thickened. Elaine stared at her hands, trying to avoid being drawn into the quarrel. Sometimes she wondered how her sister had endured living with their parents all these years. The lack of privacy would have driven her crazy ages ago, she thought.

The house was huge, of course, and when Kate and Dan had first married, both were still in school; it had seemed logical for them to make their home with her parents. While they'd been absent on their South Seas honeymoon, several rooms on the second floor had been remodeled into an apartment for the newlyweds—a pied-a-terre to accommodate them until they decided what they would do with their young lives. But somehow the couple had never gotten around to moving out.

Elaine glanced covertly at her brother-in-law. Did Dan mind being a guest in his own home, or was he too enamored of the tasteful luxury that only "old money" could provide to quibble? His own background was eminently respectable, comfortable and upper-middle-class, but on his own he never could have aspired to the standard of living he enjoyed now. Of course, on his own he never could have gotten where he was at Corminco.

Perhaps it was because she was older that Elaine had always failed to appreciate her brother-in-law's appeal. She knew Daniel Brock, Sr., was intelligent and diligent at his job, and she conceded that he was, as the cliché went, high, wide and handsome—a big, well-muscled man with hazel eyes and strong features, who worked out with near-religious zeal every day, so that at thirty-three, only his thinning brown hair differentiated him from the football team's star running back who had managed to run circles around the two younger Welles sisters thirteen years earlier.

Because Elaine had been away from Denver, finishing up her medical residency the year Jennie started college, she had never known exactly what had happened between the girls and Dan. One day Elaine received a note from Jennie gushing about the gorgeous guy who had actually asked her—a freshman—to his fraternity mixer; two months later eighteen-year-old Kate telephoned to ask if Elaine would be maid of honor at her wedding. Only when Elaine learned that Jennie had run away to New York did she realize that her two sisters had both been talking about the same man.

Carolyn pressed, "Kate, dear, are you really determined to return to college?"

"Yes, Mother, I—"

"Wait a minute," Dan blustered, "you know we haven't agreed to that."

Kate whirled to face her husband. "Dammit, I *told* you—"

Burton said quietly, "All right, you two, that's enough."

At that understated command, Kate and Dan fell silent, glancing warily at Burton like naughty children. As Kate subsided into a chair, Carolyn smiled soothingly at her son-in-law and suggested, "Why don't you fix Elaine a drink?"

Dan grimaced. "Sure, Mom. How about it, Elaine? You in the mood for a cocktail or a liqueur?"

"We just opened a new bottle of Grand Marnier," Kate chimed dutifully, her cheeks still flushed with anger. "I know you like it."

Elaine shook her head. "Thanks, but I don't really want anything right now. Maybe later."

Carolyn glanced at the Sèvres clock on the mantel. "I'm afraid there may not be time later. We're scheduled to begin eating as soon as our guest arrives, and he should be here any moment now."

Elaine stiffened. "Guest?"

"Of course, dear. Senhor Areias. He was most apologetic about being so rushed, what with his leaving for Brazil in the morning, but I assured him we'd be delighted to share any time he can spare us from his busy schedule." Carolyn hesitated. "I assumed you knew he was coming."

Reaching for the bangle that was no longer on her wrist, Elaine muttered hoarsely, "No. I had no idea."

Burton leaned forward in his chair, his brow furrowed as he regarded Elaine with the same piercing gaze he'd trained on her sister moments before. *My turn,* she thought, bracing herself.

"Didn't you and Areias go out together last night?" he demanded.

"We went to dinner and a concert. I haven't spoken to him since."

"That's odd," Carolyn noted. "Considering how perfect Senhor Areias's manners are, I would have imagined he'd telephone or send flowers. Saturday morning he sent me orchids and a note thanking me for the banquet."

Elaine shrugged airily. "Well, An—Ruy did bring me a box of candy last night."

Burton heard her tongue stumble over the name, and he pounced. "What's the matter?"

"You did have a good time, didn't you?" Carolyn pressed, looking concerned. "Surely you didn't quarrel. He seemed so taken with you."

"I had a lovely time yesterday." For once Elaine could hedge with a clear conscience. She *had* had a lovely time with Ruy yesterday. The hellish part hadn't occurred until after midnight.

Out of the corner of her eye she watched Burton sink back into his chair, still frowning. "Father, everything's fine," she insisted.

The expression in his dark blue eyes did not change. "I hope it is—" His words were cut short by the sound of the doorbell. Elaine's fingers dug into the soft leather arms of the chair. "That'll be Areias now," Burton announced as he rose.

"I'll go with you," Carolyn said, looping her arm through her husband's. As they headed toward the hallway, Burton paused. He glanced back at his firstborn, who was still seated tensely. "Listen, girl," he said, his voice low and emphatic, "even if you and Areias have had some kind of disagreement, I want you to remember that the man is my business associate and a guest in my home."

Elaine smiled primly. "I'll mind my manners, Father."

Burton nodded. Then he said, "I also want you to think seriously before you freeze him off the way you seem to do most of the men who are attracted to you. Someone like Areias shows up once in a lifetime, you know."

Elaine watched her parents disappear into the hallway. She could hear the maid at the door, shoes shuffling on marble terrazo, the splash of distant laughter. Elaine shivered. *You're wrong, Dad,* she thought fatalistically. This was the second time the man who called himself Ruy Fonseca Areias had intruded on her life, and she wasn't sure she had the strength to chase him out again.

"MY DEAR ELAINE, you should have told me you'd be here today. I would have been delighted to give you a lift."

Elaine tried not to flinch as Ruy's fingers caught her shoulders in an *abraço*, the same ceremonial hug he'd just bestowed on Carolyn and Kate. Her gaze met and locked with his as he drew her against him, his silver mustache brushing her cheek. When his lips touched her skin, Elaine jerked back. Ruy's fingers tightened, and deep in his black-gold eyes something flashed darkly, like summer lightning.

At last he released her. Aware of her family watching with benign approval, Elaine said stiltedly, "Thank you for your kind offer, but I rented a car of my own this morning."

"How fortunate for you—but how sad for me. I was enjoying our drives together."

His effusive charm made her want to grit her teeth. She wondered why none of the others could see how excessive Ruy's gallantry was, how downright insolent. Damn him, he was mocking them all, and despite her determination not to let him rattle her, Elaine felt her temper rise. Flashing a sugary smile, she retorted, "Of course I would have had to arrange my own transportation after tomorrow, anyway, wouldn't I, *senhor*? That is when you're going home, isn't it?"

Out of the corner of her eye she noticed her mother's brows lift at her tone. Abruptly Carolyn announced, "Now that we're all here, dinner is ready." Elaine accepted the diversion gratefully, but as she passed her mother, she could feel her scowling.

When they strolled into the dining room, Elaine almost groaned aloud when her mother indicated the seating arrangement. Ruy was placed at Burton's right,

Elaine beside him. The stern reproof in Carolyn's expression made protest impossible. Somehow Elaine managed not to recoil when Ruy's fingers brushed her shoulder as he held her chair for her, but it was impossible not to be aware of him, the heat of his thigh almost touching hers, the woodsy fragrance of his cologne. His lowering presence was a constant assault on her composure. Oh, God, she didn't want to be aware of him. He was her nemesis, her enemy. She didn't want to remember that less than twenty-four hours earlier she had flung herself at him. She did not want to admit that sheer luck was the only thing that had stopped her from making love again with the man who had ruined her life.

To distract herself, Elaine flashed a smile at Kate and Dan seated across the table and she asked her brother-in-law to tell her about the Broncos game he'd seen the day before. She could tell her unusual request startled him— Elaine's interest in the local football team was casual, at best—but after a moment Dan launched with relish into a play-by-play analysis of the game that kept her occupied through the soup course and the entrée. The tactic continued to work until the maid cleared the table for dessert, and Burton demanded suddenly, "Elaine, what's this Areias tells me about you turning down a chance to go to Brazil?"

Elaine started, almost choking on her coffee. Everyone stared at her as she swallowed with difficulty. Slowly she turned toward her father. She refused to meet Ruy's gaze. Setting her cup down carefully, she took a deep breath and declared, "Good grief, Father, when would I find time to go to Brazil? I have a practice here in Denver to tend to, you know."

Burton frowned. "But Areias tells me you admitted yourself last night that you could get somebody to take over for you, at least briefly."

"It's not that easy, Dad." Elaine felt herself begin to tremble. Instinctively she fumbled for the bangle. When she remembered too late that the bracelet was now at the bottom of one of her dresser drawers, she stilled her nervous fingers by knotting them around the napkin in her lap. "I have a job, you know—responsibilities. Besides, I really don't want to go to Brazil."

"Are you sure, darling?" Carolyn asked anxiously. "I've always thought Brazil would be a fascinating country to visit. Besides, I think a change of scene would do you a tremendous amount of good. You work so hard, I worry about you sometimes. I can't remember when you last took a real vacation."

The loving concern in her mother's voice tore at Elaine. "This wouldn't be a vacation, Mom," she explained gently.

"No, Mrs. Welles," Ruy's deep voice cut in. "I'm afraid if Elaine does come to my country, she may find herself working harder than she ever has before." Quickly he outlined the situation at Serra Brilhante. "But although I'm sure you would worry about your daughter overtaxing herself, you could take great pride in knowing that she is aiding people who truly need her skill and her knowledge."

Across the table Kate exclaimed, "God, sis, I think it sounds exciting. To get away from Denver and really *do* something—if I were you, I'd jump at the chance!"

Dan added thoughtfully, "And you know, Elaine, I have the feeling that having a family member on-site might actually help start the gears of this partnership turning more easily. I'll be flying down to South America periodically to check on things, but if you were there at the mines all the time, I'm sure it would mean a lot to the workers, sort of a goodwill gesture from Corminco."

Elaine's throat tightened as she listened to the arguments the people around the table were throwing at her. She felt surrounded, caught—enmeshed in a web of love and duty that was beginning to choke her. Her welling panic was only made worse by the knowledge that there was a way out, a blade that would cut her free, if only she dared use it. She stared at the faces staring at her, their various expressions imperious, urgent, sympathetic—triumphant.

Goddamn him, he knew he'd won. For some reason he intended for her to come to Brazil, and the night before, he'd used reverse psychology to make her think the trip was her own idea. The idea would have worked if she hadn't recognized his kiss. But today he was taking no chances; he was using something far more powerful even than his potent sexual attraction. He knew Elaine's loyalty to her family was so strong that she'd endure almost anything rather than hurt the people she loved by telling them who he really was.

She glared up at him, her eyes glowing in her white face. "You bastard," she whispered through frozen lips, so that only he heard her. "You bloody manipulative bastard."

"I want you in Brazil," Ruy said. Reaching for her hand, he freed her bloodless fingers from the shredded linen that had been her napkin. As he lifted her palm to his lips, he grinned winningly at the others and murmured, "Thank you all for your help. Elaine is a very strong woman. I never could have persuaded her without you."

Drearily Elaine watched the ease with which Ruy seduced her family—the same ease with which he'd seduced her twenty-two years before. Suddenly the sight was too much for her. Choking out, "I need some air," she scraped back her chair and fled the room.

The terrace looked forlorn and long abandoned, lawn chairs looming like gravestones beneath their canvas tarps, wet leaves heaped in soggy drifts against the wall. Hugging her arms to keep out the chill that penetrated her sweater, Elaine stared blindly into the night. Behind her she heard the French doors swing open as someone stepped out onto the terrace.

Ruy said, "You've upset your parents."

She did not turn around. "You've upset *me*," she retorted, "but I don't suppose that matters to you, does it?"

"It matters more than you know, my dear—not that I expect you to believe me." She heard him exhale impatiently. "Look, contrary to what you accused me of earlier, I do not enjoy manipulating people. If I could have convinced you to go to Serra Briñante without involving your family, I should have done so. But since you recognized me you've behaved as if your offended sensibilities are the only things that matter—as if blaming me for a stupid childhood affair is more important than helping women in dire need of someone with your special skills."

"Stupid childhood affair." Elaine winced. If she were a woman given to melodramatic gestures, she would have slapped him for his casual cruelty in dismissing the pivotal event of her life. Instead she fought to control the emotions roughening her voice as she turned to face him. "I'm not the only obstetrician in the world," she pointed out with as much dignity as she could feign, "or even in

the Americas. If I don't take the job, you'll find another doctor who will. I do not for one moment believe you're as desperate as you claim to be."

"Of course you don't believe me. How could you? You're a Welles." She could not see Ruy's expression, hidden by shadows as he loomed over her, but the silken scorn with which he spat the name told her her flippant tone had deceived him. "You don't know the meaning of the word 'desperate,' do you? You've never wanted for anything in your life, or been alone or afraid."

Because of you, I was so alone and afraid I almost died. Elaine wondered if the words spoken aloud would wipe that smug superiority from Ruy's voice. Maybe— but she knew she'd never speak the words aloud. The last thing she wanted or needed was his pity.

Sighing heavily, knowing he was going to misinterpret her acquiescence as some sort of personal victory, Elaine said, "All right, damn it, I give up. You're wrong about me, but I'm not going to argue anymore. You've got my family on your side, and while I can fight you, I can't fight them. I'll go."

CHAPTER FIVE

"SEJAM BEM-VINDOS A BRASIL," the Varig stewardess welcomed the passengers as the jumbo jet banked for its descent. But to Elaine, yawning and peering blearily through the window into the night, the forest of light-checkered skyscrapers and glowing highways spreading to the dark horizon beneath her did not resemble any mental image she had of South America. She'd changed planes in Miami and, worn-out by preparations for the trip, had fallen asleep almost as soon as the wheels left the tarmac. Now, many hours later, she wondered if during her stuporous slumber the pilot could have executed a U-turn over the Caribbean, so that what she was seeing was Detroit or Chicago. She tried to stroke the bangle for reassurance, forgetting in her drowsy state that the bracelet had not been around her wrist for weeks and would never be there again.

"First time to São Paulo?" the man in the seat beside her asked. Earlier in the flight Elaine had been too exhausted to notice her traveling companion. He wore a business suit and cowboy boots, and his slow Texas drawl sounded hearteningly familiar.

Elaine brushed her hair out of her eyes and straightened in her seat. Her neck and shoulders ached. A glass of Chablis sat untasted on the tray before her, alongside the customs declaration form the stewardess must have distributed while she'd slept. "My first time to Brazil, period," she mumbled as she took a sip of the wine, hoping it would ease her cramped muscles.

"Well, I guarantee you're going to love it. This is an amazing country. Take this city here—forty miles across, and most of it only dates back to the 1950s, when the Brazilian auto industry got started."

"I had no idea it would be so big," Elaine commented.

"The population's more than doubled in the past decade. I make several trips down here each year, and I swear the place is bigger every time I see it."

Elaine could tell the Texan was enjoying her interest. "You deal in automobiles?"

He laughed. "No, ma'am—orange juice. Tankers full of it. I'll bet you didn't know that half the frozen o.j. Americans drink for breakfast comes from Brazil, did you?"

"No, I had no idea. I thought Brazilians grew coffee."

"They do. Coffee and oranges, sugarcane and soybeans: just about anything you can name. As I said, it's quite a country." Pausing, the man eyed Elaine's slender form appreciatively. "And what brings a pretty little thing like you to São Paulo? I assume you're not here for a vacation, because most tourists go to Rio."

She shrugged. "Actually, São Paulo is just a stopping-off point for me. I'm a doctor, and I'm going to be working in a rural town in Minas Gerais."

Her companion's affable expression darkened as he studied her more closely, focusing on her sleek grooming and her obviously expensive clothes. "My God, honey," he muttered, his easy drawl tightening with concern, "I surely hope you know what you're getting yourself into."

"What do you mean?"

He shook his head. "Brazil may have one of the fastest growing economies in the world, but two-thirds of the people still don't have enough to eat, and they suffer from illnesses that are just memories at home, things like polio and dengue fever."

"I've seen hunger and disease in America, too," Elaine countered quietly. "Life isn't perfect anywhere. I've spent a lot of time practicing at an inner-city clinic, and believe me, in a place like that, sooner or later you come up against just about every aspect of human misery. I've learned to cope."

The man looked unconvinced. "Well, if you're sure—"

"I'm sure." She turned to gaze out the window again. *At least, I think I'm sure.*

The truth was, she admitted wryly, during the six weeks since she'd committed herself to this trip, she had deliberately allowed herself no time to think. She'd kept herself too busy to brood, because she knew that once she started debating the wisdom of her actions, she'd also have to consider the ease with which she'd allowed herself to be coerced into coming—a subject whose implications still troubled and confused her. She'd thought she had more backbone. No matter how often she told herself she was lucky to have the unique opportunity to work in a challenging new environment and assist her family as well, she was embarrassed by the uncharacteristic vulnerability she'd displayed in agreeing to come. It helped very little to remind herself cynically that successful businessmen like her father and Ruy were accustomed to steamrolling other people.

And whatever he may have been once, Ruy was now a very successful businessman. In addition to pumping

Dan for all the information he could give her about Companhia Areias e Oliveira, Elaine had made discreet inquiries outside the family. One of the hospital trustees was a banker with connections in international finance, who knew Ruy by reputation. He verified that A&O's head was admired in South American circles as a *despechante*—a facilitator, a man who "got things done."

He'd certainly gotten things done for Elaine. At the same time she was reassuring herself that Ruy's credentials were legitimate, he'd been arranging her trip. Most of the details had been handled via telex between Corminco and A&O, but in addition, Elaine had received a call from an official at the Brazilian consulate, who had thanked her for her kind interest in the welfare of his compatriots and had told her that Senhor Areias had asked him personally to assist her with the paperwork necessary for her visa. An open-ended airline ticket had arrived by mail soon after, requiring only Elaine's confirmation of her travel dates. She had also been approached by a Mrs. DaCosta, a tutor from the language department at Denver State, who said she'd been hired to give Dr. Welles private lessons in conversational Portuguese. Elaine thought she might have been very grateful for the way Ruy had taken charge of her travel plans, if only once he'd bothered to contact her directly.

É proibido fumar. The no-smoking light blinked on overhead, and the stewardess shuffled quickly around the first-class cabin, gathering glasses and cups and making sure that carry-on luggage was stowed safely for the landing. Elaine handed over her half-finished wine and tightened the safety belt across her lap. Through the porthole she could see the sparkling grid of runway lights rising to meet the jetliner; her stomach shuddered queasily as the plane descended. She wished she had time to go to the lavatory and freshen up.

"Ma'am, are you absolutely certain you're all right? You look a mite peaked."

"It's been hectic getting ready for this trip," Elaine admitted with wry understatement. She picked up the customs form and began filling it out—a simple chore since, at Ruy's suggestion, she had decided to delay most of her personal shopping until she reached São Paulo. He assured her she'd be able to find anything she needed. As a result, except for her clothes and a few pieces of medical equipment, the only item of real value in Elaine's luggage was the blue topaz bracelet, which she'd packed on impulse. Now she couldn't even remember what had prompted her to bring it.

Elaine had been grateful for Ruy's hint about shopping. There had simply been too few hours for her to accomplish all the things that had to be done in Denver. Besides contacting all her friends and closing up her condo, she'd had to arrange for other doctors to absorb her patient load for the next few months. That duty was not a small one, but it had proved easier than making those patients understand why she was going away. Many of them seemed to feel betrayed; one or two had actually cried. Although Elaine supposed those tears might be considered a compliment, a testimony to the deep bond she shared with the women she treated, they had made her feel even more uneasy. Who was she to say the women in Denver needed her any less than those in Brazil?

She'd suffered even more qualms when the neurosurgeon had kissed her goodbye. They embraced as friends now rather than old lovers, but still Elaine found herself wondering what would have happened if she'd been

married or seriously committed when Ruy had come back
into her life. Would the loving support of another man
have given her the courage to defy him? She wasn't quite
sure....

RUY WAITED RESTLESSLY at the top of the jetway. Despite the late hour, the terminal building was crowded,
and the air was stuffy and humid with the press of bodies. Around him tired children fretted due to the heat,
and their parents wilted in once-crisp summer cottons.
His wool suit felt almost unbearable. Shifting his briefcase to the arm that carried his topcoat, Ruy tugged at the
knot on his tie. He squinted down the hollow length of
the jetway. The plane had been on the ground for some
time. What was causing the delay? After what seemed
like an hour, a Varig stewardess emerged, pushing an elderly man in a wheelchair. As she trudged up the ramp,
the throng of debarking passengers crowded and stalled
behind her like jammed logs in a stream. When she
reached the top, almost even with Ruy, she turned out of
the line of traffic, and the throng broke free. People who
had been waiting behind Ruy rushed forward, weeping
and crying out names. Ruy stood like a rock in their
midst. Ignoring the mob that parted and swirled around
him, he peered narrowly down the jetway, waiting for a
glimpse of one pale head.

At last he spotted Elaine. As it had the first time he
ever saw her, her gleaming fairness beckoned to him, pale
fire shining through breaks in the crowd. He stepped
forward, ready to call her name. The word stopped in his
throat. She was strolling alongside a man dressed in a
business suit and cowboy boots, and Ruy's mouth tightened when he realized the two of them were engrossed in
conversation.

Hell, he might have known she'd pick up a man en route. The Welles women seemed to attract them like bees. According to the private investigator Ruy had hired in Colorado, none of the sisters lacked for male companionship. The little hausfrau, of course, appeared to be devoted to her children and thoroughly under the thumb of that stuffy husband of hers, but over the past ten years the actress—the statuesque beauty with the bold eyes—had flitted through one well-publicized affair after another, at least according to the supermarket scandal sheets. But Elaine—here the detective's work had been frustrated, the results superficial. Dr. Elaine Welles was a prominent Denver obstetrician who divided her practice between patients of her own social standing and others on welfare. She contributed to local charities and was a patron of both the Denver Museum of Art and the symphony. She was presumed to be heterosexual. She attended cultural functions in the company of a variety of men, but she conducted her personal life with such discretion and decorum that even close friends hesitated to guess how intimate her dealings with those men might be. However, it was common knowledge that, several years before, she had dated a fellow physician exclusively for many months. Although they were never officially engaged, he had begun to talk of marriage and a family. Nobody knew why she'd broken off the relationship.

Reading the detective's report, Ruy had thought cynically of the time she'd turned down his own proposal. He wondered if any man would ever be good enough to marry Elaine Welles.

But Elaine's marriage prospects had nothing to do with the reasons he had brought her to Brazil. There would be no husband or lover fighting for her now, when after all these years she was here at last. Separated from her family—on his home turf—she would be at a distinct disadvantage in any confrontation. In his company, she was in his power. He had plotted his strategy carefully, and he certainly had no intention of letting his plans be thwarted at the last moment by some homespun champion she'd happened to meet on the plane.

Elbowing his way through the crowd, he crossed the remaining few yards that separated them and planted himself squarely in front of Elaine and her companion. Involuntarily she jerked back, alarmed, but her face lightened with recognition when she lifted her head. "Oh, Ruy," she exclaimed, relieved, "I was just telling—" She gasped in surprise as he dropped his coat and briefcase at his feet and dragged her into his arms.

Her mouth was open as he kissed her, and he gave her no opportunity to protest before he invaded, plundering her wine-scented sweetness. When he felt her stiffen, trying to withdraw, he laced the fingers of one hand into her silky hair, holding her head immobile while he pinioned her body against his with the other. Her lashes fluttered frantically, like trapped moths. He began to move his hard lips across hers, urging then demanding a response, until at last she gave it to him. With a sigh she closed her eyes, and all along the rigid length of his body he could feel her soften, melt against him.

Ruy raised his head just enough to peek around. The cowboy was gone. Loosening his grip so that he was cradling rather than imprisoning her, Ruy brushed his lips across her forehead and murmured, "Welcome to Brazil, Elaine."

She stared up at him dazedly. "My God," she whispered, her voice reedy and breathless, "is that the way you greet all your visitors?"

"Only the beautiful ones," he quipped. He gazed into her face, noting with a hint of compunction how tired she looked. Except for the kiss-stung pink of her lips, her features were pale, her clear eyes clouded. He could count every one of her thirty-seven years in the faint lines of fatigue marring the marble purity of her skin. The realization jarred Ruy. In his mind's eye she was still fifteen.

He bent down to pick up his coat and briefcase, draping them over one arm while he kept the other anchored at her waist. He wondered if it was weariness that made her accept his touch so meekly. "So how was your flight?"

"It was pleasant enough, long but uneventful. No bad weather or hijackings."

"Thank God for that. I was worried. You look exhausted."

"It's just jet lag," Elaine dismissed his concern. "Flying always wears me out. I don't travel well."

"Like fine wine?"

She chuckled tiredly. "Right now I feel more like a flat Coke."

Ruy tossed back his head and laughed, a deep, full-bodied shout of good humor. "Poor darling," he declared, "we must do something about restoring your fizz. You don't have time to feel flat on your first visit to Brazil. There's too much to do."

"Yes, that's what—" Elaine broke off. Ruy watched her survey the crowd with a puzzled frown. "He's gone," she muttered in surprise.

Deliberately keeping his tone low and dry, Ruy asked, "Your traveling companion?" When Elaine looked blank, he continued, "The man in the boots. I saw you talking as you left the plane. I wondered who he was. You seemed quite friendly."

Elaine shrugged. "Actually, I have no idea who he was, except the person who happened to be sitting in the seat alongside mine. He wished me a pleasant trip, but we never exchanged names."

"I see." Ruy hesitated, aware that he was liable to sound jealous—or worse, avuncular. "Since you're here at my invitation, perhaps I should caution you about speaking to strangers. In general Brazilian men don't wait for an introduction to approach a woman they fancy. To some, even as innocently casual a conversation as the one you just described would be considered a blatant come-on."

As he feared, Elaine regarded him quizzically, one brow in an ironic arch. "You remind me of the house-mother in my college dorm. You don't need to tell me how to cope with alien cultures. I have lived abroad before, you know."

Ruy's mouth quirked. "So you have, *querida*, so you have—and just think what an unsavory character you became involved with that time."

Elaine tensed. She did not move, but her abrupt withdrawal was as obvious as it would have been if she had shoved him away. The easy camaraderie of the moment before had vanished. Ruy suppressed a curse. Clearly Elaine resented even the most ingenuous reference to their past.

He debated trying to cajole her back into good humor, then decided against it. Dropping his arm, he informed her brusquely, "Come along, please. There are people waiting to meet you."

Elaine struggled to stay alongside him as he stalked through the crowd. "But don't I have to go through Customs first?"

"That can be taken care of later. First I want to introduce you to my associate and his wife, before I must leave."

"Leave?" She clutched at his arm, her fingers catching in the silky wool overcoat he carried as she forced him to halt. He could tell that for the first time the significance of that coat, so at odds with the light clothes worn by most people in the terminal, had registered. "You're going away," she said hollowly.

Ruy nodded curtly. "I have business in Antwerp, at the gem exchange. My plane leaves within the hour. I should have been in Belgium days ago, but I delayed my departure in order to be here to meet your flight. I thought that on your arrival in a foreign land you might appreciate seeing a familiar face, even if only for a few moments."

"I—I do appreciate it," she stammered in confusion, licking her lips. "I appreciate everything you've done— the visa, the tickets, the language lessons—now even a welcoming committee. Thank you. I'm sorry if I seemed ungrateful. It's just—"

"It's just that you're exhausted and you didn't expect to be left on your own in a foreign country quite so soon," Ruy finished for her. "Well, don't worry. Come, let me introduce you to João and Sonia, and then you won't be alone any longer. You will stay at their home while I'm in Europe, and with any luck, by the time I return you will be rested and your old effervescent self again."

Elaine frowned. "I didn't realize you would expect me to stay with your friends. I had my travel agent book me into the Maksoud Plaza."

Trust a Welles to pick the finest hotel on the continent, Ruy thought dryly. Aloud he noted, "You should have guessed I'd see arrangements were made for the time you spend in São Paulo. The Maksoud is wonderful, of course—very modern, ultradeluxe—but I think you might enjoy the Oliveiras' home more. It was built around the turn of the century by João's wife's grandfather, a coffee baron, with every luxury the Belle Époque could provide.''

"I'm sure it's charming," Elaine said, "but I don't want to impose."

"You won't be imposing. João and Sonia have been looking forward to your visit for weeks." *Besides,* Ruy added silently, gazing down at her with silent conviction, *as long as you're with them, you're still in my power, and I have no intention of letting you slip away from me even for a few days.*

When Ruy escorted Elaine to the spot where João Santos Oliveira and his wife were waiting away from the crush, he noted with annoyance that his associate was showing the effects of the heat. Despite the fact that João's rangy body was draped in a summer-weight silk suit far more appropriate to the muggy atmosphere inside the terminal than the woolens Ruy wore, his craggy face was beaded with moisture, his thinning, sandy hair visibly damp. Ruy could see Elaine suppress a grimace as she accepted João's damp handshake. For all the man's aristocratic pretensions, he sweated like a pig.

Although Ruy knew João understood spoken English fairly well, the speech with which he welcomed Elaine was so heavily and unnaturally accented that it sounded as if he'd learned the words phonetically. Beside him his wife, Sonia, a petite, voluptuous brunette in a designer silk dress, listened in blank incomprehension. When Elaine shifted to faltering Portuguese, the woman's wary, embarrassed frown transformed into a relieved smile.

Sonia babbled an effusive greeting and hugged Elaine, touching her cheek to hers and kissing the air.

When Sonia released her, Elaine turned helplessly to Ruy. "This isn't going to work. I'd better go to the hotel, after all. At least somebody there is bound to speak English. It's very kind of your friends to welcome me, but my Portuguese is far too limited for me to possibly keep up."

"From what little I heard, you seem to be doing all right."

"Well, I'm not. If I do stay with them, I'm going to need that interpreter you promised me." She paused. "You did find an interpreter, didn't you?"

"Of course I did," Ruy said impatiently. "I'm well aware that a few lessons in conversational Portuguese will be inadequate for your work at Serra Brilhante. One of the nurses I've hired is thoroughly bilingual. She's already at the site."

Elaine sighed. "That's a relief. But it still doesn't explain how you expect me to stay with these people if I can't communicate with them."

"They do say the quickest way to learn a new language is to be thrown among people who speak nothing else."

"My grandfather tried to teach my father how to swim that way. He almost drowned."

"Somehow I have trouble imagining you getting in over your head," Ruy said. "Still, if you insist . . . João, Sonia, *a doutora* Welles—"

His words were cut short by the public-address system. First in Portuguese, then in Spanish, English, Italian, German and Japanese, a mechanical-sounding voice echoed through the terminal: "Last call for passengers boarding Flight 372 for Lisbon and Brussels" —Ruy's head jerked. Glancing at his wristwatch, he nodded apologetically to the Oliveiras, then turned to Elaine. "I'm sorry, my dear, but I'm afraid there's no time for me to help you work out your communication problems. I have a plane to catch."

Elaine stared, her eyes wide with alarm. He could almost see the blood leach from her face, taking with it the last of her flagging strength. "But you can't just go and leave me with strangers," she mouthed.

"I can and I must. The business I have to conduct in Belgium is as much for the good of Corminco as for my own company. I'll be back as soon as possible, but in the meantime I want you to rest and acclimate yourself. I'm sure you'll be able to cope better than you think. Sonia is an excellent hostess, and she may even be able to assist you with your shopping."

"I . . . see," Elaine said tiredly, her shoulders slumping. "Well, I guess it's goodbye, then."

Ruy's brows came together. "No, not goodbye— *adeus.* I will return in just a few days. Until then, take care." He wished there were time to kiss her again.

Quickly he turned to the Oliveiras, switching to his own language as he took his leave. Sonia shook his hand, and João clapped his shoulders in a hearty *abraço.* When the men's eyes met, João nodded surreptitiously toward Elaine and muttered, "*Jeito*—favor for favor?"

Ruy's mouth tightened. Perhaps he ought to have let Elaine go to the Maksoud Plaza after all; he should have known his associate would demand to be compensated somehow for taking care of her. In the years since Ruy had wrested control of A&O from the Oliveira family, the times he'd actually needed João's help had been few, but on those rare occasions when he had, the man had exploited the situation to the fullest.

In the early days of Ruy's success, João had still been the partner with the name and the connections. Ruy might have been the man with brains and ambition, but João, through his wife, Sonia, granddaughter of a coffee baron, was related to half the "old money" families in southern Brazil; one of her distant cousins was married to a member of what had once been the Brazilian royal family. All Ruy's carefully acquired culture and polish could not make up for the fact that he had no background beyond that which he'd deliberately created for himself, and in the beginning it had not been enough. Among his new countrymen, personal prestige was a significant factor in business dealings, and at the time Ruy had had little. As much as he'd despised João Oliveira, he had needed the man—and João knew it. He had never done anything for Ruy without making it more than clear that he expected to be repaid in full, sometimes with a "loan," sometimes with influence, sometimes with indefinable services such as finding a complacent husband for João's pregnant young mistress.

Ruy had gone along with the tacit agreement in the past because it was necessary; now, long after his own name and reputation had eclipsed that of his partner, he continued to use João partly out of habit and partly for convenience. Only occasionally did he ask himself if inertia was sufficient reason to allow the man to keep a hold, however tenuous, over him.

"Of course. Favor for favor," Ruy replied in clipped tones, wondering drearily what form the *jeito* would take this time. Perhaps it was time to decide once and for all whether his long-standing arrangement with his partner was really as convenient as he imagined it was....

CHAPTER SIX

"YOU WON'T REGRET buying the dress," Sonia Oliveira assured Elaine as they stepped out of the exclusive shop on the Rua Augusta. "It will be perfect for the reception tonight. It's lovely."

"Yes. *Muito bonito*," Elaine agreed, more to exercise her developing language skills rather than from any enthusiasm for the designer gown she'd just purchased. In the days since she arrived in São Paulo, she'd tried to use Portuguese as much as possible. Despite her fears when Ruy had left her alone with the Oliveiras, she and Sonia had learned to communicate with surprising success. Elaine's knowledge of the language remained shaky, but Sonia was doing her best to help her correct and refine her accent, and in a pinch they fell back on Spanish, which, Elaine had quickly learned, most Brazilians could understand even when they did not speak it.

João was the one member of the Oliveira household who did know some English, but he was hardly ever around to translate—a situation Elaine found increasingly frustrating. She had not come to Brazil to buy party dresses: she had come to work. Once she recovered from her jet lag, she'd hoped to discuss her new job with Ruy's second-in-command. She wanted to gain some insight into the people and facilities she'd be dealing with at Serra Brilhante. The opportunity had not yet arisen. João almost seemed to be avoiding her.

The one time Ruy had telephoned, Elaine had complained about her idleness. He advised her not to worry, that he'd brief her personally when he returned from Europe, which he promised to do just as soon as possible. In the meantime, he suggested, perhaps Sonia would take her sightseeing. Elaine protested, but when she telephoned her mother to let her know she'd arrived safely, Carolyn, too, seemed indifferent to her daughter's impatience. She told Elaine to relax and enjoy herself.

As a result, Elaine found herself spending all her time in the company of a woman whose main interests in life appeared to be shopping and gossip. Sonia had been raised to be a devoted wife, mother and homemaker, but now a housekeeper and cook took care of domestic details, her husband was frequently absent on business, and her only child, a daughter, was grown and worked in the civil service in Brasilia—a fact that surprised Elaine, considering Sonia's rather cloistered existence. Elaine recalled Ruy telling her that modern Brazilian women were as independent as North Americans. Liberation appeared to have come too late for Sonia. Elaine hoped the disquieting parallels with her sister Kate's situation were only coincidental.

But despite Senhora Oliveira's limitations, she had gone out of her way to make Elaine welcome in her home. Elaine tried to respond with gratitude. When Sonia suggested that Elaine might wish to attend a gem exhibition opening in a museum that evening, Elaine agreed, not because she had any real interest in jewelry but because she could tell her hostess wanted to go. João was apparently unable to escort her, and Sonia either would not or could not attend alone. But when Elaine had discovered that going to the reception required purchasing a formal gown, she'd begun to regret her decision.

Sonia was an indefatigable shopper. At first Elaine had been grateful for her help in picking up the personal items she had not brought with her from Denver, but that task had proved too mundane to hold Sonia's attention for long. Sonia loved clothes, her interest in apparel surpassed only by her complete disinterest in price tags. It took hours of deliberation in various boutiques and showrooms before she at last selected what she felt Elaine needed for her introduction to Paulista society. Elaine concurred at once. The dress was pretty and becoming, but, more importantly, buying it meant Elaine would finally get a chance to sit down. She hadn't felt this worn out since her days as an intern.

She thought she'd weep with relief when they left the dress shop and Sonia suggested, "There is a restaurant in the next block where we could stop, if you like. They have the most marvelous Viennese pastry chef. I'm ready for a break, aren't you?"

"Oh, yes," Elaine said, sighing gratefully. Although when her work demanded it, she could go most of the day without eating, she was having difficulty adjusting to the Brazilian custom of eating very late dinners. With the evening meal rarely served before 10:00 p.m., a mid-afternoon snack was almost a necessity. A break sounded wonderful.

The two women were strolling down the sidewalk, window-shopping, when suddenly Sonia touched Elaine's arm. "Stop!" she hissed. Elaine looked at her uncomprehendingly. Sonia nodded toward a group of youths lounging idly against a wall in the block ahead and whispered, "Wait a minute. Watch those boys over there."

Elaine gazed where directed, uncertain what she was supposed to be looking for.

She spotted half a dozen youngsters milling in front of a haberdashery, their ragged shorts and bare feet at odds with the formal silk evening suit displayed in the window. Their scrawny, half-naked bodies ranged in color from white to black. Although they all seemed to be less than twelve years old, a couple of them as young as seven, most were smoking cigarettes, and one shaped his fingers into a telescope and leered lewdly as a pretty girl walked by.

Several feet away another boy with a wooden shoeshine kit squatted on the sidewalk. He disregarded the others while he vigorously buffed the loafers of a portly, well-dressed man. When the leather gleamed mirror bright, the boy stood up, hoisting his kit under his arm as he meekly awaited payment. The man surveyed his shoes with approval and fished inside his jacket. The instant he pulled out his wallet, the young bootblack gave a piercing whistle and snatched the billfold out of the man's hands. He lobbed it into the cluster of other boys. As the man howled with outrage, the gang fled in all directions, their ringleader speeding after them. In seconds the only evidence that they—or their victim's money—had been there at all was the stained polishing rag lying abandoned at the man's feet.

As soon as the boys had vanished, Sonia said, "Okay, we can go now." Other pedestrians seemed to agree with her. Ignoring the red-faced man who was fuming with frustration and anger, they skirted him and resumed their walk. Elaine held back, frozen with blank astonishment. Sonia nudged her and repeated, "*Vamos.* It's all over."

Shaking her head in amazement, Elaine asked, "My God, isn't anyone going to do anything?"

"What do you suggest be done? The wallet is gone. The boys are gone. We are safe."

Elaine noticed that Sonia's handbag was firmly gripped high under her arm, and she shifted her own accordingly. "But—"

"Please, my dear," Sonia said kindly once they were out of the man's earshot, "don't concern yourself. He was a fool to display his money so openly. However, he does look as if he can afford the loss. I expect no irreparable harm has been done. Now, why don't we forget all about the incident and have our tea?"

Once they were settled in the quiet restaurant, Elaine tried to mask her anxiety, but she discovered she was too upset to do more than nibble at the food set before her. Sonia broke off in midsentence and gazed probingly at Elaine. "You're still troubled by what we saw in the street, aren't you?" Elaine nodded. Sonia said, "I'm sorry it bothers you so. Don't you have theft in the United States?"

"Of course we do," Elaine answered, thinking of the vandals who had methodically stripped her BMW of everything they could carry away. "It's just—" She shrugged helplessly. "It's just that those boys were all so young, little more than babies, and they pulled off their scam as if they'd done it a hundred times before."

"They probably have. It is because of the likes of them that law-abiding citizens must be wary all the time, even in their own homes." While Sonia talked, Elaine remembered her first glimpse of the Oliveiras' turn-of-the-century mansion. During the long drive from the suburb of Guarulhos, where the airport was located, Elaine had noticed that there was an astonishing contrast in building styles in São Paulo, so she was not surprised that the house's turrets were overshadowed by a fifty-story office building. What she had not expected to find was an armed watchman guarding the gate.

Sonia's expression was sober as she stared into her coffee cup. "Perhaps I speak too harshly. Our priest tells us it is unChristian to judge the poor by our own standards."

Elaine said, "São Paulo is such a wealthy, vibrant city that it hardly seems possible people could really be poor here."

"I'm afraid it's all too possible, and not just in São Paulo. You must realize that for several decades life in Brazil has been...unsettled. Governments have come and gone, inflation has skyrocketed. Many people with jobs do not earn enough money to survive, and the peasants who come to the cities looking for work end up in the slums, worse off than before."

"But I thought your leaders had gotten control of inflation. I know the currency has been changed, and didn't they freeze prices?"

Sonia grimaced fatalistically. "It does little good to declare prices officially frozen when many items are available now only on the black market."

Elaine frowned, made aware once again of the tremendous gap that existed between her and Sonia, despite the outward similarity of their privileged backgrounds. Like most Americans, Elaine had grown up with the tacit assumption that any necessity—or luxury—was readily available to anyone willing to pay for it. She did not understand shortages. A term like *"black market"* had no real meaning to her except as something she heard about in old war movies.

She asked, "So are you telling me that those boys we saw are stealing to help support their families?"

Sonia answered somberly, "I doubt they have any families to support. They looked like *abandonados*."

"*Abandonados?*"

"The abandoned ones." Sonia sighed. "The street children. There are several million of them. Some are orphans, some are runaways, and some—some are children whose parents simply can no longer afford to feed them."

Elaine's voice grew faint with horror. "You mean when parents can't feed their children, they just throw them out onto the street to fend for themselves?"

"The lucky ones are found and adopted. The Church tries to help others. Still others wind up in state homes. But there are so many—and yes, most of them do end up fending for themselves in the streets."

"But—but—" Elaine tried to speak and failed, choked by the images Sonia's words evoked. Millions, she'd said, unloved, unwanted, hungry and cold, ready prey for disease or for any human scum eager to exploit them. How could a country so rich, so dynamic, squander its most precious resource?

Sonia reached across the table and squeezed Elaine's hand reassuringly. "It is kind of you to be concerned, but you mustn't distress yourself. I promise you many people are working to help the little ones. Despite what you may think of us, Brazilians do love children, you know."

"I know," Elaine whispered hoarsely. The anguish in Sonia's dark eyes made her ashamed of her prejudices. She was a newcomer to this country. She did not understand its problems. She had no right to pass judgment.

For several moments the women were silent, then Sonia said, "Forgive me, Elaine. I did not mean to depress you. I'm being a poor hostess." She signaled to the waiter for two more *cafe-zinhos*. As he served the dark, sweet coffee Sonia reassured, "You know, there is no reason to assume that those boys we saw will always live in poverty. Many successful businessmen have risen from equally humble beginnings. One of our leading industrialists started out peddling sewing machines. I've heard of a former peasant who found a fabulous mine in the Amazon and now buys hotels with checks signed with a thumbprint. And while my husband, naturally, is of excellent family, the same cannot be said for his associate, the elegant Senhor Areias—"

"Ruy is hardly an illiterate peasant," Elaine cut in, a little startled by the speed with which she rushed to his defense.

Her reaction seemed to surprise Sonia, as well. Watching the woman's eyes narrow speculatively, Elaine recalled too late that as far as the Oliveiras were concerned, she and Ruy had met for the first time only a few weeks before in Denver. "I did not say the man was illiterate," Sonia declared. "Even though he does not have a university education, he is obviously well-read, with considerable native intelligence. But that does not mean he is not a peasant. Despite that aristocratic-sounding name, nobody ever heard of him until he emerged from the *favelas* of Rio."

Elaine listened in consternation. She knew nothing of Ruy's life in the period after he abandoned her in Switzerland, but she had heard of *favelas*, the notorious, noisome, hillside slums: sprawling assemblages of wretched tarpaper and scrap-metal shacks without water or sewerage, crammed so full of people that they amounted to cities within cities. She could not imagine him in such squalor. His tastes were too fastidious. Although he'd been raised in the poorer quarters of Lisbon, even as a boy he had struggled to live well, husbanding his meager waiter's pay, working double shifts—until he'd met Elaine and found a way to live well without the struggle. How could he have survived in a *favela*? How had he come to be there at all? And even more importantly, how had he gotten out?

As Elaine mulled these questions, Sonia unwittingly supplied the answers to some of them. Sipping her coffee, she flashed a smile and giggled girlishly. "He is very secretive about his background, you know," she confided, "or at least, parts of it. Ashamed, I suppose. That affected accent of his makes some people think he was born in Europe, but I am sure he acquired it deliberately to disguise his real origins. He admits freely enough that before he came to work for Companhia Oliveira, he was a gold miner, and before that he was a stevedore on the Rio docks. But there are things Ruy is not so eager to have known. When he first approached my husband for a job, João could see he had the aptitude to be an asset to the business, but still he decided to have him investigated before trusting him with a good position. And do you know what João discovered when he traced Ruy back to Rio?"

Sonia paused, her eyes gleaming expectantly, and Elaine reminded herself once again that there was no way the other woman could be aware she and Ruy had been acquainted in the past. "No, what?" she replied weakly.

Glancing around furtively, Sonia leaned toward Elaine and whispered, "Ruy may have worked as a longshoreman for a little while, but his real start was brought about by magic!"

Elaine scowled. For a moment she wondered if her linguistics skills had failed her, if the odd mixture of

Portuguese, Spanish and sign language with which she and Sonia communicated had somehow broken down. "Magic?" she repeated uncertainly, echoing the peculiar word that Sonia had spoken so matter-of-factly. "I don't understand."

Sonia edged closer. "You've heard of the spirit cults, haven't you?"

"Some," Elaine admitted cautiously. Even if Ruy had not already told her a little about his adopted country's complex religions, it would have been impossible for Elaine to remain ignorant of them once she reached Brazil. In the boutiques she and Sonia had just visited, little jeweled *figas* were displayed in glass cases alongside crucifixes; sidewalk newsstands offered posters of the deities Yemanjá and Oxalá for sale, as well as reproductions of da Vinci's *Last Supper*.

"What do the spirit cults have to do with Ruy?" she asked with spurious unconcern. "I can't imagine he's a believer."

"You might be surprised," Sonia told her. "People of all classes pray to the old gods. But what I was trying to explain was that the wealthy and esteemed Senhor Areias, who is held up as an example of success through diligence and hard work, in fact made his start as the special friend of an old witch in the *favela*. People paid her to make charms and cast spells, and everyone was afraid of her—everyone, that is, except one handsome, ambitious boy. According to some of the people my husband's detective questioned, he was her apprentice. Others were sure he must have been her—" Sonia broke off, smiling meaningfully at Elaine's expression. "After all this time, who's to say? But they would have been quite a sight, though, wouldn't they—the toothless old hag and the virile young man. No wonder she used her powers to make him prosper.''

Elaine shook her head. "You're making fun of me," she insisted, her voice suddenly hoarse. "That's a stupid story, and I'm sure you don't believe a word of it. I know I don't."

Sonia eyed her acutely. "Don't you?"

No! Elaine told herself later for the fifth time as she dressed for the evening. Sonia had sent her personal maid to help her don the slip of wispy apricot chiffon they'd purchased earlier in the day, and the woman's silent efficiency left Elaine with far too much time to think. As she sat at the dressing table, smoothing the gown's handkerchief hem over her knees while the maid arranged her hair, she tried not to remember Sonia's insinuating words. No, Elaine did not believe that ugly story, she did not believe the boy she had loved would have sunk to such depths, even if he had deliberately seduced her for her father's fortune. Yes, he'd been mercenary, even venal, but surely he would have balked at prostituting himself for a "toothless old hag." The very idea was—

"Elaine."

Sonia's quavering voice broke suddenly into Elaine's troubled thoughts. Glancing up, she saw her hostess hovering in the doorway. Her elegant red taffeta dress did not match her dispirited frown. "Elaine," she repeated drearily, "I'm afraid I have bad news. There's been a change of plans."

"What do you mean?"

Signaling for the maid to leave them, Sonia came into the room and closed the door behind her. She looked embarrassed. "I'm sorry, but my husband says you and I must not go to the reception tonight."

Elaine stared. "Why on earth not? We're both almost ready. I thought everything was arranged."

"I thought so, too," Sonia admitted abashedly, "but apparently I misunderstood. When João said he did not wish to escort us tonight, I assumed he declined because he had other plans. His business demands so much of his time, you know. Even when he is not away at the mines, sometimes he must work half the night. That's why I went ahead and made arrangements for you and me to attend without him. But when he came in just now and asked why I was dressed so formally, he became upset when I explained. He says he did not mean for you and me to go to the reception ourselves. He feels it is...inappropriate."

"Inappropriate? Why?" Elaine asked in astonishment. She noted the large diamonds glittering in Sonia's ears. "You obviously enjoy jewelry, and considering our families' ties to the mining industry, I'd think such an exhibit would be doubly appropriate. And if João is concerned about your safety, I'm sure museum security will be tight. In fact, I can imagine few events likely to be more boringly circumspect."

Although Elaine could tell that Sonia agreed with her, the other woman sighed in resignation. "*Talvez*. But my husband still forbids us to go."

Elaine stiffened. Even though so far she'd accepted without comment João's mystifying absences, the way he avoided talking to her, there was a limit to what she'd put up with for the sake of politeness. "Sonia," she declared, spacing the words deliberately, "your husband is in no position to forbid *me* to do anything."

Sonia's expression remained guarded. "That may be true, but if he says not to go, what choice do we have?"

Elaine shrugged and reached for her wrap. Originally she'd agreed to go to the reception as a favor to her hostess, but now there was a matter of principle involved. Picking up the engraved invitation that lay on the dressing table, she noted, "I'd say the choice was obvious."

Sonia's look of amazement was mirrored on João's face when he confronted her in the marble-tiled foyer, where she waited for the taxi she'd called for. His thin hair was wildly disarranged, as if he'd been raking it with his fingers. "Dr. Welles, you are going out?" he demanded, his craggy face dark with consternation.

"Yes," Elaine said calmly. "I'm sorry you and Senhora Oliveira can't come with me. I know she was looking forward to seeing this exhibit."

"You could see the exhibit some other time," João pressed.

Elaine shook her head. "No, I think not. I promised my father I'd try to learn as much as possible about the Brazilian gem industry while I was down here, and the reception seems an ideal place to start my education. I gather there will be people there who can explain to me exactly what I'm seeing?"

"Yes," João rasped, wiping a sheen of perspiration from his receding hairline. "Some great experts in the field should be in attendance at the museum. I shall be sorry to miss them. But I must stay near the telephone in case Areias calls. Did you know he may be flying in tonight?"

Elaine's eyes narrowed. "No, I had no idea. He hasn't bothered to keep me informed of his schedule."

"Well, he could be arriving home almost any moment now. Don't you want to be on hand to greet him?"

"Not particularly," Elaine said imperturbably. She'd been at Ruy's beck and call long enough. "If Senhor Areias wishes to see me—"

A security buzzer sounded. When the guard out front announced over the intercom that a cab had arrived at the gate, João hesitated. He glanced furtively at Elaine, who met his gaze squarely with cool blue eyes, silently challenging him to refuse the taxi permission to enter. "That's my ride, I believe," she said.

As she watched, João's face darkened. She thought he was going to accept her dare, but after a moment he grimaced and shrugged. "Areias shall hear of this," he muttered, barking an order into the microphone on the wall. Seconds later the taxi swung into position at the base of the front steps.

After the fuss Sonia and her husband had made over Elaine's decision to go unescorted to the gem exhibition, she half expected the museum to be located in some sordid quarter of the city, but after driving through endless concrete canyons that reminded Elaine of midtown Manhattan, the cabdriver dropped her in front of a very modern, very respectable-looking building near the Praça de República. Well-dressed people were filing through the entrance, and, Elaine noted with interest, not every woman appeared to have a man in tow. When she presented her invitation, nobody questioned her presence.

Once inside, Elaine found herself even more at a loss to understand why João Oliveira had been so opposed to her and Sonia attending the reception. The exhibit was being held in a tastefully luxurious gallery that provided a subdued setting for the display of precious stones mined in Brazil. A string quartet played soft chamber music while guests strolled quietly from one glass case to the next, admiring the impressive variety of gems, both raw and cut, that glittered like broken rainbows. Murals depicted the history of the industry from the earliest days when black slaves picked through diamond-bearing river gravel while Portuguese overseers watched closely, whips in hand. Elaine followed along with the crowd, appreciating the radiant beauty of the stones, yet remaining unmoved by them. The only piece of jewelry she had ever really cared about was the gold bangle the boy Antonio had stolen from her.

Then she spotted something that caught her interest. In a small case apart from the others a handful of gems were heaped on a plate of dull gray metal. Next to the plate lay a small sensor wired to some kind of digital gauge in the corner of the case. As Elaine watched, the device's display flashed a series of constantly changing numbers.

Her knowledge of Portuguese was inadequate to translate the caption cards describing the exhibit, and her confusion must have shown, because an elderly man standing unobtrusively to one side spoke up. When Elaine replied haltingly, she was relieved and surprised to hear him switch to English. "Avram Steinberg of Steinberg e Filhos, jewelers. Formerly of the Lower East Side—as if you couldn't guess," he added with a heavy New York accent. After Elaine introduced herself, Mr. Steinberg said he was serving as docent for the evening and offered to explain the display to her.

"The instrument in the corner of the case is just a little Geiger counter, to show that the stones on the lead plate are radioactive."

"Radioactive?" Elaine repeated. "That sounds dangerous. What happened?"

"These gems have been irradiated, only not very well, by people who didn't know what they were doing. Instead of just enhancing the color with gamma rays, they managed to bombard them with neutrons, rendering them—"

Elaine held up her hand. "Please, Mr. Steinberg," she said with a laugh, "I'm an obstetrician. I don't know anything about nuclear physics."

The man smiled wryly. "I'm sorry, doctor, I didn't mean to get technical. Let's try again. Do you know about the four C's that determine a gemstone's value: color, clarity, cut and carat?" When Elaine nodded, Steinberg continued, "Well, the cut of a stone is something that can't be changed. Either it's well done or it's not. And you certainly can't make the carat weight bigger. But since the beginning of time men have known that there are ways to improve the color and clarity of inferior stones. There are ancient recipes for brightening emeralds by baking them in fig cakes—or whitening pearls by feeding them to chickens. And of course, you can always shine stones with colored wax, or dye them." He paused, clucking. "In fact, not long ago one of the major auction houses in New York was all set to sell a large flawless pink diamond, when somebody noticed that the stone was in fact an inferior yellow one that had been coated with nail polish!"

"You're kidding," Elaine exclaimed.

Steinberg shook his head. "No, it's true, I swear—but that little episode was the result of a series of almost unbelievable blunders. Nowadays anyone really trying to raise the value of mediocre stones has to use modern technology—lasers to burn out imperfections, heat to improve clarity. And, of course, irradiation."

"You mean exposing stones to some source of radioactivity?"

"Yes. Around the beginning of the century one gemologist discovered that if he buried ordinary corundum
in radium salts for a month, it turned emerald green, just
as diamonds could be changed to blue-white or tourmalines to deep pink. Unfortunately, stones treated so
crudely also end up radioactive, not exactly a desirable
quality in jewelry! Some cases of skin cancer have even
been linked to tainted gems from those days. That's the
point of the display in this case here. Nowadays, anyone
wanting to irradiate stones can use an electron accelera-
tor or some other method that doesn't cause contami-
nation."

Elaine frowned. "But no matter how it's done,
wouldn't the whole matter of treating stones be considered unethical, like trying to pass off an artificial diamond as a real one?"

Steinberg shrugged. "Yes and no. A perfect natural
stone is always going to be far more valuable than one
that's been enhanced, and some of the international jewel
exchanges refuse to deal with any but the real thing. But
as long as you don't try to defraud your customer—as
long as he is aware of what he's getting—there's nothing
wrong with selling treated stones. Luckily, most countries have very strict codes regarding disclosure, and
would-be crooks get caught sooner or later."

Elaine nodded thoughtfully, peering once again at the
glittering gems in the glass case. It was difficult to imagine anything so pretty being dangerous, but then, she
admitted ironically, it was also difficult for her to imagine anyone coveting the stones so much that they'd re-
sort to deception or international fraud to get them. She
supposed she just had a blind spot where jewelry was
concerned.

Noticing that other people were trying to approach Steinberg, Elaine realized she'd monopolized the man's attention long enough. It was time to move on. She wondered what she should do now that she'd seen all the exhibits in the gallery. Apart from trying the refreshments, she seemed to have exhausted the possibilities for the evening. After a glass of champagne and a nibble of caviar, she'd have no choice but to take another cab back to the Oliveiras' home and face her host's displeasure. Smiling her thanks to Avram Steinberg, she stepped back.

As she edged her way through the crowd, watching her feet in order not to step on any of the long, flowing gowns a number of women wore, all at once she collided with a hard male body. She recoiled, and strong hands reached out to steady her. Silently cursing herself for her clumsiness, she blushed and mumbled, *"Desculpe-me. I* wasn't looking where I was going." She tried to pull away, but the hands did not release her. Jerking up her head, she said more forcefully, "Senhor, please...." The words faded.

Beneath the silver mustache Ruy's lips were curved into a lopsided grin. His dark eyes gleamed. *"Querida,"* he murmured, a low rumble of amusement sounding deep in his throat, "I warned you that Brazilian men will take advantage of any opportunity that's offered them." And before she could voice her astonishment, his mouth closed hotly over hers.

CHAPTER SEVEN

"FOR GOD'S SAKE, Ruy!" Elaine laughed breathlessly, trying to break free. "Remember where we are!"

He released her, but the quirky grin remained in place as he drew her away from the crowd. They began to stroll around the gallery, and a number of people addressed Ruy by name, the men hugging him, the women pecking his cheek. "You see?" he said, chuckling, when he and Elaine were alone momentarily. "Nobody in Brazil minds a public embrace. The *beijinho*—the 'little kiss'—is a standard form of greeting."

"There was nothing 'little' about that kiss you gave me," Elaine countered, touching her lips with her fingertips. "My mouth is still stinging."

"Sorry," he murmured unrepentantly. "I'll try to be more careful next time."

There's not going to be a next time, Elaine told herself, but even as her mind formed the words, she knew she was lying. Whoever he was, whoever he'd been, the man who had once called himself Antonio held a sexual attraction that she was as helpless to resist now as when she'd been a girl.

Despite the stories Sonia Oliveira had whispered about his past, there was no trace of the *favelado* in him now. He looked every inch the influential, affluent socialite, entirely at home in their elegant surroundings. Elaine found herself trying to reconcile the imposing image he presented with that of the boy she'd known so long before. Antonio's features had been attractive but immature, his aquiline nose still too softly defined to be called hawkish, his short upper lip as naked and exposed as his smooth cheeks. Even the eyes had seemed gentler then—black-gold irises veiled behind lashes as long as a girl's.

Or perhaps it had been his shabby clothes that had made him so poignantly appealing to a girl with Elaine's compassionate nature, from her privileged background. Now he was dressed in impeccably correct evening clothes, but then his wardrobe had consisted of a single pair of worn corduroy slacks and two ill-fitting shirts, which he washed by hand in a rusty basin in his room. Once, after they'd made love, Elaine had tried to demonstrate the depth of the bond she felt for him by ironing one of his shirts. She'd scorched the frayed collar. She had offered to buy him a new shirt, but he'd refused huffily. The next day in the dining hall at the school, when she'd seen the burned collar under his baggy white waiter's jacket, she had almost wept.

Odd about memories. Even now, when she knew that Antonio's actions had all been calculated, his every declaration a sham, the recollection of the defensive dignity with which the boy had worn that unprepossessing uniform still had the power to tie her in knots.

Ruy scowled. "What's wrong, Elaine? You seem troubled."

She recalled herself to the present with an effort. Searching his dark face, she noticed for the first time that the lines etched along his eyes, his nose, seemed deeper than usual. "I was thinking how tired you look tonight," she said.

He exhaled wearily, and his shoulders sagged. "I am tired. I just flew in from Belgium, and when I staggered into my flat an hour ago, all I wanted was a shower and a drink. I certainly wasn't expecting to have to change into my tux and dash over here—not that I mind, of course, when I see how very beautiful you look tonight. That's a charming gown." His gaze traveled deliberately over Elaine's slender body, veiled in silk chiffon, and she could feel her skin tingle as if he'd touched her.

Irritated by her instant response to his inspection, she countered, "You didn't have to do anything. I told your business partner I was quite capable of attending this function on my own."

Ruy shrugged. "Unfortunately, João didn't see it that way. I could hear my telephone ringing off the hook even before I stepped out of the elevator. It was still ringing when I let myself into the apartment. As soon as I picked up the receiver, he began yelling that you were running around the city alone, and if I didn't take you in hand at once, your uncontrollable behavior was liable to jeopardize the consortium with Corminco."

Elaine's oath was short and pungent. Ruy smiled sympathetically. "I'm sorry, my dear, but you have to realize that my associate is something of a throwback, even by South American standards. He still thinks a woman's place is in the convent or the kitchen."

"He sounds as if he'd get along beautifully with my father," Elaine muttered. She sighed heavily. "God, I wish I'd never agreed to stay with the Oliveiras. I should have gone to the Maksoud Plaza as I originally planned. Sonia is congenial enough, but keeping up with her is like living in a hamster's cage, running around in circles and getting nowhere."

"I can only say once again that I'm sorry you're dissatisfied with the arrangements. When we made them, they seemed practical and convenient. But since they're not, I promise you will not have to endure the situation much longer.''

Elaine remained unmoved by Ruy's apology. "Exactly how much longer?" she demanded. "When do we go to Serra Brilhante?"

"You are so impatient to begin your new job? Burton and Carolyn suggested you might enjoy some time off."

"Ruy," Elaine retorted emphatically, "my parents never listen to me, but I expected better of you. How many ways must I say it? I did not come to Brazil for a vacation or to shop or even to learn Portuguese. I came here to work. I left my practice in Denver, and patients I care deeply about, because you convinced me that there are women here who need my medical skills even more than the ones at home do. If that's true, then who's looking after them while I waste my time here eating caviar and hobnobbing with wealthy Paulistas? Why am I not in Minas Gerais right now, taking care of those women?"

Ruy's eyes narrowed. "Then you want to go at once?"

"Yes, yes, *yes*! The sooner the better."

He nodded tersely. "Very well, it shall be as you wish. We'll go tomorrow. Let me have a decent night's sleep to recover from my jet lag, and then you and João and I shall fly to Serra Brilhante tomorrow afternoon."

IT WAS DIFFICULT to imagine a more startling contrast than that between the megalopolis of São Paulo and the state of Minas Gerais. As the A&O company plane headed northeast, carrying Elaine and the two men away from the vast mantle of steel and concrete that shrouded the earth to the horizon, she gazed down at the forested foothills and undulating plateaus passing beneath her, and she sighed with relief. Despite its excitement, its energy and its luxury, she had found the huge city oppressive.

But the quiet beauty and diversity of Minas Gerais appealed to her. The weather remained clear during the three-hundred-mile journey, and Elaine, who had never flown in a propeller-driven plane before, was fascinated by the panorama unfolding a couple of thousand feet below her. Despite the loud whine of the twin engines, João spent most of the flight buried in a briefcase full of papers, but Ruy pointed out sights to her, yelling his comments and smiling indulgently at her enthusiasm. She could see people moving about the small farms that dotted the countryside and tending endless rows of coffee trees in vast plantations. Sleepy-looking villages centered around pretty colonial churches contrasted with enormous open-pit mines where ultramodern equipment gouged out the landscape and sent up roily clouds of dust. When Elaine noticed a sizable airport in the distance, Ruy said it belonged to Belo Horizonte, the third largest city in Brazil. But the landing strip where their plane touched down consisted of a short gravel runway cut through the middle of a cornfield and a single hangar of corrugated metal, with the letters A&O painted on the roof.

The propellers were still turning when the pilot lowered the folding steps. João immediately jumped from the plane and loped toward the hangar. Ruy stepped down and offered his hand to Elaine. "Watch yourself," he said. After hours of shouting over the roar of the engines, his voice boomed in the sudden quiet.

"I'll be all..." Elaine's voice trailed off as her high heels dug into the gravel, making her sway drunkenly. Ruy caught her by the waist.

"Dizzy?" he asked with concern.

"A little," she gasped. "I'm not used to being bounced around in a small plane." She took a deep breath to clear her head. The air was warm, perfumed with the tangy scent of growing crops. As she grew steadier, she muttered, "But I think the real problem is my shoes. I should have had sense enough to wear flats."

He glanced down at her trim Italian footwear. "No," he conceded amiably, "pretty as they are, I don't think Botticelli pumps were really meant for a mining community."

"Fortunately, I do have sandals in my luggage," she noted. "As soon as I get to my quarters and can unpack—" She broke off with a quizzical frown to survey her surroundings. "By the way, where are my quarters? For that matter, where is Serra Brilhante and the mines? All I see is farmland."

"We're on a mesa here," Ruy explained. "You can't see the edge because of that little rise there, but there's a river at its base." He nodded toward a rutted road that disappeared around a small knoll. "If you'd looked in that direction as we approached the runway, you might have noticed a small building where the road skirts the edge of the bluff. That's the top of the winch housing. The whole cliff is crisscrossed with veins of pegmatite, and the mine is dug into the side of the bluff and in the alluvial deposits at its foot." He pointed to the right. "The settlement is about two miles in that direction, beyond those trees and away from the noise and dirt. The site office and the school and your clinic are all in a complex in the middle of the settlement. You will be lodging close by. We'll head over there just as soon as transportation arrives." He glanced at his wristwatch. "João went into the hangar to call the manager for the

Jeep, but since this is the middle of lunch, it may be a while before someone comes."

Elaine said, "Considering that both you and your partner were arriving today, I'd have thought your manager would have had someone here promptly to welcome you."

Ruy smiled ironically. "My dear, promptness is not a virtue we Brazilians value highly—it implies servility. On the other hand, even though we may be casual about both time and work, one thing we never take lightly is the long lunch break. The manager may be digesting a delicious meal or making love to his wife or doing any number of things more agreeable than dashing out here to the airfield." He paused, squinting into the distance. "On the other hand, it looks as if the man decided to interrupt his lunch, after all. Perhaps his wife had a headache."

Moments later the manager, Senhor Cruz, a slight, dark man in a sport coat and tie, pulled his station wagon, a Brazilian-made Volkswagen "Kombi," to a halt alongside the plane. After shaking hands with João and Ruy, he turned to Elaine, eyeing her curiously while Ruy made introductions in English and Portuguese. As soon as Ruy interpreted Cruz's greeting, the man nodded and presented Elaine with his business card; he waited expectantly. After a tiny hesitation, Elaine murmured, *"Obrigada, senhor,"* and fished into her handbag for one of her own cards. With the formalities completed, Cruz relaxed and smiled. As he escorted Elaine the few feet to the Volkswagen and settled her into the back seat alongside João Oliveira, his words sounded warm and welcoming, even though he spoke far too rapidly for her to follow them.

Taking his position beside the driver, Ruy leaned across the back of the seat and translated, "Cruz says I

should tell you how very happy everyone is that you've
come. Not only is it an honor to have a member of the
Welles family herself on-site, but it will be a great relief to
all, especially the women, to have a doctor available. Up
till now we've only been able to secure the part-time services of a physician whose regular practice is in Diamantina, about an hour's drive away. He conducts clinics here
once a week, and he does rush over for emergencies, but,
as Cruz points out, babies eager to be born are noto-
riously stubborn about waiting for the doctor."

Elaine nodded. "Please tell Senhor Cruz that I feel
privileged to be able to come to Serra Brilhante, and I'll
do everything in my power to provide the very best medical care people here deserve."

While Ruy relayed her message to Cruz, the car headed
across the top of the mesa in the direction of the trees
Ruy had indicated earlier. Elaine settled back in her seat
and tried to relax. She was here. At last. After the frustration and boredom of her life in Denver, whatever
happened to her now would seem like an adventure. She
shivered with anticipation.

At her side João noticed that faint tremor and murmured, "Are you regretting your decision already?"

Elaine scowled, surprised not so much by the waspish
tone of that muttered remark as by the fact that João had
spoken to her at all. Since her arrival in São Paulo the
man had ignored her whenever possible. Although he had
proved a punctilious host, Elaine had become convinced
that he had never wanted her involved in his business—
which was ironic, considering how she had tried to resist
Ruy, her parents, her whole family, when they had insisted she come. Now, perversely, the knowledge that
João did not welcome her made her determined to succeed at this assignment.

Pointedly flashing a smile, she said, "Of course I don't regret coming to Serra Brilhante, senhor. Even if I did, I would never go back on the promise I made to your associate. Besides, it's going to be fun."

João's jaw tightened, and he returned his attention to the papers in his briefcase.

As the station wagon bounced along the road that threaded through the woods, Elaine leaned forward, straining for her first sight of the community. All at once the vehicle climbed a rise and burst through an opening in the trees, and below them was Serra Brilhante.

Beyond a graded field marked with surveyor's stakes, encompassing an area at least as large as the established part of the town, the community spread before them with monotonous regularity, raw and spartan. From a central complex of larger buildings the narrow blacktop streets extended in an unvarying grid, studded with little concrete boxes with red tile roofs. White wooden fences divided the tiny patches of seedling lawn that surrounded each house; identical carports shaded the same corner of each yard. Elaine frowned. Ruy had warned her in Denver that the facilities would seem primitive, but still she'd expected something a little less regimented. The barrackslike rigidity of the scene disturbed her.

Then she looked again, more closely. As they drove through the rows of drab little cement boxes, faces peered out from between pretty curtains. Women worked in flower beds that sported tropical blooms. In the carports teenagers proudly washed late-model vehicles. Television theme music poured through open windows, and while Elaine saw no antennas, the large satellite dish atop the highest roof in the central complex made her suspect that the town had some kind of cable system. As the car drew nearer to their destination, she glimpsed the school; children of all colors filed out, abandoning their books as they dashed toward a shimmering swimming pool.

She remembered something else Ruy had told her in Colorado: "Most of the miners of Serra Brilhante have come there straight from the farms or the slums, and we are providing free medicine, free housing, free education and entertainment. For them it's an improvement in their standard of living beyond anything in their wildest dreams." He had spoken the words quietly, without conceit, a simple statement of fact.

Leaning forward, she touched Ruy's shoulder. When he turned his head, she smiled and said, "It's beautiful."

His dark eyes narrowed and he searched her face, as if he doubted her sincerity. At last his gaze softened. "Thank you, Elaine," he whispered, laying his fingers over hers. Despite the awkward position he did not release her hand until the station wagon pulled to a halt in front of the central complex.

THE MOMENT OF SERENITY shared by Elaine and Ruy did not last long.

While João and the manager conferred in the company office, Ruy showed Elaine to the medical facility. The waiting room was empty, and a sign on the door indicated that the nurse was away on her lunch break. When Ruy used a master key to let them in, Elaine could see at once that the place was comfortable, sanitary and far better equipped than she had expected. In addition to an office, which she would have to share with the doctor from Diamantina when he held his weekly clinics, there were two treatment rooms and an operating room that could be set up for surgery or delivery, depending on the need. There was also a four-bed ward, which, Ruy noted, was hardly ever used. Whenever possible, the townspeople preferred to recover in their own homes, and those who were so ill that they could not be treated on an outpatient basis were usually transported to a larger hospital elsewhere.

While Elaine was admiring the compact, convenient layout of the clinic, the nurse returned. She was a bright, competent-looking woman somewhere in her twenties, her auburn hair and buxom figure set off well by her starched white uniform. When Ruy introduced her as Consuelo Gomes, she greeted Elaine pleasantly in Portuguese. Shaking her head, Elaine said in English, "I'm very happy to meet you, Consuelo. I know we'll work well together if you'll just be patient while I get the hang of how things are done around here. I'm really going to need your help, especially with the language...." As Elaine had spoken, the younger woman had seemed to grow increasingly consternated. Confused, Elaine turned to Ruy and said, "I'm sorry. I assumed Consuelo was the bilingual nurse you promised me."

Ruy frowned. In rapid Portuguese he tossed a question at Consuelo, who replied at length, her indignation obvious. Placating her with a conciliatory gesture, Ruy sighed and glanced down at Elaine. "I have bad news, I'm afraid."

"What kind of bad news?"

"There's been some kind of mixup. The obstetrical nurse I hired to serve as your interpreter suddenly changed her mind about working here. Consuelo says the woman had seemed happy enough, then all at once she declared she couldn't stand it any longer here in the boondocks. She hitched a ride to Diamantina the last time the other doctor was here, and by now she's presumably back in Rio, or wherever it was she headed.''

Elaine felt her stomach lurch. "And Consuelo doesn't speak any English at all?" The nurse shook her head. Elaine hesitated. "How about Spanish?" she ventured hopefully. "French?" Consuelo's expression remained blank. Letting her breath out with a hiss, Elaine turned away. "Goddammit all to hell," she groaned, "how am I supposed to manage without an interpreter? I'm learning the language as fast as I can, but I can't afford mistakes in translation when I'm treating patients!"

"I know," Ruy commiserated, "and I promise I'll find help. I know there are English-speaking nurses at the Hospital Samaritano in São Paulo. Perhaps if I offer enough money, they'll spare one for a few days, at least until we think of some other solution." He spoke again to Consuelo, who chewed her lip before replying. Ruy told Elaine, "She says she's willing to chance it if you are."

Elaine smiled gratefully to the nurse. "Thank you, Consuelo," she said in halting Portuguese. "I appreciate your cooperation. It's not going to be easy, but maybe if we're lucky no emergencies will arise before we get the situation straightened out."

The other woman nodded her understanding. She started to speak, but suddenly she broke off, jerking her head toward the door. Elaine listened intently. Somewhere far in the distance a high-pitched horn bleated an alarm. "What is it?" she demanded.

Ruy swore grimly. "That's the signal that tells us there's been some kind of accident at the mine. If it's serious, you and Consuelo will have to take charge until the other doctor arrives." He glanced down at Elaine, his lips twisted into an ironic smile. "I'm sorry, darling, but it looks as if that luck you hoped for may have run out already."

"ONLY ONE MAN INJURED," João judged with satisfaction. "A minor incident."

Ruy's eyes darted toward the door through which a man on a stretcher had just been carried, moaning with pain. Although Ruy knew he might be needed in the treatment room at any moment to provide translation for Elaine, he elected to stay out of the way until she summoned him. "I doubt the victim considers the incident a minor one," he noted to his partner. "At the very least he must have several broken bones."

João remained imperturbable. "Bones mend. It could have been worse."

"According to Cruz, it could have been much worse," Ruy countered grimly. "He says it's a miracle the man wasn't killed in that rockfall. What I want to know is, why was he burrowing back into that crevice in the first place? That part of the cliff hasn't been reinforced yet."

"Who knows? Perhaps he hoped to find a new vein. Many of the men, especially the ones who are as small as this guy is, try to worm their way into parts of the hill that have yet to be explored. They think that way they will have a better chance of finding big stones, the bonus stones." Ruy snorted, and João pointed out, "They all know that once the new equipment arrives from the Americans and we begin processing ore by the ton instead of shovelfuls, the odds of any one man making a fabulous strike will be reduced to almost nothing."

Ruy sighed tiredly. "How many times do we have to explain it to them? Once our expansion is under way, output is going to increase so much that everyone will profit. Even if individuals are less likely to receive bonuses for finding fancy stones, they're also less likely to endanger their lives looking for them. Why don't they understand?"

"They are peasants." João shrugged, and Ruy had to turn away to hide his anger.

He knew the comment was directed as much at himself as at the workmen. All his life he'd been scorned by people who thought their names or their money made them better than he was. From the time he was a barefoot urchin in the back streets of Lisbon, surviving on bread and olives and the grudging charity of an aunt resentful of her dead sister's bastard, it had never mattered that he was smarter and worked harder and was more ambitious than most. All anyone ever noticed were his shabby clothes, his street dialect. During the several years he'd knocked around Europe, after running away from Portugal at the age of fourteen, he had deliberately set out to educate himself, reading, aping the diction of actors he watched on television and dressing as well as his meager resources would allow—but somehow it made no difference. He had gone to Switzerland looking for work in a bank or a counting house as a clerk, office boy or general flunky—it didn't matter how menial the job was as long as there was some chance for advancement. Instead he found himself a servant to the pampered offspring of the superrich, ignored by those to whom he was not simply invisible. And the one person who had seemed to notice him, had pretended to care for him as a human being, had turned out to be the worst of all. It had not been enough to despise the base waiter who had dared to aspire to her lofty family: that family had set out to destroy him.

Ruy threw a sidelong glance at the man standing beside him. João Oliveira would like to destroy him, he knew. He hated Ruy for having bested him, for having taken over his company. Ruy had always been aware of the man's resentment, but it did not bother him. João was ineffectual, a weakling. If he were stronger, he would not now be only a figurehead in the mining company founded by his great-grandfather. No, João's hatred had always been too impotent to be more than an annoyance. It did not hurt.

It was the hatred of the Welleses that hurt, even after more than two decades. For twenty-two years their scorn had stung like a thorn in his pride, and Ruy knew at the deepest level of his subconscious that the strongest motivation for his success had always been the desire to someday make them—her—regret that they'd despised him.

But now, just when revenge was at hand—so simple, so easy—why did it seem so pointless?

"Areias—" The finger prodding Ruy's shoulder returned his attention to the present. He looked blankly at his partner. "Dr. Welles wants us," João said. He nodded toward the door where Elaine waited. She had donned a long white coat over her dress, and around her neck hung a stethoscope. Her face was grave. Ruy started. He had never seen her in her work clothes before, and he was stunned by the difference the uniform made in her. She looked aloof, imposing and untouchable.

Shaking himself, Ruy strode across the room. "What's wrong?" he demanded. "The workman, is he—"

"He'll recover," Elaine assured quickly. "According to the X rays, he had a broken arm, a broken ankle and three cracked ribs. They're all simple fractures and should heal cleanly."

"Thank God!" João intoned piously.

Ruy relaxed. "That's a relief." When Elaine's somber expression did not change, he asked worriedly, "What else is wrong? You're not telling us everything."

Elaine said, "Something has arisen that I don't know how to deal with. I think you and Senhor Oliveira need to take charge." Turning away, she led the two men down the short corridor. At the door of the treatment room, she paused. "I've just given him a shot, but he's still in a lot of pain. He's also frightened and very nervous. I don't want either of you saying anything to upset him."

Puzzled, Ruy glanced at João, who signaled his own bewilderment. They followed Elaine inside.

The man lying in a half-raised position on the table in the center of the room watched their arrival with wary black eyes, alert despite the drug that was beginning to cloud them. The women had removed his shirt, and the wide strips of bandage that strapped his gaunt chest looked startlingly white against his hairless, coffee-colored skin. His left forearm was already immobilized, while Consuelo, her pretty face thunderous, methodically wrapped plaster-impregnated gauze around his ankle. His baggy trousers had been cut away from his leg, and despite the cast, there was no disguising the adolescent thinness of his limbs. Ruy studied the "man" with dismay. He suspected the sweat beading that unlined forehead was caused less by pain than by stark, gut-wrenching fear.

In a tone as gentle as he could manage he asked, "How old are you, *jovem*? The truth, please."

"*A verdade?*" the boy repeated, peeking sidelong at Elaine for reassurance. She patted his dark head. Reluctantly he looked up at Ruy again. "*Treze,*" he mumbled, his voice cracked and sulky. "I'm thirteen."

CHAPTER EIGHT

RUY STARED at the injured youth, whose beardless chin was quivering. "What's your name?" he asked, striving to keep his voice low and nonthreatening.

The response was grudging. "Vadinho."

"What are you doing here, Vadinho? Where is your family?"

The boy's eyes grew hooded. He did not answer. João barked, "You heard the boss. Speak up! Tell us what you've been up to. What do you mean, trying to pass yourself off as a miner?"

At the harsh words, Vadinho flinched, reaching instinctively for Elaine with his good hand. "Hey, doc," he whimpered, "you said they wouldn't bug me."

She caught his fingers in her own, and he clutched at her as if she were a lifeline. "Nobody's going to bug you," she murmured, glowering challengingly at Ruy and João.

Ruy's brows lifted. The boy had addressed Elaine in her own language. "Where did you learn English?" he demanded.

Again Vadinho glanced at Elaine and Consuelo before replying. Ruy was almost amused by the way the women moved imperceptibly closer, two lionesses sheltering a cub. He tried again. "I'm amazed at how well you speak English, Vadinho. Where'd you pick it up?"

"From the tourists," the boy muttered, his face mutinous and wary. "They like it when you talk their lingo. It makes 'em more comfortable and they tip you better, especially the Americans. I know a little Japanese and Italian, too."

"That's very impressive." Ruy's suspicions were quickly taking shape, but he knew that if he tried to bully the information from the youth, the women would unite against him. In the few minutes they'd spent alone with Vadinho they'd obviously appointed themselves his protectors. Mildly he asked, "So where were these tourists who were so generous to you?"

"The coast."

"You mean Rio? That's over two hundred kilometers from here. What brought you to Serra Brilhante?"

"Rumor around the *morro* was that there were jobs here. I was tired of hustling, and I liked the idea of having food and a bed. So two months ago I beg—I scraped together enough money for a bus ticket to Belo Horizonte, and I hitchhiked the rest of the way—"

"And then you got a job by lying about your age," João accused.

The boy sniffed cynically. "Hey, man, I can do the work. If the foreman thinks I'm eighteen, that's his problem."

Ruy could sense João about ready to erupt. Squelching him with a look, he continued to speak in the same soothing manner. "And what about your family, Vadinho? How do they feel about your taking off the way you did?"

This was the question Ruy guessed the boy did not want to answer. The chapped lips began to tremble, and behind the defiance in the swimming eyes Ruy could see the pain and bewilderment of a hurt, frightened child. He pressed, "Vadinho, where are your parents?"

All at once Vadinho exploded. Levering himself upright on his one good elbow, he swore at Ruy, cursing him in a mixture of languages with every gutter oath he could think of. Consuelo gasped, and Elaine, her face ashen, caught the boy by his shoulders and tried to push him back against the pillows. As suddenly as it had begun, the stream of filth was choked off, and Vadinho buried his face in Elaine's coat, sobbing. "Damn you, I don't know where they are!" he wailed. "They threw me out when I was ten."

As she comforted the weeping child, Elaine glared across the room at the two men, her own eyes glossy with tears. "Get out of here, both of you," she ordered them. "I will not permit you to harass my patient."

Ruy bowed his head. "I'm sorry. I did not mean to harass him, but I had to find out if there was anyone we should contact. Under the cirumstances, I suppose the boy will be our responsibility until we decide what to do with him."

João insisted, "It's obvious what to do with him. As soon as his injuries have healed, we must send him back to wherever he came from. I agree it's unfortunate the youngster appears to be one of the abandoned ones, but if the state won't take over his care, then he'll have to fend for himself. It is not up to us to cure the ills of society."

Ruy muttered, "We'll discuss this later, my friend." He addressed Elaine. "Is there anything you need, any way we may help you?"

"I think the two of you have done quite enough already." She was gazing at the boy, her caustic words at variance with her soft expression as she stroked him. His eyes drooped shut; he appeared to have succumbed at last to the injection she'd given him earlier. Elaine said, "Go away. Consuelo and I will be able to manage."

Ruy hesitated, stunned by the look on her face. He had thought her a cold woman, but when she held the hurt child, she glowed with a warmth, a tender compassion he'd never seen in her before. She glanced at Ruy, her eyes veiled with long, wet lashes. "We don't need you now," she whispered. "Please, just go."

Her beauty took his breath away. "Very well—but I'll be back."

When Elaine stepped out of the clinic, the sun was sinking toward the mountains in the west, bathing the little town with a golden glow. The tropical warmth of the late afternoon felt good on her bare shoulders, making her grateful that when she had removed the white lab coat she wore while treating Vadinho, she had not once again donned the thin cover-up that topped her sundress. Anyway, the people of Serra Brilhante did not seem likely to be offended by bare shoulders. Now that the men had come home from work, she spotted adults, singly and in couples, gravitating toward the recreation facilities in the central complex. A family—parents and four children— trooped by, dressed for the pool. The mother and oldest daughter were wearing the skimpiest bikinis Elaine had ever seen. She sighed. A swim sounded wonderful, but she had no bathing suit in her luggage. For that matter, she had no idea where her luggage was. The incident with Vadinho happened so soon after her arrival that she hadn't even seen her quarters yet.

"Elaine—"

She whirled around. Ruy was lounging against a stone planter beside the door, smoking a long, thin cheroot.

Like her, he had abandoned his jacket. The sleeves of his white shirt were rolled up over his elbows, revealing tanned, sinewy forearms. His tie was gone, his shirt was open at the collar, and in the dark V at his throat Elaine could see the string holding his *figa*. As she stepped toward him, he crushed out the cigar and dropped the butt into the planter.

"I didn't know you smoked," she said.

"I don't, at least not very often." He tapped his front teeth with a fingernail. "Stains the caps."

Admiring the perfection of his dental work, Elaine smiled reminiscently. "That's right: when we were kids you had a big chip out of that one tooth there. It made you very self-conscious. I'd forgotten."

Ruy's eyes darkened. "I'm surprised you could forget a thing like that. It seems to me I managed to bite you with that tooth more than once."

Elaine looked away, trying not to recall the rough, greedy kisses that had alarmed as much as they had aroused. He'd been a bumbling lover who had attempted to please, yet had been made clumsy and inconsiderate by the sheer force of his youthful hunger. Her own complete ignorance had not helped. She sighed. "That was a long time ago. I don't remember much about it."

"Really? I remember everything."

The words dissipated unanswered into the warm air. Ruy tried again. "Tell me, how is Vadinho?"

"Resting comfortably. Consuelo and I moved him into one of the beds in the ward. Since I'm not familiar with the clinic yet, she's agreed to sleep over to keep an eye on him. I'll take the shift tomorrow night."

Ruy frowned. "It's not too late to have him transported to a hospital, you know. That would relieve you
and the nurse of the burden of watching him."

Elaine shook her head. "No. Vadinho is already
frightened and upset enough without being packed off to
strangers. At least he knows us. If you want the other
doctor to confirm my diagnosis when he comes for the
weekly clinic, I don't mind a second opinion, but I really
don't anticipate any complications. He's strong and surprisingly healthy, considering his background. In a couple of days he should be improved enough to move out
of the ward. Even though he'll be able to get around on
crutches, he obviously can't return to the dorm with the
other unmarried miners, but Consuelo says she knows a
family who can take him in temporarily."

"For two women who don't speak the same language,
you and Consuelo seem to communicate remarkably
well," Ruy observed.

"We try. I flounder around with a Portuguese-English
dictionary in hand, and she very graciously declines to
laugh at my pronunciation. Besides, half the time we
don't use words. Consuelo is an excellent nurse—highly
skilled, very professional. While we were treating Vadinho, most of the time she knew exactly what I wanted
before I even asked. That kind of teamwork is rare."

Ruy said, "Well, despite the disappointment the other
nurse turned out to be, I'm gratified that at least one of
my choices was a success."

"A great success," Elaine amplified. "I can tell already that Consuelo is going to be a real pleasure to work
with." She paused for emphasis. "But, Ruy, no matter
how well Consuelo and I muddle along, it is imperative
that you find someone who can translate for me, as soon

as possible. I simply must be able to speak with my patients."

"Of course. I'll get on it the moment I return to São Paulo tonight."

Elaine felt her spirits deflate. "You have to go back so soon?"

"I'm afraid so. There's a great deal of paperwork from the trip to Antwerp that I haven't even begun to deal with. It should keep me busy for days. In the meantime, João will remain here at the site to make preparations for the arrival of the men and equipment from Corminco—we have to get started constructing the new housing. While he's here he'll be able to help you if any crisis arises. You needn't worry about being a stranger in a strange land."

Aware of the teasing note in his last words, Elaine protested without heat, "I'm not worried. I just— I just wish you could stay longer."

Ruy made a resigned gesture. "I know, *namorada*, I know. The thought of climbing into yet another airplane is singularly unappealing to me, too." He glanced at the darkening sky. "I expect the pilot will want to depart within the hour, while there's still daylight left for the takeoff—our landing strip has no lights. So, in what little time we have, why don't I at least show you to your quarters? You must be exhausted."

"It has been an eventful day," Elaine agreed, curling her arm through his. "I'll be glad for some rest."

They strolled together across the compound, past the crowded recreation hall and swimming pool, past a small chapel to which, Ruy explained, the diocese sent a visiting priest at intervals to hold Mass. They were headed for a cluster of houses located behind the central complex, houses fashioned of the same concrete block as the

trees framing the front porches. "Obviously intended for
the upper echelon," Elaine noted dryly when Ruy un-
locked the front door of one of the bungalows. Holding
his arm, she was surprised to feel him tense when he ushered her inside.

Although the gathering twilight made the interior of
the house shadowy, Elaine saw at a glance that her quarters, while not spacious, looked comfortable and attractive, decorated with vivid fabrics that offset the dark teak
furniture. When Ruy flicked on a lamp beside the couch
in the living room, a spray of green orchids picked up the
light and glowed their showy splendor. The house was
spotlessly clean—thanks, Ruy said, to a local woman
who came in once a day; if desired, the woman would
cook, as well. Elaine said she'd consider it, but for the
moment she thought she'd be content with the basket of
fruit centered temptingly on the small dining table.

As soon as she'd made sure that her luggage had been
placed in the larger of the two bedrooms, Elaine returned to the living room and sat down on the couch, inviting Ruy to join her. "This is lovely," she commented.
"When I agreed to come here, I never envisioned anything so nice."

"We could hardly expect a Welles to make do with less
than the best Serra Brilhante has to offer."

Elaine glanced sharply up at him. Hovering above her,
his expression was cryptic. She ventured, "You know,
Ruy, I'm not quite the pampered, frail little blossom you
seem to think I am. I may have money, but I learned a
long time ago to cope with the harsh realities of life."

"Yes," he admitted, his strained posture slackening as
he sank onto the bright cushions beside her, "I'm just
beginning to appreciate that. I was very struck by the way
you handled Vadinho. The boy responded to you at once,

as if he recognized instinctively that you were someone he could depend on."

"I think that poor child would respond to anyone who showed him a little kindness," Elaine declared sadly. She shuddered. "Abandoned on the streets when he was ten—my God, I can't even begin to imagine what his life has been like these past three years."

"I can," Ruy mused. "Although I was a bit older than Vadinho when I left home, big enough to fend for myself, I've never forgotten the loneliness and desperation, the sort of soul-grinding despair that would overcome me whenever something happened to remind me that the world simply did not recognize my existence. But you're wrong if you think that kind of isolation makes one more likely to trust people. Quite the contrary."

He grew quiet for a moment, framing his words. "Did you hear Vadinho say that he came to Serra Brilhante because he heard on the *morro*—the hillside—that there were jobs here? I'm almost certain he was referring to one particular Rio slum that overlooks Guanabara Bay. It may be somewhat improved now, but years ago it was a warren of shanties with no water, no power and no sewers—just dogs and pigs and thousands of people the rest of the world considered of no account. Most of the inhabitants were decent and resourceful and lived as well as their poverty and ignorance allowed them to, but still they were wary of strangers. There was no telling who might be one of the criminals who hid in the *favelas*—or worse, an informer for the *Esquadrão da Morte*, 'the death squad'. . . the vigilantes who used to track them down." Ruy paused, glancing sidelong at Elaine. "If I seem to know a lot about the place," he said deliberately, "it's because once upon a time I lived there myself."

Falling silent again, Ruy awaited Elaine's reaction to his revelation. When she sat calmly, her expression composed as she gazed at him, he muttered incredulously, "I expected you to be shocked."

"By what?" Elaine asked, her brow furrowing. "By the news that you lived in a *favela* when you first came to Brazil? I already knew. Sonia told me."

Ruy's face darkened. "Sonia Oliveira does not know as much about me as she thinks she does," he muttered grimly.

"I'm well aware of that." Elaine dismissed the woman with a wave of her hand. "She assumes you and I met for the first time in Denver. But she did say you once lived in the Rio slums."

"What else did she tell you?"

Elaine searched his strong features, wondering about the secrets that lay hidden behind them. She had no intention of revealing what she'd heard about the old woman he had lived with—the witch or priestess or whatever she was. If he wanted her to know, he would tell her himself. Lightly she replied, "Sonia didn't say much, other than she thought you worked on the docks before you went prospecting for gold in the Amazon. That was about it."

"And none of these revelations—that I used to do menial labor for pennies, that there was a time in my life when I was grateful for a crust of bread or a lean-to of battered tin to keep the rain off me—knowing these things does not bother you?"

"Of course it bothers me!" Elaine exclaimed. "It bothers me like hell to think that you—or Vadinho or anyone else, for that matter—should be hungry and homeless. It bothers me more than you'll ever guess that some of us have so much while others have nothing."

Ruy stared at her, his lionlike eyes intent beneath hooded lids. He drawled, "Unfortunately not everyone is fated to be born into an aristocratic family like the Welleses of Denver."

Stung by his mockery, Elaine jumped to her feet. "Sorry to disillusion you, Ruy," she tossed back bitterly, "but the much-vaunted 'Welleses of Denver' are only hardscrabble Missouri farmers who happened to get lucky a few generations back. If my great-grandfather hadn't stumbled across the Copa de Oro, we'd probably still be trying to scrape a living from a little spread outside Joplin. In fact, considering the plight of the American farmer these days, we might be out on the streets ourselves."

She stalked through the archway to the dim dining area, where she picked up the basket and began to finger the luscious mangoes, oranges and other fruit that filled it. She selected a peach and sank her teeth into the ripe, juicy flesh. The flavor was delectable, but she was so angry that she could not appreciate it fully. Suddenly Ruy's grip closed over her upper arms. She jerked with surprise, dropping the peach; it rolled across the tabletop toward the edge. Elaine scrambled to catch it. "Allow me," Ruy muttered, reaching past her to grab the fruit before it pitched to the floor. Retrieving the peach, he set it carefully on the table. His arms wrapped around Elaine's waist, and he drew her back against the length of his body.

"Let me go," she said.

"No." Pale curls fluffed softly against his cheeks. Through her flimsy sundress he could feel her fine bones. Because of her tremendous emotional strength, it was always a surprise to hold her and realize how delicately made, how fragile she was...how easily hurt. Holding her reminded him of a time in the Amazon goldfields when, buried to his waist in mud, he had stopped for a moment to wipe the sweat and grime from his eyes. While he'd paused, to his amazement, a butterfly had fluttered out of the steaming sky to rest on the end of his pick handle. He had stared transfixed as the iridescent blue wings had slowly opened and closed, revealing their ethereal beauty. As he'd gaped, a large dirty hand had suddenly reached across the staked line separating his claim from the adjacent one and had snatched the butterfly from its perch, crushing it. "Hey, man, snap out of it," the miner next to him had laughed. "Has the sun got to you or something? There's no profit in bugs!" Ruy had stared in horror at the shining, broken wings littering the ground, fragments of heaven lying in the muck.

Elaine could feel tension vibrating in the lean body wrapped around hers. His fingers splayed open until his thumbs rested tantalizingly at the base of her rib cage. "Let me go," she whispered again, hoarsely.

His lips moved caressingly over her hair. "Please. I have to leave soon. Let me hold you, just for a moment." Nuzzling her ear he murmured, "I'm sorry I was sarcastic about your family. Forgive me. I suppose I was frustrated and irritated by the thought of you and Sonia gossiping about my past."

"Sonia was gossiping," Elaine corrected breathlessly, "I just listened. Even if I had wanted to gossip, except for those few months in Switzerland, I know nothing about you."

Ruy's mouth found the vulnerable curve of her neck. The silky brush of his mustache made her skin prickle. She reached up to shield her shoulder with her hand, trying to flick his mouth away. Instead he licked her fingertips. "You taste of peaches," he murmured. Suddenly the bodice of her dress felt very tight.

His hands inched higher. "I'm sure I told you about my background when we knew each other before," he insisted quietly. "I must have."

She shivered. "You told me lots of things. I—I just never knew which ones t-to believe."

She could feel his frown. "I told you I loved you."

Elaine said sadly, "I believed that least of all—"

Before the words escaped her lips, he whirled her in his arms. Pushing her back against the edge of the table, his mouth ground down over hers, only to be met by an answering force of her own. Hungrily they collided—teeth meeting, nipping; tongues dueling with an almost painful ferocity. She wove her fingers into his thick silver hair, while Ruy's hands skimmed upward and closed at last over the breasts that ached for his touch, the layer of fine fabric no barrier to the press of her tender, puckered nipples. Mewling deep in her throat, Elaine arched against him. He was fiercely aroused. The evidence of her power over him made her shake.

She caught Ruy's hands in her own. Thinking she was about to push him away, he groaned against her lips, "For God's sake, not yet—"

She moaned. Carrying his fingers to her shoulders, she looped his thumbs through the narrow straps of the sundress. "Undress me," she whispered.

Ruy lifted his head, searching her face. Even in the failing light he could see the flush of red on her cheekbones, her throat. "What did you say?"

"Undress me," she repeated urgently. "Not all the way, but enough so I can feel your skin against mine." She began unbuttoning his shirt.

His hands moved along her arms, peeling away the dress. Her naked breasts gleamed pearly and inviting. Awed, he cupped his hands around the taut flesh that was fuller than he remembered, the areolas darker. "*Deus*, Elena—"

"No, not Elena!" she cried. "I'm not a girl anymore. I'm Elaine—a woman—and I'm too old to be coy about what I want." Her tone softened slightly as her fingers burrowed under the lapels of his shirt and slid downward through the wiry hair on his chest, tracing his flat stomach, loosening his belt buckle. "Don't worry, *querido*," she soothed, "I don't expect declarations of love from you. What I want is you inside me—here, now, as fast and as deep as possible." She found the impressive evidence of his desire. Smiling whimsically, she added, "And unless I've been away from medical school too long, that's what you want, too."

"My God, you amaze me," he said thickly, quaking at her touch. He lifted her onto the edge of the table and brushed her skirt aside. She leaned back and propped herself up on her hands, watching with glowing eyes while he stripped away the undergarments that hindered them and spread her legs. When his fingers touched her moist, scented softness, he almost lost control. He could feel sweat bead his forehead.

Her voice was a croak of emotion tearing the heated silence. "Now," she choked. *"Now!"* Cupping her bare bottom, he surged against her, filling her. She locked her legs around his hips and dug her nails into his shoulders as she clung to him. The table bounced, spilling the basket of fruit onto the floor, perfuming the air with the fragrance of mangoes and peaches. Ruy and Elaine did not notice. Together they writhed and whimpered with a passion in which an anguished past and an uncertain future were powerless against the explosive, irresistible force of the present....

SHE WAS STILL CLINGING to him when he carried her into the living room and they sank onto the sofa. She lay across his lap, her head snuggled against his chest as she listened, dazed, to the deep throbbing sound of his heart beneath her ear. When he caressed the sleek line of her bare thigh with long, soothing strokes, she sighed contentedly.

"Did I hurt you?" Ruy asked suddenly.

Elaine lifted her head, blinking in bewilderment at his worried expression. The feeling of drowsy satisfaction cushioning her at the moment was so complete that a word like "hurt" was meaningless. "I don't understand."

"I must have hurt you," he murmured, half to himself, "mounting you like a rutting stallion. You're so delicate. You need delicacy."

"I need exactly what you gave me," Elaine insisted as she pushed herself upright and stretched lazily. She watched his eyes grow murky again as he gazed at her full, womanly breasts. Reluctantly pulling the sundress back up over her shoulders, she said, "Accept it, Ruy. I'm a mature adult now, with adult needs and desires. Whatever you may have known about me when I was a teenager is irrelevant." She paused, pursing her lips. "For that matter, I know nothing about what you want, either. If I disappointed you—"

He gave a shout of laughter. "You didn't disappoint me... far from it. You astonished and delighted and rejuvenated me—I thought I was well past the age for sexual gymnastics."

Elaine smiled teasingly. "Well, maybe neither one of us is quite as old as we feel sometimes."

All at once Ruy's expression sobered. "There's one thing we're both definitely young enough for," he said seriously. "Elaine, my darling, you made me so crazy with wanting you that I didn't even think about taking precautions. Are you going to be all right?"

The acceptance of her sterility was so deeply ingrained in Elaine's being that it took her a moment to realize what he was talking about. She gazed blankly at him. Then suddenly the afterglow of their lovemaking dissipated completely, overwhelmed by pain and loss. She looked at Ruy Fonseca Areias and remembered who he really was, how he had used and abandoned her, and at what cost. She remembered her lingering qualms about his business ethics, his intentions toward Corminco. She slid off his lap and turned away, trembling with revulsion. Her foot kicked an orange that had rolled into the living room. She bent to pick it up. The golden fruit had split in the fall, and the juice ran thin and sharp over her fingers.

Ruy stared at her back, her hunched shoulders. He said, "You must know, if there are any consequences of our carelessness, I'll make sure you're all right. I'd never let you down."

"Oh, no, of course not," she agreed, wincing at the irony. She could not face him. She swallowed thickly. "Thanks for the offer, but you needn't worry, Ruy. There's no chance I'll get pregnant."

"Then what's wrong?"

Slowly she turned. The flush of passion had faded from her cheeks, leaving them marble-pale. She glanced at her wristwatch. "It just occurred to me that it's past time for you to find the pilot and leave for São Paulo," she temporized. "I wouldn't want you to be late...." Her voice faded. Then testily she blurted, "Oh, hell, I guess I'm just not as crazy about quickies as I thought I was!"

He stood up. As he straightened his clothes, his eyes never left her face. She was blinking back tears. "The next time will be no quickie, Elaine," he said gruffly, drawing her into his arms to kiss her goodbye. Her lips were gentle, but he could feel her withdrawal. Releasing her, he sighed. "The next time, we'll have all the time in the world. I promise."

CHAPTER NINE

As HE HOBBLED back and forth between the kitchen and the dining area, noisily setting the table for lunch, Vadinho chattered. "You know, doc, according to some of the people around here, Saci has taken up residence in the mine."

Elaine lifted her head from the sofa cushion. She'd been awake since 3:00 a.m., when a set of twin boys had decided to make their appearance into the world. Despite the multiple birth, both babies topped six pounds, and now mother and sons were safely ensconced at home, resting. Elaine was trying to do the same.

"What on earth are you talking about, Vadinho?" she asked groggily. "I don't recall anyone around here named Saci."

In the weeks since Elaine arrived in Serra Brilhante, she had learned to recognize most of the inhabitants of the small community, and she could greet many by name. They, in turn, were always unfailingly courteous to her. Their formal politeness only emphasized the distance between her and them. Although the mine workers and their families came from a variety of backgrounds, Elaine was something altogether different: a foreigner, a woman doctor and the daughter of a rich industrialist. She knew the people were curious about her, but those same qualities that intrigued them also made her unapproachable. Despite Ruy's warnings, even the men treated her with aloof respect. While she thought she was very slowly beginning to win the confidence of their wives, whom she attended professionally, she doubted anyone would ever regard her as anything but an outsider.

Except for Vadinho. He had adopted Elaine on sight. As soon as the doctor from Diamantina had replaced the original cast on his ankle with one suitable for walking, the boy began to limp after her on crutches wherever she went, a faltering shadow. He lingered in the waiting room of the clinic while she was on duty, and he tagged along when she went to the commissary daily to purchase bread and sugar. Elaine knew he was only responding to her kindness, but his constant attention worried her. He belonged in school, he belonged with other children. To this end, Elaine had made arrangements for him to move in with the family Consuelo had suggested. The mother, who was pregnant, was grateful for the money Elaine paid for his board and care—and warily Vadinho had allowed himself to be assimilated into their household. The children in the family included a boy Vadinho's age, and Elaine hoped his companionship would eventually break through Vadinho's reserve, but for the moment she was fearful he was becoming overly dependent on her. Moreover, she had already realized that in many ways she was dependent on him.

The other youngsters in the settlement were still busy with the final weeks of the school year, which would break for the summer at the beginning of December. As soon as they departed for class, Vadinho would hobble over to Elaine's quarters. He had made himself her guide and interpreter, and had become her houseboy and her friend. The ingratiating personality that had allowed him to wheedle a living from tourists now made him indispensible to her. He performed errands, he prepared light meals when the housekeeper was absent, he passed on the latest gossip and told her jokes in English. With him at her side, Elaine could relax from the constant strain of trying to cope with what was still a very alien world.

How alien it all was, was reinforced when Elaine asked again in confusion, "So who is this Saci you're talking about, and what's he doing living in the mine? I can't believe Mr. Cruz would allow such a thing."

Vadinho laughed heartily. "Fooled you, didn't I, doc? Saci-Pereré isn't a 'who,' at least not really. He's a story, a—a fairy tale. He's supposed to be a little black guy with one leg—" Glancing ruefully at his cast, Vadinho noted, "I guess that makes him a lot like me, except he uses a pipe, and I prefer cigarettes."

"Vadinho..." Elaine chided. They'd already had several mild arguments about his smoking.

"Sorry," the boy muttered, unabashed. "I promise I'm trying to quit. But anyhow, as I was saying, Saci goes around causing trouble for people. Sometimes he just plays jokes on them, like spooking animals or making food go bad, but other times his tricks get kinda scary."

Elaine nodded soberly. "I see. But what does this Saci creature have to do with the mines?"

Vadinho frowned. "A lot of country people believe in him, you know—of course, country people are awfully superstitious, not like us guys from the city—and they say it's Saci's fault men have been getting hurt lately—the way I was...."

His voice trailed off, and despite his alleged skepticism, Elaine saw his thumb slip between the fingers of his fist, forming a *figa*. She pretended not to notice. Instead she commented, "I wasn't aware there had been any more accidents among the miners."

"Oh, yeah, especially since the new equipment arrived from America. One guy nearly overturned a bulldozer, and another got his arm caught in the vibrating table that shakes the dirt off the stones. Took a lot of stitches to sew him up. I guess that must have been when the other doctor was on duty, or else you'd know about it. Maybe you were busy delivering a baby."

"Maybe," Elaine agreed dubiously. She had scheduled her office hours not to conflict with the other physician's weekly visits, and the two of them met to confer only when cases required it. Still she found it hard to believe she'd heard nothing. "I'd think one of the nurses would have mentioned the incidents."

Vadinho shrugged. "It'd be pretty hard for Consuelo to tell you anything, not speaking English, and as for the new one—" He broke off, making a face.

Although Elaine said nothing, she sympathized with Vadinho's disdain for the second nurse who had recently arrived from São Paulo. She did not care for the woman, either. Surprisingly, it had been João rather than Ruy who had finally located an obstetrical nurse with interpretive skills, but Elaine was less than thrilled with his choice. From the moment Magdalena had reached Serra Brilhante she had made it clear that she considered the town a wilderness, its inhabitants ignorant yokels she deigned to work with only because of the inordinately high salary A&O offered. She performed her medical duties with the same pained precision she used to translate, but her manner was so off-putting that Elaine worried her patients might keep silent rather than relay their symptoms and concerns through the unsympathetic woman. Outside office hours Magdalena remained sequestered in her quarters, associating with no one. Assuming she had heard about trouble at the mine, it was little wonder she'd failed to pass on the news.

Elaine let Vadinho prattle on while they ate lunch, but later, after her clinic closed for the day, she cornered João in the mine office, conferring with Senhor Cruz. Although the general manager was in charge of the day-to-day operation of the mine, since the new equipment had begun arriving from Corminco, João had flown into Serra Brilhante each week to oversee its installation. This was in keeping with his role as A&O's head of production; Ruy, the more cosmopolitan and diplomatic of the two men, handled marketing and the financial aspects of the business.

Elaine would have much preferred to discuss her apprehension with Ruy, but he had not returned to the site since he had brought her to her new "home." At first he had telephoned daily, but after that paroxysmal passion on her dinner table, Elaine could think of little to say. Ever mindful of Vadinho's constant presence, as well as the listening ears of the switchboard operators who put through calls, she had always made excuses to hang up. After a week or two her phone had stopped ringing. Now, when she needed to talk to him, she understood he was overseas once more.

Reluctantly she voiced her uneasiness to João. Dismissing Cruz, he stared pointedly at her and said, "Dr. Welles, while I appreciate your interest, I must suggest you devote your attention to the women and infants you were brought here to care for. Don't think your father's role in our business gives you more influence than it does. Other arrangements have been made for the men. Job safety is not your concern."

Struggling to maintain her temper, Elaine retorted, "You're wrong, Senhor Oliveira. My father's financial stake in this operation has nothing to do with my concern for the men. It's my patients I worry about, especially the pregnant ones. If they are constantly anxious about the welfare of their husbands, their health can be affected, and that of their babies. And neither of us wants anything hurting babies, do we?"

Under the heat of her anger, João looked away, his expression sullen. "No, of course not," he agreed grudgingly. "Very well, I will concede there have been one or two trivial incidents concerning our workmen. Mining is a hazardous business at best, and much of our equipment is old."

"I thought Corminco was contributing state-of-the-art technology to this project."

"It is. It has. But our labor force remains unskilled in its use. Most of our miners come straight from the farm or the slums. They do not understand modern work methods and they are unused to the routine safety precautions that are second nature in more developed countries. Some of them even regard minding the rules as a sign of effeminacy. I expect they will learn better, in time. But until they do, the occasional accident is inevitable."

"So you say the injury rate is due to inexperience, and not the pranks of some malicious spirit," Elaine concluded.

João looked at her as if she'd suddenly grown another head. Grimacing with distaste, he dismissed her impatiently. "I leave spirit worship to the peasants—and my business partner. Now, if you'll excuse me, doctor, I have work to do."

ELAINE TURNED OVER on her towel and stretched languidly in her shorts and halter top, praying the tropical sun would bake some of the tiredness from her weary muscles. For several days the clinic had been bustling with activity. There had been a constant stream of patients demanding her attention—for minor aches and pains, prenatal checkups, inoculations and general baby care. To most of the parents in Serra Brilhante, many of whom had never received regular medical attention prior to moving to the settlement, having a doctor routinely check the progress of an infant who was not obviously ill was a novel and rather bewildering concept. But once Elaine and Consuelo were able to convince them of the idea's importance, they began flocking to the clinic. Elaine was truly pleased to be playing a small role in improving the health of the next generation, but lately the unending flow of people through her treatment room had begun to sap her energy.

Then, late the night before, just as she was preparing for bed, Senhor Cruz had banged frantically on her door. The pregnant wife of a nearby farmer had gone into convulsions, he gasped, and it seemed unlikely the woman would survive the long drive to the closest hospital. Could Dr. Welles be so kind as to look at the woman, even though she was not, in fact, one of the good doctor's patients? Elaine had tossed on her bathrobe and run barefoot across the compound to the clinic, where she found Consuelo waiting in similar dishabille. By the time Magdalena arrived, fully dressed, Elaine had already diagnosed the woman as suffering from severe pre-eclampsia; her blood-pressure readings almost shot off the top of the scale. When the convulsions did not respond to drugs, Elaine had had no choice but to perform an emergency C-section. Providentially, both mother and child survived the difficult birth. A helicopter arrived at dawn to transport them to a maternity hospital in Belo Horizonte.

Elaine had had time for only a brief nap, and then the morning deluge of patients had begun again, and she was as busy as she'd been before the emergency—busier, because the women all wanted a few extra minutes to gossip about the uproar of the previous night. For once she had been almost grateful that Magdalena's imperious manner discouraged small talk. Then, after a lunch break during which Elaine felt far too exhausted to eat, she returned to her office to discover that the rush was over. No one waited in the clinic. Limp with relief, she closed early and sent her staff home.

And now she lay warm and languid on the tiny patio behind her bungalow, enjoying the solitude as she basked like a lizard in the somnolent silence. Even Vadinho was gone. She had sent him to join the other children. It was the first week of December, and the school year had finished a few days before. Elaine wanted the boy to spend more time with youngsters his own age; he was a child and he needed to learn once again to act like a child. Sometimes Elaine thought he must be a thousand years old.

Yawning, she fumbled behind her back to untie the strings fastening her halter. While she knew she'd never have the nerve to wear a *tanga*, the outlandishly minuscule bikini favored by Brazilian women of all ages and sizes, as long as she was alone she saw no reason to encourage strap marks. Sitting up, she dropped the top onto the concrete beside her and began to slather sunscreen over her pale skin.

"You missed a spot," said a voice behind her.

Elaine jumped. Instinctively crossing her arms over her naked breasts, she jerked her head to stare over her shoulder. Ruy was standing in the doorway, gazing down at her. Beneath the luxuriant mustache his lips twitched at her defensive posture. "When did you get here?" she gasped breathlessly.

"Just now. There's a shipment of stones ready to be taken to the gemologist for sorting and grading. Since the plane was coming this way to pick them up, I thought I'd hitch a ride." His glance caressed the soft flesh only partly shielded by her hands. She reached for her halter. His eyes grew murky. "No, don't. It's been too long since I've looked at you."

"I—I need to cover up," Elaine stammered. "Th-the sun's too strong."

Dropping onto his haunches beside her, he mused, "Why are you out here at all? I thought nowadays doctors disapproved of tanning."

"I always time myself carefully, and I use a strong sun block," she replied automatically. She regretted the words when Ruy picked up the tube of lotion.

"Then we'd better make sure you've reached every spot, shouldn't we?" He squeezed a line of cream into his palm. The fragrance of cocoa butter filled the air, warm and sweet.

"Please, no."

Ruy smiled, ignoring her feeble protest. He caught her shoulder and eased her backward until she lay supine on the towel.

The sunlight stung her bare breasts. He loomed over her, a dark silhouette against the sky. Her words were a strangled groan. "Please..."

"Relax, darling," Ruy murmured. When he slid his hand along the line of her breastbone, through the layer of silky lotion she could feel the rough callus on his palms. There was something deliciously seductive about the contrast. Elaine closed her eyelids, shielding them with her forearm against the light that filtered through.

With long, hypnotic strokes Ruy smoothed cream into the hollows at her throat, the sensitive flesh under her arm, the slope of her breast. Though she was slipping into sleep, she could feel her nipples crinkle when his fingertips brushed them.

Ignoring the evidence of her arousal, he noted, "You needn't be afraid I'm going to make love to you here on the patio. I promised that next time we'd be comfortable and at our leisure. I'm too old not to appreciate the charms of a good bed, even if you do make me feel like a teenager again."

Elaine shifted drowsily. "I'd never survive being a teenager again," she said, yawning, "it almost killed me the first time."

His hands stilled. "Me, too," he declared brusquely. She could sense his brooding gaze on her, suddenly intent.

She was too tired to question his abrupt change of mood. Sinking deeper into the torpor that overwhelmed her, she had to struggle to hear him when he began speaking again. "I understand there was some excitement here last night."

"Uh-huh. It's all over now."

"Cruz says it was pretty dicey. He's tremendously impressed by the way you handled the situation."

"Any competent doctor could have done it."

Ruy pressed, "According to Cruz—and a lot of other people—you saved the woman's life."

At last his words cut through Elaine's fatigue. Rousing herself with difficulty, she lifted her lashes and squinted up at Ruy. His expression was unreadable. She forgot her nakedness as she levered herself up onto her elbows and shook her head to clear it. She said seriously, "I didn't perform any miracles last night, Ruy. The operation was a routine cesarean section. Of course, with a little routine prenatal care the need would never have arisen in the first place.''

"Here in the backcountry, medical care is never 'routine.' Much of the time it's simply unavailable. Maybe the miracle is that you were here at all to help that woman.''

Elaine exhaled windily. "Maybe so, but what about in a year or two, when she's pregnant again? For that matter, what about other women who aren't lucky enough to just happen to have a company doctor close at hand? What do they do?''

"Sometimes they die.''

The grim fatalism in his voice made Elaine shudder with frustration. "Please don't think I'm knocking Brazil,'' she said plaintively. "All the time in my own supposedly enlightened country I encounter women who never see a doctor until they start labor—or something goes terribly wrong. Some stay away because they think they can't afford prenatal care. Others simply don't know any better. And still others—usually no more than babies themselves—won't get help because they're too scared....'' The memories, both professional and very personal, aroused by her words made Elaine feel sick. She buried her face in her hands.

Ruy watched compassionately, a little surprised at the protective feelings her distress aroused in him. She cared. A Welles actually *cared*.

Laying a comforting hand on her shoulder, he reminded her, "Elaine, nobody can save the whole world. Last night you managed to save a woman and child who might not have survived otherwise. Isn't that enough?''

"I don't know,'' she said glumly.

He captured her chin in his fingertips and searched her features. Despite the faint blush of pink tingeing her nose, her expression remained wan. "You're becoming sunburned," he murmured. Then, bracingly he declared, "It seems to me, my dear, that what you need right now more than anything is a little rest and recreation. As far as I know, you haven't had a break since you first arrived in Serra Brilhante. You should go away. How would you like to go to Rio tonight?"

Elaine blinked. "Just like that?"

"Just like that," Ruy assured her. "If we commandeer the company plane, we can reach the coast in no time." He hesitated. "Unless, of course, there are any more babies you expect to deliver within the next twenty-four hours?"

After a moment's consideration, Elaine shook her head. "No, I think things have settled down for a while."

"Bom," Ruy declared. "In that case, while you pack a few things—you might want to bring that dress you wore to the gem exhibition in São Paulo. We can change at our hotel—I'll tell your staff you'll be gone until tomorrow evening. Cruz can notify the doctor in Diamantina that he's on call. And then there will be nothing to prevent you from having your night in Rio—" He broke off, puzzled. "You have the most peculiar look on your face. Is something wrong?"

Elaine flashed a whimsical smile. "I was just thinking how ineffably romantic 'a night in Rio' sounds, like strolling in the moonlight along Copacabana Beach with samba music playing in the background. Wasn't there some classic movie from the thirties by that title?"

Ruy shrugged. "I wouldn't know, I'm not a film buff. But if you want a walk along Copacabana, we'll take one. If you want samba music, we'll find a nightclub." His gaze drooped to her sun-kissed breasts. "And if you want romance . . ."

IT WAS TWILIGHT when the small plane crested the coastal mountains on the western side of Rio de Janeiro. They were heading for Santos Dumont Airport, located in the heart of the central district on a finger of land extending into Guanabara Bay. Elaine gasped. The light-spangled city lay in a long curve in the shadow of the mountains, facing the most beautiful harbor she'd ever seen. In the water could be seen the reflection of the red beacon that gleamed on Sugar Loaf, the shadowy, hump-shaped mountain that loomed like a sentinel over the entrance to the bay. Inland, atop a higher peak, a huge statue of Christ bathed in green floodlights overlooked the highways and skyscrapers. His arms were outstretched to embrace the populace. "Oh, Ruy," Elaine gasped.

"Corcovado. The first sight is always breathtaking," Ruy agreed quietly. "I'll never forget mine. I arrived here on a coffee freighter, after the most wretched journey of my life. I'd been miserable and seasick the whole time. Returning to Europe was impossible, but I was scared witless at the thought of what was waiting for me in Brazil. But one day while we were still far out to sea, someone hollered and I stopped vomiting over the railing long enough to look up. There hovering in the clouds above Rio was the Christ, with His hands held out in welcome. I knew then that I'd survive."

Elaine regarded Ruy curiously. "I had no idea you were religious."

"I'm not," he said lightly. "But I recognize the power of symbols. Brazilians are very fond of symbolism, as you can see by the statue on Corcovado or the futuristic architecture of the government buildings in Brasilia—"

"Or the *figas* people wear," Elaine added.

He fingered the little charm through the fabric of his shirt. "Yes, those, too," he murmured dryly. He glanced at Elaine's lap. "Is your seat belt fastened? We're about to land."

Much, much later in the evening, after they had dined on lobster cooked in tomatoes and coconut milk, and listened to haunting, seductive music performed by an expert *sambista*, Ruy and Elaine strolled arm-in-arm in the moonlight along the mosaic sidewalks edging Copacabana Beach. An ocean breeze fluffed the apricot silk of her dress as he suddenly returned to the topic they'd been discussing on the plane. "You're curious abut the *figa*, aren't you? You want to know about the woman who gave it to me."

"You know I do," Elaine said, her grip tightening. Beneath the sleeve of his dinner jacket she could feel the muscles of his arm, reassuring in their strength. She was going to need reassurance if he told her he'd been an old witch's gigolo.

"Where to begin?" Ruy wondered aloud. "Her name was Dona Maria, she must have been about seventy years old—although she never admitted her exact age, if she even knew it—and the first time I ever saw her she was being beaten by a couple of thugs." He frowned in distaste at the memory. "Not that the sight of a battered woman was new to me—far from it. In Lisbon my uncle used to abuse my aunt with tiresome regularity. But that day when I took a shortcut through an alley and discovered two hulking men pounding their fists into this tiny, wizened woman, something in me exploded. I don't know why. I'd never seen any of the three of them before. Perhaps I was only looking for an excuse to vent the fury and frustration building in me ever since I arrived in Rio. Now I had a chance to take direct action against something. But I yelled at the men to stop hitting her, and when they ignored me, I picked up a piece of lumber I found lying nearby, and I went after them.''

"And you drove them away?" Elaine prompted, intrigued by the scene Ruy described. Even as a boy he had never impressed her as a brawler.

He chuckled wryly. "They ran—but in retrospect I'm sure they were far more afraid of Dona Maria than they were of me. One of the two claimed he had lost his woman to a rival because of a love charm Dona Maria had made, and he and his brother had dared attack her only after heavily fortifying themselves with *cachaça*, a sugarcane liquor that's almost pure alcohol. By the time I blundered onto the scene swinging my two-by-four, they were beginning to sober up enough to realize how dangerous it is to anger an Umbanda priestess."

"What happened then?"

"I could see Dona Maria was badly bruised and shaken, and I wanted to take her to a doctor, but she refused. Instead, she asked me to help her home. She directed me to a little hut in the middle of the slum overlooking the railway station, and when I took her inside, I saw a poster of Yemanjá tacked to the wall, with flowers and candles arranged in front of it. That was when I first suspected she was something besides just a pitiful old woman. She thanked me for bringing her home, and then she offered me a shot of *cachaça*, the first I'd ever tasted. After I recovered from the drink— for a few moments I thought my throat had been burned away—she told me she had a gift for me, something to protect me from devils, and then she gave me the *figa*.''

"And you've worn it ever since?"

"I have to," Ruy said. "If you lose a *figa*, all the bad luck it's warded off will come back to you. Besides, giving me the charm was the first unselfish thing anyone ever did for me."

Elaine flinched. Turning her head, she stared out at the moonlit ocean while she blinked back the tears that stung her eyes. Once upon a time she had given him her love unselfishly—too unselfishly, without a thought for her own protection. Her whole life since had been prejudiced by that girlish altruism, and now he didn't even credit her with caring. His skepticism hurt.

But the question was, she admitted candidly, did she have any right to feel hurt when it was only her own stubborn pride that prevented her from telling him what had happened?

After twenty-two years she still didn't know the answer.

Forcing a laugh to disguise the huskiness in her voice, Elaine queried brightly, "So you and Dona Maria became fast friends?"

Ruy frowned, puzzled by her unnatural tone. After a moment he shook his head and said, "We were more than friends. She became my confidante, my mentor...my mother. Everything I am today I owe to her. I loved her."

That simple statement of emotion shook Elaine. She hadn't known he was capable of deep feeling. Aware that Ruy would relish the irony of Elaine Welles being jealous of a pathetic old crone from a Rio slum, she suggested, "Maybe you'd better tell me more about her."

"I'm not sure I know how," Ruy said. "I've never told anyone about her before." They walked in silence for several yards before he continued. "The day after Dona Maria and I met, I went back to the *favela* to check on her. To my surprise, almost immediately she asked me to move in with her. I assumed she was afraid that the men who'd attacked her might return, and she wanted some protection. After the flophouses I'd been sleeping in, her little shack seemed almost an improvement, so I accepted the offer. It was only later that she explained she'd cast my fortune and discovered the gods had great plans for me: I was to be a man of wealth and power. To see that their bidding was done, she made me educate myself, and when the gold rush began in the Amazon, she used her meager savings to help me stake a claim. The only thing she asked in return was that after I became rich, I should make sacrifices to the gods in her honor."

"And did you?"

"Did I what?" Ruy echoed. "Become rich? Beyond Dona Maria's—and my own—wildest fantasies, although it didn't happen at once. After two years in the goldfields, I thought I'd failed. I found a few nuggets on my claim, but I never made the fabulous stike I hoped for. What I did have was a number of shares in other miners' claims that I had either bought or won gambling. Still, I wasn't happy. But my disappointment seemed petty compared to what I found when I came back to Rio. My friend was dying."

When he paused, Elaine could hear the real pain roughening his voice. "I'm sorry," she said.

He sighed. "There's no reason to be sorry. She was an old woman, and by her lights she'd lived a good life. All that mattered to her now was that I remember my vow to make offerings in her honor. When I told her I'd failed to get rich, she became very agitated. The gods never lied, she insisted. They had promised me both wealth and power, and if I didn't have the money yet, that meant I must have the power, even if I didn't realize it. It was up to me to figure out what it was."

"Obviously you did work out the puzzle eventually," Elaine noted.

Ruy nodded. "After Dona Maria died, I suddenly realized that a substantial portion of those shares I held were in the forms of IOU's cosigned by João Oliveira, of the prestigious Companhia Oliveira. It seemed he'd had grandiose plans of cornering the gold market, but his scheme backfired and he'd overextended himself. Since there was no longer any reason for me to stay in Rio, I traveled to São Paulo and confronted João. I demanded either payment in full or an executive position in his firm. He gave me the job—"

"And you took his business away from him," Elaine concluded.

Shrugging, Ruy said, "It wasn't quite that cut-and-dried, but essentially you're correct. I acquired a majority of A&O's stock, and my first million, before I was thirty—" He broke off, smiling ruefully. "Of course, at the same time I also acquired this head of gray hair."

Elaine glanced up, admiring the sheen of moonlight on his silver locks. She reached up to stroke back a strand that had fallen across his forehead. "It really is very distinguished-looking gray hair," she said.

His mouth quirked. "I'm glad you approve."

They stood in silence for several moments as Elaine gazed into the shadowed recesses of Ruy's face, wishing she could read the thoughts hidden there. She realized that for perhaps the first time she was truly seeing him not as the boy Antonio but as the man he'd become since. Slowly she said, "Thank you for telling me about your friend. I wish we could have met. In a funny way she reminds me of my great-grandmother. I think I'd have liked her."

"I think she'd have liked you, too." He bent his head to hers, and their lips met with a gentle passion that transcended their earlier hunger. There was a kind of fierce tenderness new to their kisses. A party of teenagers swirled by them on the sidewalk, giggling and making smacking noises as they passed. Reluctantly, Ruy and Elaine ended the embrace. His arm tightened around her waist and with one mind they turned, striding purposefully along the mosaic tiles to the privacy of their hotel.

CHAPTER TEN

FROM THE BALCONY on the thirtieth floor of the Meridien Hotel, Elaine sipped a goblet of mango juice and watched a pair of hang gliders dip and soar like tropical moths high above the white beach and the jade-green waves. The morning sun sent their long shadows dancing across the facades of the hotels lining the waterfront. Despite the early hour, she could see people already darting through the traffic on the Avenida Atlantica to spread their vivid towels on the sand and venture into the surf. Joggers stitched lines of footprints in the slick area just below the high-water mark, and parties of sleek, bronzed men strung up volleyball nets. Elaine tugged her negligee close about her shoulders and sighed.

Behind her she heard the rustle of linen as Ruy slipped from the bed to pad barefoot across the thick carpet. "Room service already brought up breakfast," she called without looking around.

"I'll eat later," he grumbled. She could feel his nearness before he touched her. She set her glass on the railing as he slipped his hands beneath her arms. He urged her back against the naked length of his torso, molding her breasts through the fine lace of her gown. "Why so dejected, *namorada*?" he asked as he teased her earlobe with his lips.

She shivered and wrapped her arms over his, tightening the embrace. They had come together repeatedly during the night, but she could not get enough of him. His warm breath against her neck, the brush of his mustache, was seducing her yet again. Her skin felt prickly, charged. When he wriggled his fingers, she arched tremulously, galvanized by the brush of his thumbs across her nipples.

"Elaine, tell me what's bothering you," he ordered. He seemed to be under control, yet his words were a husky rumble deep in his throat.

Her own voice sounded reedy and unnaturally high. "You bother me," she said faintly. "We bother me."

His hands stilled. "Why? Don't try to convince me you haven't enjoyed our lovemaking. I felt your response. My God, I felt my own! It has never been like this for me before."

"Not for me, either." Elaine shuddered deliciously, remembering the sweet madness he roused with his hands, his mouth, his lean, powerful body.... "I had no idea I could be this way," she admitted candidly, "and that's what's wrong. You and I make no sense. How can we be such amazingly compatible lovers? We don't love each other. Sometimes I'm not sure we even like each other very much."

Gently Ruy turned her in his arms. His expression was unfathomable as he gazed down at her. "Has your life been so blameless—or so blessed—that you've always loved the men you've gone to bed with?"

She hedged, "I've always trusted them. I was never afraid any of them would deliberately try to hurt me."

"But you're not sure about me."

The words were spoken without rancor, a simple statement of fact. Elaine decided to answer with the same frankness. "No," she said calmly, "I'm not sure about you."

His lips pressed into a thin line. "I see. May I ask why you distrust my motives?"

She shrugged. "I'm not a fool, you know. I've been aware from the beginning that something is going on that I don't yet understand. You've never explained the real reason you bulldozed me into coming to Brazil, just as you've never explained how it 'happened' to be my father's company you approached about your consortium. It's a long way from São Paulo to Denver. You may have been looking for foreign investors, but it couldn't possibly have been a coincidence that Corminco was the one you chose."

"Burton seems happy enough with the arrangement," Ruy pointed out.

"My father doesn't know who you are."

Ruy's face hardened. Releasing Elaine, he turned and stalked across the room to the breakfast cart. Pouring himself a cup of coffee, he rasped, "It always comes back to that, doesn't it? No matter what I've done with my life, no matter how I've improved myself, in the final analysis you still see me as a fortune-hunting guttersnipe with designs on your family's money."

"Am I wrong?"

As she watched, the muscles in his shoulders stiffened, causing little ripples of tension beneath the golden skin on his back. His voice sounded strained. "I've told you before, Elaine, I happen to be a very wealthy man now. I don't need the Welleses' money."

"Then what do you need from us?"

Slowly he turned. His face was composed, but the little white lines feathering from the corners of his eyes looked deeper, as though they'd been engraved with a heavy hand. Tightly he suggested, "Perhaps it would be more to the point for me to ask what you need from me. You claim to distrust my motives in inviting you to my country, yet you've come anyway. You've put yourself at a definite disadvantage. Why?"

"Why not?" Elaine countered. "In the first place, I don't consider that I am all that much at a disadvantage where you're concerned. I may have been a trifle disoriented when I first arrived in Brazil, but I know how to take care of myself. I'm here to do a job, and I'm not going to let you—or João or anyone else—intimidate me into giving less than my best." She paused, allowing her gaze to move slowly over his naked body; her eyes widened with frank appreciation. "As for the other reason I'm here—bluntly, I enjoy your company and your caresses. In my work I deal with birth and death on a daily basis, and I know how fragile life is—so fragile that I'm not about to waste any of the good things while I quibble about motives."

Ruy's features relaxed into a piquant smile. "And my lovemaking qualifies as one of the good things of life?"

"The best," Elaine said, heaving a delicious sigh. "I'll always be a little amazed—and grateful for the time we've spent together."

"Then what's wrong? Why did you sound so dispirited a few moments ago, when I first woke up?"

Elaine gestured helplessly. "I suppose it's because in some ways I'm a fraud. No matter how pragmatically I try to live or what compromises I've made, at heart I'm still a romantic. I want to believe there can be more to a relationship than good sex. I want to believe that love and lovemaking go together."

Crossing the room in long strides, Ruy drew Elaine into his arms. He could feel the faint tremor in her body as he held her close, pressing her cheek against his shoulder while he stroked her pale hair. "Elaine, my darling," he said huskily, "I wish I could reassure you about love, but I can't. I never knew the answers to questions of that sort. I can't even assure you with any certainty that I'll never hurt you." He captured her chin with gentle fingertips and lifted her face to his. As his lips brushed over hers he murmured, "The only thing I can promise you is that I'll never hurt you like this...."

LATE THAT EVENING, when the Volkswagen Kombi pulled to a halt at Elaine's bungalow, she and Ruy found Vadinho slumped forlornly on the front porch, a tangle of thin, ungainly limbs made even more awkward by the casts. At the sound of the vehicle, he jerked his head up, and his dark face glowed with relief. "Oh, God," Elaine breathed, stricken with compunction as she watched him struggle to pull himself up with his crutches, "he didn't think I was coming back."

Ruy patted her hand. "But you did come back. That is what is important." Signaling the driver to leave the motor idling, Ruy climbed out of the station wagon and held the door for Elaine. Before they could walk the few feet to the door, Vadinho hobbled out to them. "Hi, doc, hi, boss! How was Rio?"

As Elaine hugged the boy in greeting, her eyes flicked upward, meeting Ruy's gaze then darting away. She could feel a tingle of warmth in her cheeks. "Rio was wonderful. The most beautiful city I've ever seen."

Now that Elaine was safely home once more, Vadinho's air of youthful bravado returned. "Aw, doc, Rio's okay," he informed her loftily, "but I bet it can't compare with cities in America. One of these days I'm going there myself."

"You do that," Ruy agreed, nodding. He held out a small parcel to the boy. "Here's a little something we found this afternoon while we were poking around at Disco do Dia. We thought you might like it."

"A present? For *me*?" Vadinho's astonishment was almost painful to behold. Elaine wondered if anyone had ever given him a gift before. Holding her breath, she watched him eagerly tear into the wrapping paper to reveal a small transistorized cassette player and a collection of tapes featuring both North and South American rock groups.

"At home I know most boys your age prefer to lug around the big blasters," Elaine explained, "but we thought that as long as you're on crutches, a little player like this would be easier for you to manage. You can clip it onto your belt."

"There are also headphones so your music won't deafen everyone," Ruy added dryly.

Vadinho blinked hard, clutching the player and plastic cassette boxes to his chest. "*Obrigado, muito, muito obrigado!* I-I don't know how I can ever pay you back...."

Ruy said, "Just keep looking after the doctor for me the way you've been doing, that's all I ask."

"Sure thing, boss, you bet!" Smiling blearily, the boy bore his treasures into the house. Moments later raucous music blared through the open door.

Elaine's brows lifted as she muttered, "I hope my eardrums are up to that."

"Make him use the headphones later," Ruy said. "For the moment, just let him enjoy himself."

Elaine nodded. "You're right. This seems to have been a big moment for Vadinho. Thank you for remembering him."

"The idea was as much yours as mine...." Ruy's voice trailed off, and all at once they fell into each other's arms. Their mouths blended with breathless intensity—wet and hungry, their lips slid and sucked, until reluctantly, the lovers parted, dazed. Elaine stared up at him with murky eyes. Now the only sound was the purr of the car's engine. Sighing heavily, Ruy said, "Darling, I have to go. I left the pilot waiting at the landing strip."

Her glum expression mirrored his. "I know. But that doesn't make it any easier to say goodbye."

"Not goodbye, Elaine," he countered, "never goodbye. *Até logo*—I'll see you soon."

"How soon?"

"As soon as possible. The weekend. Sooner. And when I return, nothing is going to keep us apart."

After the lights of the station wagon disappeared into the woods above the settlement, Elaine trudged into her bungalow. Vadinho was in the kitchen, his eyes closed in rapt appreciation as he swayed back and forth on his crutches in time to the music playing over his headphones, which he seemed to have figured out with little problem. Elaine had to tap his shoulder to get his attention. Regretfully he switched off the player.

"Well, Vadinho," Elaine asked with a wan smile, "how have things gone while I was away? Did anything exciting happen?"

The boy shook his head. "One kid slipped on the wet concrete by the pool and tore his knee a little, but Consuelo stitched him up and he's fine now. Other than that, it's been pretty quiet. You and the boss picked a good time for your trip." He paused, and when he spoke again, his voice sounded unusually serious. "Doc," he probed carefully, "does going away together like that mean that Senhor Areias is your man now?"

Elaine considered the question. Was Ruy her man
now? She liked the boy's forthright phrasing, so refresh-
ing after the coy terminology currently in vogue among
people of her own background. Ruy was not her boyfriend or her "significant other," just as he was not her
husband or perhaps even her lover in the truest sense of
the word. But, yes, he was her "man," the most influential male figure in her life. She supposed he always had
been.

She said, "Yes, Vadinho, Senhor Areias is my man
now."

"That's good," the boy judged firmly. "It's not right
for a nice woman like you to be alone."

RATHER TO ELAINE'S SURPRISE, the other residents of
Serra Brilhante accepted her relationship with Ruy with
the same ease Vadinho did. The two of them did not
flaunt their liaison, but the workers and their families
noticed immediately that Senhor Areias was flying up to
the mines at far more frequent intervals than before.
They also observed that the comfortable house reserved
for the boss's use went unoccupied, while he spent most
of his time at the doctor's bungalow. When Elaine worried about the townspeople's reaction, Ruy reassured her,
and in fact knowledge of the affair seemed to increase
Elaine's esteem. Many of her patients who had been
somewhat standoffish suddenly opened up to her, chat-
ting more freely, offering sympathy whenever Ruy had to
return to São Paulo. Elaine had thought it was Magdalena's curt manner, or her own foreignness, that had
made the women seem so remote. She had not realized it
was her unattached status they distrusted.

She also had not realized how much she lived for his
visits. Saying goodbye grew harder every time. It was not

just the sex she yearned for when Ruy was away, although the sight of his empty pillow beside hers made her weak with frustration; Elaine missed the opportunity to talk to him. It was such a relief to be with someone familiar with her own language, her own culture, who could discuss people and events that took place in a world not constricted by the woods and the river at the foot of the bluff. As interesting as she found her work in Serra Brilhante, sometimes Elaine felt cut off from everything she held dear.

The feeling of isolation was reinforced when she received mail from home. The first letter she opened was from her father, a stiff little communiqué on office stationery. Burton said he hoped Elaine was enjoying her time in Brazil. Through his correspondence with A&O, he understood she was working hard. He was glad to hear the news, and he was sure Elaine would never forget she was Corminco's de facto representative in South America. The note was signed "Your father." Wondering wistfully how much effort it would have cost him to pen "Your loving father" or even just "Love," Elaine set the paper aside. It would have been out of character for Burton to express his emotions. At least he'd written—even if the letter had obviously been dictated to his secretary.

Her mother's letter was more cheerful, full of news about Thanksgiving at the family's chalet in Aspen, where they all gathered each year. A predicted blizzard had failed to materialize, and skiing conditions had been so perfect, Carolyn and Kate and the children had spent virtually the whole weekend on the slopes. The twins were both progressing well, but Danny was turning into a regular little hot dog; he'd be ready for the Olympics by the time he reached college. Dan, Sr., had put in a few hours on the runs, but Burton had remained indoors immersed in paperwork, surfacing only for the holiday meal, which had consisted of trout quenelles and medallions of venison instead of the traditional turkey dinner. The food was wonderful and Elaine should have been there; it wasn't the same without her. Jennie should have been there, too, but of course she was busy with her own life in New York. In a postscript Carolyn noted that if Burton didn't mind, she thought she might take a few days at Christmas time and fly east to see her youngest daughter.

Reading her mother's letter, Elaine realized with shock that she'd skipped Thanksgiving altogether. Since the Brazilian celebration of the Proclamation of the Republic on the fifteenth of November was also election day, that holiday had been hard to miss, but the American feast later in the month had slipped her mind completely. Her forgetfulness surprised her. The annual ski trip to the chalet was the one family outing she usually enjoyed. She supposed it was impossible to think of snow when the thermometer was climbing toward eighty degrees.

And Christmas—good God, the holiday was less than three weeks away and she hadn't even begun her shopping. If she didn't make her purchases immediately, there wouldn't be enough time to ship them back to the United States. As she quickly formulated a gift list in her head it suddenly occurred to her that for only the second time in her life, she wouldn't be with the family on Christmas morning to see those gifts unwrapped. The first time had been when she was fifteen. She'd been scheduled to fly home for the holidays, but Burton had canceled those plans when the headmistress of the boarding school had reported that his daughter's grades had taken an abrupt and inexplicable nosedive.

The shopping was carried out almost too easily: leather goods for the men, handmade lace for Kate and Mom and a *tanga* for Jennie—the only person Elaine knew with the nerve to wear one. Within a matter of days all were shipped by air express, leaving Elaine with too much free time. There were only so many hours she could fill with work, and the charms of reading or watching television soon palled. Helping Vadinho construct a crèche and Christmas ornaments with craft materials borrowed from the school occupied a couple of afternoons, but since Elaine was actively encouraging the boy to spend more time with other children, she knew she could not bank on him to keep her amused.

Another day she hiked across the top of the mesa to the bluff overlooking the mines. From the rim she watched curiously as bulldozers cut terraced steps into the side of the cliff, while men with jackhammers followed to carve away the last of the stone overlying the gem-rich pegmatite veins. At the foot of the bluff still other men sifted through the alluvial debris the river had mounded there over the centuries. Elaine observed unhappily that few of the workmen deigned to wear hard hats, and a number of those digging in the muck near the water actually appeared to be barefoot. She shuddered with apprehension. Given the lack of routine safety precautions, it was no wonder accidents occurred—even if the townspeople did prefer to blame the mishaps on some malicious spirit.

Elaine did not realize her little excursion had been observed until Ruy returned the following weekend. Late in the evening, he and she lay curled together on the couch, sipping Grand Marnier and enjoying a classic Villa-Lobos recording Ruy had located in São Paulo. The lamplight cast a rosy glow over them as his fingers stroked Elaine's breast in time to the music. As they basked in the sultry prelude to passion, suddenly he said, "João tells me you've been snooping around the mining operation."

Lifting her head from his shoulder, Elaine frowned her confusion. "I haven't been 'snooping' anywhere. I was walking the other day and out of curiosity I headed in that direction. I'd never been to the mines before. I watched for a few minutes and then I left."

"Well, apparently the foreman on duty spotted you and didn't like it. He complained to the general manager, who complained to João—who, naturally, could not wait to relay their gripes to me."

Elaine asked, "But why should anyone mind if I take a look? I stayed well away. I wasn't interfering with anything."

"Perhaps not, but as a rule the women of Serra Brilhante show little interest in the actual operation of the mine. The men reasoned your presence had to be due to something other than mere inquisitiveness. Since you're a Welles, the most logical assumption is that you're a spy for Corminco."

"I'm not into industrial espionage," Elaine declared impatiently, "although I do get the impression my father wouldn't object if I were. But frankly, it's a good thing for everyone concerned that I'm *not* a spy for Corminco. Dad would have a fit if he saw what I did the other day. The safety standards here are appalling."

"They're not as bad as all that. Good Lord, when I remember what conditions were like when I was a boy in the Amazon goldfields—"

"I don't care what it was like in the goldfields," Elaine snapped. "You're not a boy and this isn't the Amazon!"

"It's not the United States, either," Ruy retorted. "You have no right to make judgments about things you don't understand."

Elaine said grimly, "I understand when people get hurt. I understand when accidents could be prevented but aren't—" She broke off, recalling what João had told her about the miners' ignorance and disdain for routine precautions. "Oh, hell," she grumbled, slumping back against Ruy's shoulder, "maybe I don't understand, after all. The idea of refusing to wear a hard hat because it's an affront to your machismo is totally incomprehensible to me."

Her bewilderment touched Ruy. "It's frustrating, isn't it, trying to save people who don't know they need saving?"

"Their wives know it," Elaine said glumly. "A lot of them think the mine is bad luck. They say there's an accident every time someone makes a big strike."

Ruy's expression was quizzical. "They say that, do they? How interesting..." His voice trailed off, then he hugged her bracingly. "If it's any comfort, sweetheart, I personally don't have problems with wearing a hard hat and steel-toed boots. When I'm at the diggings I always try to set a good example by using whatever safety gear is available. And," he bantered, "when any of the men make comments, I remind them that dangers like rockfalls are trivial when you compare them with the real threats to masculine pride."

Elaine's spirits perked at his teasing. "And what, may I ask, do you consider a real threat to the fragile male ego?"

"Oh, lots of things. A man has to worry about keeping his good name, keeping his family fed—" his eyes danced "—keeping his woman satisfied...."

"In that case, your ego must be pretty much unassailable," she drawled, "considering you created your name out of whole cloth and you don't have a family."

Ruy murmured, "But what about my woman?"

Elaine's throat tightened. "You mean, is she satisfied? You know the answer to that question already."

"But I want to hear it again," Ruy said roughly, his voice suddenly harsh with need. His nostrils flared, and the olive skin stretched over his high cheekbones looked tight, feverish. Elaine could see a vein throbbing in his temple. He growled, "I want you to tell me what I do to you, Elaine. I want you to say it with words, and with actions, and with those soft little kitten cries you make whenever I'm inside you. I want you to make love to me."

Holding her breath, Elaine stared hungrily at Ruy. Light from the lamp on the table behind him caught in his silver hair, creating a shining corona whose delicate glow enhanced the strength of his dark, craggy features. He sat motionless, vibrant with tension as he peered at her through hooded eyes. Elaine lowered her lashes. She let her gaze skate down the length of his beautiful body, from his broad chest with the wiry tangle of hair just visible in the open neck of his shirt, to his lean waist and hips, to his sturdy thigh muscles and his legs, which were surprisingly long for his height and were delineated through the fine summer-weight gabardine of his slacks. Elaine looked at him and wanted him and at last admitted to herself that the insatiable craving she felt for this man had nothing to do with unbridled lust, and everything to do with love.

"Touch me, Elaine," Ruy ordered, his voice a strangled croak.

She exhaled wheezily. "Yes. Oh, yes." With a surgeon's skilled fingers she swiftly unbuttoned his shirt, spreading the wings of fabric wide. She could feel the pulsing rhythm of his heartbeat. The *figa* gleamed ghostly white against his tan. Impulsively she pressed her lips against the little amulet.

He gasped. "Don't do that. You don't believe."

"If you think the charm helped you, that's all that matters," she whispered. Her lips slipped away from the *figa* to glide moistly over his chest. She licked at his shoulder blade, then his breastbone, savoring the salty-sweet taste of his skin. When she burrowed through the thicket of iron-gray curls to find his flat nipples, she nipped delicately at the sensitive nubs of flesh, and he jerked as if jolted by an electric shock. Gurgling with delight, she moved lower.

Her hands were a little less steady as she unfastened his belt buckle. He was already fiercely aroused, and the pressure made her fumble. Ruy groaned. "*Deus*, Elaine, I didn't mean—you don't have to—"

"I don't have to do anything," she agreed dizzily, inhaling his musky, intensely masculine odor. "But I want to."

He wove his fingers into her hair and eased her face away from his lap. Elaine craned her neck to look up at him, her eyes glazed with excitement. She said, "Darling, I really want to do this. I want to please you."

"I want to please you, too," Ruy echoed gruffly, so suffocated by his need for her that he was amazed he could speak coherently. "Why don't we go to bed, where we can share our pleasure?"

BRILLIANT SUNBEAMS WERE LEAKING in around the edge of the window shade when the noise of fists pounding on wood awakened Elaine. Startled from her dreams, she tried to bolt upright, but Ruy's arms restrained her. "No, don't go," he mumbled, his eyes still closed as he clutched her naked body closer to his and drew her deeper into the honey-scented tangle of sheets. "You feel so good...."

Elaine prodded his bare shoulder. "Sweetheart, please," she begged. "Somebody's banging on the front door. I have to see who it is. It might be an emergency."

Reluctantly he released her and lifted his head, blinking groggily. He scowled at the oblique angle of the light. "What time is it?" he muttered, yawning.

"I don't know, but we must have overslept." As she spoke the words, Elaine's eyes met Ruy's, and she caught her breath at his expression. No wonder they overslept. They had not rested until dawn.

The noises at the door sounded again. "Hey, doc, are you okay in there?" Vadinho yelled through the door. "Hurry up! You got company."

"Oh, hell," Elaine grumbled, stumbling to her feet, "that's all I need right now." She snatched up her bathrobe and tossed it on, cinching the tie belt around her waist. As she padded barefoot toward the front door, she hesitated long enough to call over her shoulder to Ruy, "I don't know who this is, darling, but you probably ought to get dressed, too." Scraping her hair away from her face, she squared her shoulders and reached for the doorknob.

The late morning sun blazed directly into her face, momentarily dazzling her. Black spots swam before her eyes. Squinting against the glare, she griped, "Vadinho, who on earth—"

A petite figure with soft brown hair rocketed across the porch at Elaine with a force that staggered her. As she lurched backward into the house, struggling to keep her balance, loving arms wound around her and hugged her ferociously. "Surprise, surprise, surprise!" her sister Kate cried.

CHAPTER ELEVEN

ELAINE BLINKED. As her eyes cleared, over Kate's shoulder she could make out the hulking figure of Dan Brock. "My God, what are you two doing here?" she gasped.

Kate laughed archly as she kissed her sister. "Now, is that any way to greet us after we've flown halfway around the world just so you won't have to spend Christmas alone?"

"Christmas? But I sent your—I didn't expect—of course—I'm sorry—great to see you," Elaine stammered in confusion, still fuzzy with sleep. She scrubbed her face with her hands, yawning windily. When she felt slightly more alert, she addressed her brother-in-law. "Welcome to Brazil, Dan dear," she said, standing on tiptoe to press a *beijinho* on each cheek.

His startled reaction made her realize suddenly how foreign the gesture must seem to them. He hugged her awkwardly. "You're looking good, Elaine. Nice tan."

She shook her head. "I'm a mess. I haven't even combed my hair." Rubbing her eyes, she gulped. "Oh my, you'll have to give me a moment to collect myself. I can hardly believe you're both really here. It's as if I'm still dreaming."

"Yes, it's obvious we've woken you up," Dan observed. "I'm sorry. We should have let you know we were coming, but the trip was rather spur-of-the-moment. I need to talk to Areias. But when we arrived in São Paulo yesterday, his partner told me he was up here in Minas Gerais."

"They each do a lot of commuting between their head office and the mines," Elaine explained, wondering what topic of discussion was so portentous that it could not be handled via telephone or telex. "I'm surprised João couldn't help you."

Dan said darkly, "I don't know whether he could or not. This was something Burton asked me to take up directly with Areias. In any case, Oliveira offered the use of the company plane to bring us today. By the time arrangements were made, there was no time to telephone, and besides, Kate wanted to surprise you." He frowned at his wife. "I told you I didn't think much of that idea."

"No, no, it's perfectly all right," Elaine cut in. "There's no need to apologize. It's a wonderful surprise, and I should have been up hours ago, anyway. Thank God I don't have the clinic today." A noise on the porch distracted her. Turning, she saw Vadinho balancing unsteadily on his crutches as he struggled to drag several large leather suitcases into the house. She exclaimed, "Vadinho, for heaven's sake, leave those alone! You'll hurt yourself."

"Not to mention my new Vuitton luggage," Dan muttered, scowling. "Who's the kid? He acts like he owns this place."

"He's a friend." Elaine regarded the boy with fond impatience. "Honestly, you know you're in no condition to carry those bags."

"But, doc, the driver said this stuff all belongs inside. Where do you want it to go?"

"I'm not sure yet, but we'll figure something out. The second bedroom, I suppose...." Elaine's voice trailed off.

As if conjured by her thoughts, the door to the first bedroom opened, and Ruy emerged.

He was fully dressed, groomed with his customary precision—the quintessential imperturbable businessman—but when he looked at Elaine, his gaze was heavy with banked hunger. "Good morning, darling," he murmured.

Out of the corner of her eye Elaine saw Kate go white, then fiery red. Dan's flabbergasted glance was quickly averted. Suddenly aware of her dishabille, Elaine pulled the lapels of her thin robe closer together. "Good morning, Ruy," she echoed throatily.

Slipping his arm around her waist, Ruy kissed Elaine lightly. Then he held out his free hand to Dan. "Welcome to Serra Brilhante, Brock! This is a most unexpected honor. I didn't anticipate seeing you until after the first of the new year."

She had to give her brother-in-law credit for recovering quickly, Elaine admitted. He shook the hand Ruy offered. "Some matters have come up between Corminco and A&O that require immediate attention."

"Of course. We'll get to them at once." Ruy addressed Kate. "Mrs. Brock, I can't tell you what a delightful surprise it is to meet you again—not only for your sister but for myself, as well."

A smooth wing of Kate's hair fell forward, hiding her face as she stared at the floor, but the back of her neck was blotchy with embarrassment. "Dan was right," she mumbled in strangled tones. "We should have warned you we were coming."

"Nonsense," Ruy asserted briskly. "You are Elaine's family. Her door is always open to you."

He glanced past the Brocks to the entryway where Vadinho hovered, listening in openmouthed fascination. At

Ruy's signal, the boy approached. In quiet Portuguese Ruy instructed, "I'd like you to locate my housekeeper and tell her there are going to be four for lunch."

"At your place?" Vadinho whistled. "She's not going to like it. All she does these days is play cards with her friends. She hasn't had to lift a finger ever since you and the doc—"

"Vadinho," Ruy warned.

"Okay, boss. Lunch for four at your place." The boy limped away, grinning.

Ruy looked down at Elaine, still pressed against him in the curve of his arm. From her relieved expression he could tell she had been able to comprehend most of that murmured conversation, and he knew he had guessed right: even though a blind man could see the two of them were lovers, Elaine was not ready to announce to her family that they were practically living together. *"Obrigada,"* she mouthed.

He nodded his understanding. "You're welcome, *querida*." Switching to English, he addressed Dan again. "I've just arranged for us to lunch in my quarters a little later on. While we're waiting, Brock, why don't I show you around Serra Brilhante? I'm sure Elaine would love a few moments alone with her sister, to catch up on news of the family." So tactfully that Dan seemed unaware of what was happening, Ruy ushered him out of the bungalow.

After the door banged shut behind the men, Kate regarded Elaine with wide amber eyes. After a long, pregnant silence, she asked, "How long has that been going on?"

Good question, Elaine thought ironically, wondering how her sister would react if she answered, "A lifetime." Shrugging, she replied noncommittally, "Oh, a while."

"You mean it started in Denver?"

Elaine shook her head. "No, that's not what I mean."

Recognizing the evasion, Kate conceded, "Well, nobody can fault your taste. He's extremely attractive."

"I think so."

"I don't suppose you're planning on getting married, are you?" When Elaine didn't answer, Kate fell silent again. Then she declared pithily, "Father will have a fit."

"What makes you say that?"

"After the way he carried on about Jennie and her movie star, are you kidding? You really think he's going to sit back and watch his daughter sleep with his new business partner?"

"Unless there's a video camera hidden someplace around here," Elaine rejoined calmly, "nobody's going to watch anything. I'm not into exhibitionism."

"Don't be glib," Kate chided. "Father's bound to find out, somehow. For one thing, that cranky associate of your lover's obviously knows something's going on. Dan said he seemed really pissed off about the amount of time Areias is spending out here."

"As far as I can tell, being pissed off is the normal state of João's temperament," Elaine observed scornfully. "The man has one of the most negative personalities I've ever encountered."

"Maybe so, but if he should spill the news to Father—"

"Damn it, don't lecture me!"

Kate blanched. Stiffly she said, "I'm sorry. I don't mean to interfere. It's just that you're my big sister and I love you and I worry about you."

Elaine relented. "I realize that, and I appreciate your concern. But believe me, there's nothing to worry about. I know what I'm doing."

"Are you sure?"

"Positive," Elaine declared flatly. She glanced down at her skimpy robe. "And what I'm doing right now is getting dressed. If you want to come into the bedroom, you can talk to me while I take my shower."

Kate followed Elaine into the larger bedroom and halted abruptly at the doorway, transfixed by the sight of the wildly disarranged bed, the coverlet that had been kicked onto the floor, the tangled sheets and the suggestively stacked pillows. Whistling through her teeth, she drawled, "Wow! I'm beginning to suspect you have hidden depths."

Rummaging through her dresser drawers, Elaine paused long enough to acknowledge the accolade with a saucy bow. "One does one's best...." She carried fresh lingerie into the bathroom and turned on the shower.

As Elaine tested the water, Kate called through the half-closed door, "You know, hon, if this guy is what you want, then I'm very happy for you. But I can't help feeling you're acting way out of character."

Elaine poked her head through the door. "What do you mean?"

Kate gestured helplessly. "Well, good grief, Elaine, you must realize a torrid affair seems totally unlike you. You're the beautiful but unnerving Dr. Welles, whose life is devoted solely to the welfare of her patients. You're the woman whose energy and selfless dedication to her work is so formidable that strong men weep at the prospect of trying to keep up with you."

"Who said that?" Elaine asked, crinkling her brows.

Kate shrugged sheepishly. "Actually, it was Dan. It's silly, but I think he's always found you a little...alarming. I suppose because you're so intelligent and so determined to do things your own way. I know he didn't mean anything by it, but once he called you Attila the Nun."

Closing her eyes, Elaine counted to ten. "Kate, darling," she said with an explosive sigh, "you may inform your husband for me that not all men are intimidated by intelligence. I have never pretended to—nor needed to—live like a nun."

Kate glanced at the bed again. "Obviously not."

Elaine slammed the door and jumped in the shower.

When Elaine emerged from her bathroom, Kate had disappeared into another part of the bungalow. Slipping into a crisp sleeveless cotton blouse and skirt, Elaine went looking for her. She found her on the patio. Kate's straight brown hair shimmered like silk floss in the noonday sun as she huddled on the chaise lounge, her shoulders slumped with dejection, her face in her hands. She had looked that way when she was five and she was the one girl in her ballet class to have been rejected when dancers had been chosen to portray Mother Marshmallow's children in an amateur production of *The Nutcracker*. All Elaine's sisterly sympathy reached out to her. "What's wrong, Katie?" she asked gently.

Reluctantly Kate lifted her head. Her amber eyes were forlorn. She said, "I've made a terrible mistake in coming here."

Elaine plopped onto the end of the chaise lounge. "You mean because of Ruy? I wish you wouldn't feel that way. I realize you were embarrassed, walking in on us like that, but I honestly don't mind you knowing."

"I wasn't talking about you two," Kate said, sighing, flicking her hair from her face. "Frankly, if I feel anything about you and him, it's probably envy. Seeing the way he looked at you, the way he couldn't keep his hands off you, only emphasized how bleak things are between Dan and me these days. My husband hardly even talks to me anymore."

Elaine scowled. "I don't understand. Before I left Denver, I suspected you two were going through a rough patch, but I thought things must be getting better. I don't remember him ever bringing you along on a business trip before."

"He didn't bring me along!" Kate snapped. "I invited myself. When he said he was coming down here, I made up that excuse about keeping you company for Christmas and nagged him until he finally gave in." She paused, faintly abashed. "There I go putting my foot in my mouth again," she muttered. "I do want to be with you, Elaine. Please don't misunderstand. It's just, well, I hoped that if Dan and I could get away from the house—and the folks—a few days, maybe we'd have some time for each other, for a change. Since you left, everybody we know has talked about how lucky you are to be in a romantic country like Brazil. I thought that if we were lucky, too, a little of the romance might rub off, and maybe—maybe this trip could turn into a second honeymoon. We could certainly use one! It's been months since we—" She broke off, shamefaced.

Elaine tried to hide her dismay at her sister's choked-off remark. If Kate and Dan weren't sleeping together, then their marriage had deteriorated even more than she'd suspected.

Suddenly Kate wailed, "Oh, God, I don't know what I'm going to do! I want this marriage to work, but I don't see how it can if Dan won't admit there are problems, or rather, he won't admit there are problems *on both sides*. When I've tried to explain how very stifled I feel, he accuses me of being jealous of you and Jennie. He says any real woman would know that having a home and two beautiful children is more important than a so-called 'exciting career.' He claims if I go back to school or get a job, I'll just be 'denying the opportunity to someone less fortunate who really needs it.' He thinks—''

Elaine cut in impatiently. "Enough of what Dan thinks! What does Kate think?"

Her sister shuddered with repressed fury. "I think," she spat savagely, "that my husband isn't nearly as interested in the needs of the less fortunate as he is in avoiding having to make any adjustments in his own life-style! I think if he doesn't shape up soon, he's going to get a surprise that'll knock his socks off!"

As soon as the words left Kate's mouth, her face turned white, and Elaine realized that she was not the only one to have been caught unaware by the thought that had just occurred to her sister. "Are you talking about divorce?" she asked gently.

Kate stammered, "I—I guess I must be. But—but Dan and I—we've been married thirteen years. He's—he's the father of my children."

"Do you love him?"

Kate's eyes grew round. "I don't know," she whispered faintly, her voice tinged with panic at the realization. "Oh, my God, I don't know if I ever loved Dan."

"Then why did you marry him in the first place?" Elaine asked reasonably. She was astounded when Kate's sickly pallor changed before her eyes to a chagrined flush.

Tittering nervously, Kate admitted, "I married Dan because Mom and Father made us get married. They—

they came home early from a party one night and caught us in bed together."

Elaine stared. "You, Kate?" she gasped. "I don't believe it! The pride of Miss Washburn's deportment class, the girl who thought *The Sound of Music* was suggestive, you actually got caught in the act of screwing your boyfriend?"

"He wasn't even my boyfriend," Kate said drearily. "He was Jennie's. You wouldn't know about any of this because you were off at medical school, but I had a mad crush on Dan from the time we met in my freshman year. My sorority and his fraternity always held functions together. Dan was a junior, the rising star of the varsity football team, and even though we were sort of friends, he never paid any real attention to me. Then when Jennie started college the following year, he took one look at her and flipped. I couldn't stand it. Ever since we were tiny, Jennie was the pretty one, Jennie was the talented one. I was 'sweet little Kate,' the wallflower. So when she stole the guy I wanted, I decided I wasn't going to be sweet anymore."

"What happened?"

Kate shrugged. "Nothing extraordinary. One night when Jennie was expecting Dan to come by, I lied and told her he'd called to cancel the date. She went to the movies with girlfriends, and I stayed home—'to do my homework,' I said. When Dan showed up, we were all alone. I said Jennie was out with another guy, and then I tried to 'comfort' him. I succeeded." She paused, smiling ironically. "I was about as inexperienced as it was possible to be, but I discovered it's not really very hard to seduce a guy that age if you're obvious enough. I must remember to warn Danny about conniving women when he's a little older."

Elaine was having difficulty envisioning her strait-laced sister as a femme fatale. "And Mom and Father walked in on you two that night?"

"Not that very night," Kate corrected. "But within two weeks. And you know the rest."

Elaine nodded. "You and Dan had one of the fanciest weddings Denver's ever seen, and Jennie ran away to New York City."

Sighing dispiritedly, Kate said, "I hurt her, Elaine. My own baby sister, and just for spite I genuinely, truly hurt her. I'll always feel guilty about that."

"You were a kid, Kate," Elaine said firmly. "We all do things when we're young that make us cringe in later life. That was a long time ago. You and Jennie are both grown women. Instead of berating yourself for your teenage sins, you should be concentrating on the problems you have now."

"Like a husband who doesn't touch me anymore."

"There must be something you can do, Kate. No matter why you and Dan became involved in the first place, obviously you two clicked. You didn't rape him. After all," Elaine pointed out dryly, "he came back willingly enough for the 'comfort' you were dispensing."

Just for a second Kate's brown eyes grew hazy with warm, very personal memories. "Yeah, he did," she breathed, her lips curving in an intimate smile. Then she blinked, and her tone grew harsh. "But, as you just pointed out, that was a long time ago. Nowadays, when I try to be romantic with Dan, instead of being aroused by my company, he acts as if I get on his nerves. He resents me taking even a little time away from his precious Corminco. All he cares about is work, work, work."

"Perhaps that's to be expected. In some ways, Dan is very much like Father."

"Maybe so—but goddammit, Elaine, I refuse to end up like Mom!"

"YOU NEVER DID tell me what was so important that Dan had to make a six-thousand-mile trip just to talk to you personally," Elaine observed, watching the setting sun turn Ruy's profile to copper. A warm breeze feathered around them as they stood on the bluff overlooking the deserted mine. All the workmen were either at home, enjoying the temperate Sunday evening with their families, or sitting around the pool or in the chapel where a priest was saying Vespers. At the airstrip the company pilot waited to ferry Ruy back to São Paulo. When Ruy suggested that Elaine borrow Senhor Cruz's VW to drive him to the plane, she had assumed he wanted a few moments of privacy for their goodbyes. But now as they stood on the rim of the cliff, staring at distant mountains silhouetted in black against the ruddy sunset, he smoked in silence and made no attempt to touch her.

"Darling, what's wrong?" Elaine asked again. "You've been brooding ever since you talked to Dan."

Ruy sighed. "Your brother-in-law relayed your father's anxiety about the quality of the stones in the first shipments we sent to the United States. Apparently Corminco's gemologists disagree with the way ours graded them."

"And this is a serious problem?" Elaine questioned, confused. "So serious that it requires face-to-face negotiations to settle it?"

"Since the entire structure of A&O's consortium with Corminco is based on equal division of the products of the Serra Brilhante mines, naturally it is of grave concern to everyone that those stones are evaluated correctly. Disputes are bound to crop up occasionally.

However, because your family is new to the gem trade, I think they are more sensitive than most to any appearance of duplicity. I told Brock that any problems with the stones would be corrected at once, and I asked him to relay to Welles my personal assurances that the incident would not be repeated."

Elaine eyed Ruy speculatively. "You know, it sounds to me as if it wouldn't be very difficult for you to take advantage of my father's inexperience in this field."

"It wouldn't be difficult," he agreed, "not difficult at all."

Taking one last drag on his cigarette, Ruy let out the smoke in a long plume. He dropped the butt on the ground and crushed it with his heel. When he turned to Elaine, it was not the sunset that made his eyes smoulder. "I didn't arrange for these few minutes alone so that we could spend them discussing business," he declared raspily, reaching for her. She flew into his arms.

For mindless moments they clung together, their bodies fashioned into one form, one will. Tongues and teeth pantomimed deeper intimacies while hands searched and clutched and grappled, frustrated by the barrier of their garments. By the time their mouths parted reluctantly, Elaine was shaking with longing, and she could feel the impressive evidence of Ruy's desire straining against her as he molded her softness to his strength. He groaned, "*Deus*, I need you. You're like a craving, an addiction. Every time I have you, I want you more!"

"I can never get enough of you, either," Elaine admitted weakly. "I want to be with you all the time. It's hell whenever you have to leave me to go back to São Paulo."

Ruy laced his fingers into her pale hair and lifted her face to his. "And what exquisite torment do you think these past two nights have been, with your insistence that we keep to our own quarters? How could I rest alone in my bed knowing you lay not a hundred meters away?''

"Do you think that empty bed was any less painful for me?" Elaine cried. "I've tossed and turned so much my sheets are threadbare. But I could hardly ask you to stay over, with my sister and her husband in the next room. The walls are like cardboard."

"It never occurred to you that perhaps your sister and brother-in-law might enjoy some privacy themselves?"

Remembering the unhappy bickering that filtered through the connecting wall each night, Elaine said, "Frankly, no. I think they preferred to have me around to referee their spats. But regardless of their problems, you could scarcely expect me to flaunt our relationship in front of them."

"Why not? They already know about us."

Elaine exhaled wearily and shook her head. "No. I'm sorry. I realize I'm being hypocritical, but there's just no way I'm going to tell my family, 'Excuse me while I sleep with my lover.' "

Shaping the delicate oval of her face with his palms, Ruy peered searchingly at her. Beneath the lustrous mustache his lips barely moved as he asked, "Would you feel the same if you were sleeping with your husband?"

Elaine gulped. "What did you say?"

He declared urgently, "I wanted to marry you when we were children. You laughed at me, but I was not joking then, and I am not joking now. You are my woman, Elaine. It is pointless to pretend otherwise."

Elaine's heart shriveled a little at that passionate yet chilly ultimatum. She did not know how to respond. As she gazed into the lionlike eyes she had loved since she was a girl, the dark, beautiful features, she knew that he cared about her. There was too much tenderness in his lovemaking to be mere sexual obsession. Ruy Fonseca Areias was fonder of Elaine Welles than he was willing to admit—even to himself. Wistfully she noted, "Most proposals at least mention the word love."

"When I was nineteen, I told you I loved you. If you refused to believe me then, why should it be any different now?" His expression hardened. "Elaine, there are forces binding us that are stronger than love, stronger than the romantic conventions that precipitate most proposals. Desire and pride make us one. You want me. I want the right to proclaim to the world that you are my wife."

Of course, she thought drearily. Marrying her would be a way of resolving the conflict that had existed between them since adolescence, a method of healing the wound she had inflicted on his self-esteem when she'd spurned him with a deliberate cruelty by saying he wasn't good enough to marry a Welles. Marrying her would prove to the world—and, more importantly, himself— that Ruy was indeed good enough.

She felt torn. Although she supposed she ought to declare herself mortally offended and fling his offer back in his face, she did not. At her age, with her experience, Elaine was realistic enough to believe that compatible sex and a certain mental rapport could provide a sound basis for a marriage, as long as both parties approached it openly. She and Ruy certainly shared those qualities, and she'd admitted to herself before she'd ever left Denver that she'd like to be married. Accepting him on his terms might provide an easy cure for the emotional malaise that had troubled her lately, she thought.

And yet ... and yet she did not think she was ready to settle for a marriage of convenience, especially since she still entertained nagging doubts about Ruy's motives. As much as she loved him—or, more accurately, because she loved him—she could not commit herself to a lifetime with a man she did not trust. Moments earlier he had accused her of making him suffer by insisting on separate beds. What kind of refined torture would it be to marry him, love him, and then discover that he had made her his wife as part of some elaborate scheme to avenge the wrongs he perversely blamed on her family?

She needed time to think. Evasively she said, "Please, darling, you must realize I can't just give you an answer on the spur of the moment. As much as I want to be with you, I don't know if I'm capable of the kind of adjustments our marriage would require. I assume you'd expect us to live in Brazil. I have friends in Denver, not to mention a career that is very important to me."

"There are always jets to the United States and intercontinental telephone calls," Ruy pointed out. "There would be no need to abandon your friends. And contrary to the impressions you may have drawn from the Oliveiras, even in Brazil women who wish to do so may have a career and a husband and children, as well."

I can't, Elaine thought poignantly, realizing with a stab of guilt that there were issues about which she had not yet been open with him, either. How could she expect Ruy to be straightforward with her if she lacked the courage to tell him about the baby she had lost? Until she found that courage, she could not consider marriage.

"Will you give me a little time?" she asked, gazing up at him with pleading eyes.

Ruy nodded curtly. "As you wish. I'll be back here for Christmas, and you can give me your answer then." His arms tightened around her. "But, *namorada*," he murmured, his breath tickling her lips as he lowered his mouth to hers, "never forget that in the end there is only one answer to all our questions...."

CHAPTER TWELVE

"BUT, DOC," Vadinho pleaded, "what's Christmas without fireworks?"

Elaine was leaning against a shaded wall outside the clinic, taking a breath of fresh air while Consuelo was setting up the treatment room for the next patient. The weather was muggy, the air inside the facility hot and close. Magdalena had departed by bus two days before to spend the holiday with her family in São Paulo, and her absence had left Elaine and Consuelo shorthanded and shorter-tempered. When Vadinho poked Elaine in the arm and repeated his question, she regarded him impatiently. "Is this a riddle? I give up. What *is* Christmas without fireworks?"

The boy, unused to anything but tolerance and sympathy from Elaine, grew sulky. "Don't make fun of me, doc. Maybe it's different in America, but in Brazil for the holidays you're supposed to have fireworks and boat races and picnics and roast pig and shrimp and presents and candy and Christmas trees and—"

As Vadinho eagerly rattled off the endless list, Elaine's expression softened. He was a child, she reminded herself, a child of the streets who very possibly had never enjoyed even a single one of the delights he was now enumerating with such wistful relish. To an *abandonado*, whose whole existence was a grim struggle for survival, simple pleasures like picnics or roast pork must seem the essence of unattainable luxury, Elaine thought guiltily. She said, "Look, Vadinho, I promise it's going to be a wonderful Christmas. We'll have a tree and candy and good food and lots of gifts. I expect we can even arrange a picnic, if you want one. My sister and her husband might enjoy an opportunity to see some of the countryside. But you're going to have to accept the fact that there won't be any fireworks. Tomorrow night is Christmas Eve, and nobody has time to drive to the city to buy some."

"But that's just it: we don't need to buy anything," the boy insisted. "My buddy Luis knows all about it." Luis was the oldest son in the household where Vadinho lived when he wasn't tagging after Elaine; the boys were the same age, and in the past few weeks they'd become fast friends. "Luis says all we need is a little black powder— they have lots of it lying around at the mine—and some chemicals from the school science room."

Elaine paled. "Good Lord, Vadinho, do you have any idea what you're suggesting? People get killed playing with homemade fireworks!"

"Luis says—"

Angrily Elaine ordered, "You tell your buddy Luis for me that there is no way on earth I'm going to let either of you mess with explosives. Tell him if he won't listen to me, I'll tell his mother. She's one of my patients, and I know she wouldn't approve, either. Tell him—" Vadinho muttered something unintelligible. Breaking off in midsentence, Elaine demanded, "What did you say?"

The boy's mulish frown deepened and his lower lip protruded. "I said, you can't order me around. You're not my mother."

Elaine stared at Vadinho, her heart in her throat. He was right: she wasn't his mother. She was his doctor, his patron, perhaps his friend. But she was not his mother.

She wondered how long ago she had begun to pretend otherwise, without even realizing what she was doing. In the weeks she'd been in Serra Brilhante, it had been very easy to indulge that particular fantasy, given the boy's dependence on her and his puppylike devotion to anyone who showed him a little kindness. His easy, undemanding affection had touched her spirit in a way that all of Ruy's passion had so far failed to do. But no matter how lonely she was, it was wrong to take advantage of Vadinho's vulnerability. She didn't know yet what her own future held. It was unfair, if not downright cruel, to let the boy assume he might be a part of it.

"I'm sorry," she whispered humbly. "I shouldn't have been bossy. It's just that I don't want you to get hurt. I care what happens to you."

She knew her fears were justified when he demanded, "Do you care enough to take me with you when you go back to America?"

Oh, God, what have I done? she asked herself guiltily, seeing the pathetic eagerness that brightened his face. How could she make him understand that life was not simple; how could she explain the plethora of complex issues—issues she wasn't sure she had the courage to confront—that would be raised if she, a single woman, attempted to adopt an adolescent boy of another nationality and race? Despising herself for her spinelessness, Elaine equivocated. "I don't know if I am going back to America."

Vadinho exclaimed with surprise and pleasure, "Does that mean you're going to stay in Brazil and marry the boss?"

"I don't know that, either," she said drearily.

As Elaine watched, the happiness that had lighted the boy's features faded and was replaced by a shuttered mask. She could feel his abrupt withdrawal. "Oh. I see," he said, his voice cracking. "Well, I gotta go now. Luis is waiting." He turned and stomped away.

Elaine's gaze followed him as he hobbled out of view, his skinny body rigid with hurt and betrayal. She wondered how many times he had been betrayed in his wretched young life. Elaine sighed remorsefully. Was she just another in a long line of adults who had shammed interest in Vadinho and then discarded him when his presence became inconvenient? "I see," he had muttered, his tight-lipped words rough with pain. The awful part was, she thought perhaps he did see.

"'SLEEP IN HEAVENLY PEACE,'" Elaine sang as the clock struck midnight. Her rather thin lyric soprano harmonized inexpertly with Kate's richer alto. "'Sleep in heavenly peace.'" As the sisters finished the carol, they glanced at each other across Elaine's living room and giggled. Elaine turned to Ruy and Dan. "Okay, guys, there's no reason to look so smug. I know our singing is a little off-key, but it would help if you joined in."

On the couch next to his wife, Dan groaned contentedly. "Sorry, but I'm too stuffed to sing."

Ruy added, "I'm afraid I don't know the song. Besides, I thought you sounded charming."

"Come on, Ruy, you know too much about music to believe that," Elaine scoffed genially.

He shook his head. "No, my dear, I'm quite serious. I enjoyed listening to you and your sister sing. I enjoyed watching Vadinho open his presents. I enjoyed the food. This has been one of the most—no, *the* most delightful

Christmas Eve I've ever spent. Thank you for allowing me to be part of it.''

You're a part of everything I do, Elaine telegraphed across the room, her eyes slumberous with pleasure. She knew exactly how he felt. Despite her fears that she would be lonely away from her family, the festival had turned out to be a good one, celebrated with a mixture of Brazilian and American customs. She, Ruy and the Brocks had crowded into the chapel for late Mass, along with all the miners and their families who had remained in Serra Brilhante for the holiday. Afterward, Vadinho had joined the adults and they'd returned to Elaine's bungalow for dinner. Knowing how short the supply of meat was in the cities, she had chosen not to question where Ruy had obtained the succulent Virginia ham he'd brought with him when he'd flown north from São Paulo that morning; instead, she'd simply enjoyed the meal the housekeeper had prepared of it, with its unusual accompaniments of fried plantains and shrimp patties cooked in palm oil. When everyone was replete, they had retired to the living room to watch Vadinho tear into the gifts piled beneath a wild orange tree ornamented with tinsel and lights.

After the boy had departed, bearing away his treasures to show his friend Luis, the adults had sat quietly, sipping *batidas*, potent cocktails of passion fruit and sugarcane liquor which were supposed to aid digestion. Elaine and Kate had sung a couple of Christmas carols, and then they, too, had fallen silent, listening to the sounds of frolicking children outside.

After a while Kate noted with a pensive sigh, ''It's going to seem strange not being with the twins tomorrow morning.''

"I know what you mean," Dan agreed somberly. "I was really looking forward to seeing Danny's expression when he opens that computer I got him. A telephone call just won't be the same. Still, business does come first, and we'll be home in a few days, anyway."

Elaine asked, "Then you've worked out the problems that brought you here in the first place?"

"I think I can report back to Burton that the situation has been resolved. Don't you agree, Areias?"

Ruy said, "You have my word."

Dan nodded, then his expression darkened. "Of course," he added with a frown, "even though it's gratifying that we've been able to come to an understanding so quickly, there are still other issues I think need to be addressed. I can't pretend I'm happy about the number of accidents that have occurred in the mines."

Ruy glanced sharply at Elaine. "You told him?"

"I had to find someone who would listen to me."

Ruy's mouth tightened as he leaned forward in his chair. Propping his chin on one hand, he addressed Dan. "I'm sorry Elaine has chosen to involve you in this, Brock. Although I have tried on more than one occasion to make her understand that the situation here at Serra Brilhante is not as straightforward as she chooses to see it, she prefers not to believe me. My associate Oliveira also failed to convince her. So now I must appeal to you."

"Appeal to me for what?" Dan asked, puzzled.

Ruy said, "I want you to help your sister-in-law see that mining is, by its very nature, hazardous. Even though no one likes his workmen to be hurt, the simple fact is that a certain percentage of accidents are bound to occur. I suppose it is Elaine's vocation that makes her so sensitive to the pain of others. Naturally she wants to do all in her power to prevent that pain. But the truth is, we at A&O are already doing all we can. By Brazilian standards the Serra Brilhante mines are models of occupational safety."

Irritated by his patronizing tone, Elaine asserted, "I don't believe that! If you were doing all you could, you'd upgrade your security, insist on better equipment and training—"

"Training that the miners would probably choose to ignore," Ruy reminded her tightly. "How many times must I explain? In this country, most men are willing to take a few risks in order to have jobs. If safety measures were to slow down production and reduce their earnings, they'd rather do without them."

"Of course, it's only incidental that slowing production would also cut into your profits," Elaine insinuated.

"Yours, too," Ruy rejoined. "Before you become sanctimonious, shouldn't you remember that you and your sisters each hold fifteen percent of your family's stock in Corminco?"

Elaine stilled. "How did you know that?"

"Shareholder lists are a matter of public record," Ruy dismissed.

Public records you just happen to be familiar with, Elaine accused silently. She wondered when he had apprised himself of the exact extent of her personal wealth. Before he had approached Corminco? Before he'd proposed? Aloud she said, "You have no right to drag my sisters and me into—"

"Oh, for God's sake, Elaine!" Dan exploded. "The man has been trying to explain things to you. You could at least do him the courtesy of hearing him out." Shaking his head with exasperation, he gibed, "Women!

Whatever makes them think they understand business...." He patted Kate's hand. "You don't understand business, do you, dear?"

Kate looked askance at her husband. "In case you've forgotten after all these years," she muttered, "I was an economics major in college when we met."

Elaine watched her sister's mutinous expression deepen; she saw Ruy's lowering scowl. In a matter of moments the happy rapport of the evening had been spoiled, sullied by resentment and doubt. She jumped to her feet. "Will you listen to us?" she declared breathily. "We're squabbling like children, and here it is Christmas! Let's have a little peace and goodwill, shall we?" Without waiting for the others' response, she stalked across the room to the open window.

Although the hour was well after midnight, the air was warm and the noise of celebration still reverberated throughout Serra Brilhante. Someone nearby was playing a guitar and crooning a plaintive ballad; farther away could be heard the throbbing beat of a bossa nova. Senhor Cruz, the mine's manager, stood at the top of the steps leading into the recreation center and declaimed poetry to admiring listeners, while a group of very young children danced in a circle and clapped their hands in time to some rhyming game. The happy sounds that had given Elaine so much pleasure earlier in the evening now nagged at her. Heaving a futile sigh, she listened in vain for sleigh bells or strolling carolers singing "White Christmas." She had never felt so out of her realm in her life.

Concentrating intently on the sounds filtering through her window, she did not hear Ruy's approach. When he slipped his arms around her waist, she started. "What's wrong?" he asked, pulling her tense body back against him. For a long moment she stood rigid, unyielding, then all at once she relaxed into the cradle of his embrace, her eyes still focused on the darkness outside. Ruy repeated, "What's wrong, Elaine? Why the sigh?"

She said, "I don't think I belong here."

Ruy frowned. "You don't belong where—in Brazil? In Serra Brilhante? In my arms?"

Her voice sounded dull and dejected. "All of the above, I guess."

"But why? Why should you suddenly—"

He never finished the question. As they gazed into the night, suddenly there was a muffled boom, and the boxy roof line of the recreation center stood silhouetted black against a burst of magnesium-white light. Sparkles of fire shot up into the sky and fell back, still burning. A thin, boyish voice shrieked out in pain and terror. Elaine tore herself from Ruy's arms, almost leaping through the window.

"*Vadinho!*" she screamed.

"WE'RE GOING TO NEED more burn packs," Elaine assessed as she delicately and precisely positioned the sterile dressing over the charred flesh that had been a boy's forearm. Blinking against the harsh fluorescent light, her eyes flicked upward to the bottle of intravenous solution dangling over the operating table. She looked at Ruy. "Please ask Consuelo how the supply of D5W is holding out. He's going through it fast."

Ruy translated the question with difficulty, hampered by the unfamiliar medical terms. Fortunately Consuelo understood him, perhaps because of the natural empathy that existed between her and Elaine, which transcended words. Ruy watched in awe as the women interacted, methodically, meticulously, dispassion-

ately—never permitting their anxiety for the injured
teenager to interfere with their treatment of him.

A snuffling noise behind Ruy reminded him of the
three people watching from the corridor. A stocky man
in a festive shirt stared into the operating room with bewildered, tragic eyes. One arm was wrapped protectively
around his wife, who looked about seven months pregnant. She whimpered wordlessly and clung to him, ashen
and afraid. The man's other arm rested absently on Vadinho's shoulders.

Engraved forever in Ruy's mind was the moment just
after the explosion when Elaine had first seen the boy
writhing in flames on the ground and had realized he was
not Vadinho, but Vadinho's friend Luis. Incredulity had
twisted her features, followed in the space of a heartbeat
by relief and then guilt at her relief, as she'd watched two
men fall on the flailing youth and smother the fire. She
had twirled her head frantically, searching for Vadinho,
and had finally seen him huddled against a wall, gibber-
ing with fright yet unhurt. Then she had relaxed visibly.
All expression had been wiped away as she'd sunk to her
knees beside Luis, already reaching into her medical bag
for a drug to dull his agony. From that moment on her
face had remained impassive—an ivory carving—as she
worked.

"Were you able to contact the emergency services in
Belo Horizonte?" she demanded abruptly. "The boy is
stabilized for the moment, but all Consuelo and I can
really do here is keep him sedated and try to prevent in-
fection."

"The hospital burn unit is on alert," Ruy said,
"awaiting Luis's arrival. Unfortunately, the helicopter
pilot disappeared somewhere to celebrate the holiday...."

At last emotion glinted in the pale blue eyes above the edge of the mask that covered her mouth and nose. Ruy could see her slim figure shake with anger. "Let's hope the pilot's celebrating doesn't cost a life!" she snapped bitterly.

Although Elaine spoke in English, her tone communicated itself to the people standing in the hallway. Ruy heard Luis's mother give a loud wail. Studying her with concern, Elaine murmured to Ruy, "Can you please try to convince her to lie down somewhere? She needs to rest."

Ruy glanced over his shoulder. "You're right. She's in no condition to be watching all this. Do you want me to ask her to go home?"

Shaking her head, Elaine said, "No. She'll want to stay close to her son. She can use any of the beds in the ward—or, on second thought, perhaps you should send her into one of the examination rooms. I think I ought to take a look at her. I don't like her color."

Elaine's fears were justified. Before Ruy could speak to Luis's mother, she uttered another shrill, keening cry, and this time Ruy could hear the physical as well as emotional pain edging her harsh moan.

"Oh, my God," Elaine whispered, watching the woman's eyes widen with shock as she doubled over, clutching her belly.

Her husband tried to hold her, but she lashed out at him, made hysterical by her panic. *"Não, não, não,"* she sobbed, *"demasiado cedo, demasiado cedo!"* Instinctively Elaine reached out, but Consuelo waved her back, gesturing toward the injured boy. Instead, the nurse jumped into the fray, and together with Ruy and Luis's father she was able to subdue her. The woman thrashed against the three of them, her eyes wild with fear and despair. Then suddenly she fell limp, all fight gone. As they carried her into the treatment room, her anguished lament echoed throughout the clinic: "Too soon, too soon, too soon...."

SQUINTING INTO THE RISING SUN, Ruy and a crowd of onlookers watched the emergency helicopter lift off. When the aircraft was only a dot in the lightening sky, they disbursed somberly to their homes. Ruy lingered long enough to confer with the priest for a moment, then he went searching for Elaine.

He had not seen her for an hour, not since she had escorted Father Figueiredo into the quiet room where the bereft parents had waited for him to baptize the still, pitifully tiny figure who hadn't had a chance to live. When the priest had opened his prayer book, Elaine had slipped away. Ruy presumed she had returned to Luis's side, but before he could locate her, the trauma team had arrived at last. From that point on, there had been no room for anyone in the clinic except medical personnel.

He found her sitting on the back steps of the recreation center, her knees hunched under her chin as she gazed broodingly into space. She was still wearing her surgical scrubs, the shapeless pants and baggy smock of faded green cotton hanging limply from her fragile frame. She looked like a waif. Ruy stared at her delicate, despondent face and wondered how he could ever have pretended, even to himself, that he'd wanted to hurt her.

At the sound of his footsteps she lifted her head. Rubbing the knotted muscles at her nape, she smiled wanly and said, "Oh, hi. I was just thinking about you."

"Pleasant thoughts, I hope."

She shrugged. "Do you have a cigarette I could borrow?"

Ruy's brow furrowed. "You don't smoke."

"It seems like a good time to start."

Despite the flippant words, her voice sounded plaintive, deeply depressed. "Are you all right?" Ruy queried. "Is there anything I can do for you? I know you must be exhausted. You've been up all night."

"So have you. So has half the town."

"Would you care for something to eat?" When Elaine shook her head, Ruy thought of the Brocks. Aware that they'd only be in the way, Kate and Dan had remained in the bungalow when the excitement began. "Perhaps you'd like me to get your sister?"

"No, thank you." She glanced at her wristwatch. "It's still very early. Let her sleep." She paused, tilting her head quizzically. "Oh, my, I just remembered: it's Christmas morning."

"So it is. *Feliz Natal*—although I suppose this isn't going to be one of your happier, more memorable Christmases."

"I'm afraid that to Luis's family it will be all too memorable," Elaine said drearily. "From now on, the season of joy will always remind them of the time they lost one child and another was maimed or at least permanently disfigured."

Ruy shoved his hands deep in his pockets. "Elaine, I promise I'm going to use every means at my disposal to ensure that Luis gets the best possible medical attention, including rehabilitation and plastic surgery, if necessary. There is no way I will permit him to be permanently crippled."

Elaine was silent for a moment. "Thank you, Ruy. That's very kind." She exhaled windily. "It's just too bad you can't help the baby, too."

"Darling, I'm not God." His lips thinned. "Perhaps you should remember that you aren't, either."

For some reason the comment appeared to annoy her. She rose stiffly to her feet and began to pace the narrow width of the top step. "I've never aspired to godhood," she declared edgily. "Few things irritate me as much as doctors who get delusions of divinity. I've lost patients before—everyone does. It's never easy, but you learn to accept that in the natural cycle of things life must have an end as well as a beginning. But there was nothing natural about the senseless tragedy we just witnessed. It could have been prevented!"

"You mean that the baby might have been saved if we'd been able to get to a fully equipped medical facility?"

Elaine nodded curtly. "Perhaps. The neonatal crisis unit at my hospital in Denver has saved preemies half the size of the one we just lost—newborns so small they could lie in my hand. There's no guarantee of success, but at least there's a chance, a chance we didn't have here. But that's not the point."

Seeing her pallor, the feverish glow in her blue eyes, and watching her spasmodic, increasingly fidgety movements as she stalked back and forth, it occurred to Ruy that all the emotion Elaine had dammed inside her while she'd treated her patients was now welling up, demanding to be released. If it spilled out unchecked, catching him in the flood, he did not think he was going to enjoy it. Gingerly he asked, "What is the point you're trying to make?"

Elaine stated flatly, "Everything that happened last night was your fault."

Ruy stared, stunned. "What the hell are you saying?" he gasped.

He could see the tremor in her hands as she gestured fitfully. "I've been thinking for hours," she claimed, "and I keep coming to the same conclusion. We may have lost the baby because its mother was shocked into premature labor by her son's accident, but ultimately the baby's death and that boy's injuries were both precipitated by the same cause—"

"Yes, of course," Ruy cut in. "A childish prank that went disastrously wrong."

"No!" Elaine exclaimed. "Everything that happened, happened because you didn't care enough to employ standard safety measures around the mine. How do you think Vadinho and Luis got hold of the black powder they used in that damned skyrocket of theirs? For God's sake, man, the shed where explosives are stored wasn't even locked!"

Although he knew it was her pain that was making her lash out at him, Ruy could feel his temper rise. "Elaine, you're tired. You—"

She waved aside his protest. "I warned you," she ranted, her eyes glossing with bitter tears. "Repeatedly I said that if you didn't institute a few routine precautions, something terrible was going to happen. But you wouldn't listen to me. No, you told me, I was just a silly woman, and a foreigner at that, and I didn't understand that your workers didn't mind taking some risks as long as there was a steady paycheck involved. Well, guess what, Ruy, it wasn't one of your big macho men that got hurt! Does it really take *children dying* to prove to you that no amount of money is worth people's lives?"

Ruy's own control dissolved. Infuriated by the injustice of her accusation, he shot back, "Only someone who's always been rich can afford to be so noble."

Elaine recoiled. Her face reflected her disillusion as she whispered, almost choking with dismay, "I was right about you all along, wasn't I? From the time we were teenagers, the Welles money was the only thing you wanted."

His eyes were hooded. "Oh, I wouldn't say the money was the *only* thing I wanted," he drawled, allowing his gaze to slide insinuatingly over her slender body. He stared at her deliberately until her moist lips parted and faint flags of pink appeared in her cheeks. Then he sniffed and turned away. Over his shoulder he tossed obscurely, "You know, *querida*, your beloved Welleses haven't always been as upright and humane as you pretend. I know of at least one instance when the family put a very specific price on a person's life."

"Just what is that crack supposed to mean?" Elaine demanded.

Ruy shrugged. "Ask your father."

"I will," she retorted hotly as she glared at the wall of his back. "I'll ask him as soon as I go home." She paused, seething. "And by the way, *senhor*," she added, biting off the words, "I do hope you're making some progress in locating a Brazilian doctor to take over for me! I don't know if I can stand a few more months in this place. I think I'll go crazy if I don't get back to civilization soon."

Slowly Ruy turned. He peered at her in silence for several long, speculative moments. Then he let out his breath with a hiss. His eyes were opaque, unreadable, as he rasped, "If that's the way you feel, Elaine, maybe you'd better not wait any longer. After all, we wouldn't want the magnanimous Dr. Welles to suffer because of her charity to the benighted peasants, would we? If you start packing now, you can leave with your sister and her husband. We don't need you here.''

CHAPTER THIRTEEN

"WE DON'T NEED YOU HERE." Of all the equivocal statements Ruy had made in his checkered career, none had ever been more true—or a bigger lie—he thought as he watched Elaine's luggage being loaded onto the company plane.

He had regretted the rash words the instant they'd been spoken, but pride would not permit him to disavow them. Even when she'd stared blankly at him and asked "You're not serious, are you?" his overweening vanity had refused the out she'd offered.

"I'm very serious, Elaine. If you're unwilling to accept me and my adopted country on our own terms, then you'd better go home."

"But what about my patients?" she appealed.

He had been incensed—irrationally, he now conceded—that her first question had not been "What about *us*?" and his anger had sharpened his words as he shot back cuttingly, "I won't have any trouble finding a Brazilian obstetrician to replace you."

"Overnight?" she questioned. "Kate and Dan are flying to Rio on the twenty-seventh, and if you want me to go with them—"

Ruy shrugged. "You're familiar with that wonderful American invention, the checkbook? We have them here, too. If I begin telephoning the major hospitals later today, I'm sure in one of them I'll find a doctor willing to

curtail his Christmas holiday and move to Serra Brilhante—for a substantial incentive, naturally.''

Elaine protested, ''But the reason I came to Brazil in
the first place was because you insisted there were no
doctors available, for love or money.''

''I wouldn't know about love,'' Ruy retorted, ''but for
the right amount of money, there are always people
available. Even you—''

She gasped indignantly. ''I've taken no money for
working here!''

''I'm aware of that. For you, 'no money' is the right
amount. You probably would have refused to come at all
if I'd offered you a salary. You like seeing yourself as the
kindly philanthropist, dispensing benevolence to the
downtrodden, don't you? That image flatters your ego
and makes it unnecessary for you to take the people you
work with seriously. It reaffirms your conviction of how
inherently superior the Welleses are.''

The hurt in her eyes tore at him. She said stiffly,
''That's neither fair nor true, Ruy, but I'm not going to
try to reason with you. If you really see me as the con-
ceited, condescending, self-righteous little prig you just
described, then no argument on my part is going to convince you you're wrong. My only question is why you
ever wanted me here at all.''

He laughed. ''I should have thought you'd known the
answer to that one from the beginning. Surely you must
realize it's all been a Byzantine plot to have you at my
mercy. I was certain that if I lured you away from the
protective arms of your family, here in my mountain
fastness I could seduce you into marriage and finally get
my hands on the fortune you denied me when we were
children.''

The tic at Elaine's temple told Ruy she was holding her temper stubbornly in check. "Of course. I thought as much," she acknowledged laconically. "How fortunate for me that Kate and Dan arrived in time to distract me before I did anything stupid, like saying yes."

Ruy nodded ironically. "I suppose I'll never know how close to success I was, will I? But then, what is it you Americans say? 'Close only counts in horseshoes'?"

Idiot! he cursed himself, watching the pilot stow the last of the Brocks' Vuitton suitcases into the luggage compartment, under Dan's grumbling orders. How could Ruy have stood there Christmas morning mouthing dreary platitudes when what he should have said to Elaine was that he was sorry for telling her to go and would she please, please disregard his stupidity and stay with him? But no: after the hideous night he and she had just endured, they'd both been too exhausted and overwrought to think rationally. Instead of falling into each other's arms and consoling their grief with murmured endearments, with the healing balm of their caresses, they'd confronted each other on the steps like duelists, hurling spiteful, sarcastic accusations until a chasm of pain and resentment yawned between them, too wide to bridge with mere words. Now the woman he loved stood a few feet away, speaking a few last words to Vadinho before she climbed into the plane and raced the sun northward, back to her snowbound aerie in the Rockies. There was nothing Ruy could think to do to prevent her from leaving.

He gazed hungrily at her face as she talked with hushed urgency to the boy. In the forty-eight hours since that dismal encounter on the steps, he'd seen very little of her. Taking him at his word, she had spent her time in her bungalow packing, or else in the clinic updating her patient notes in preparation for handing over the files to her successor. Her actions had left Ruy no choice but to chain himself to the telephone while he made pressing calls to hospitals in all the major cities, searching for her successor. The size of the task forced him to include João in the quest—reluctantly. Ruy knew that, as usual, the man would demand to be repaid generously for the favor, and Ruy would have preferred not to incur further obligations until he'd clarified some things with his associates. Although the *jeito* could be very handy as a way of doing business—clearing away red tape and expediting tiresome details—it was not without its drawbacks.

But Ruy had not earned his reputation as a *despechante* for nothing; somehow within the absurd time limit, a replacement for Elaine was found. Ruy's sources informed him that a gynecologist in Bahia had expressed an unexpected urge to relocate his practice. The doctor was a young bachelor with impressive credentials: intelligent, up-to-date, well loved by his patients— too well loved, which explained his sudden wanderlust. Ruy interviewed the man by telephone, and after pointing out that the miners of Serra Brilhante were unsophisticated country people who took a blunt approach to men who messed with their womenfolk, he hired him. The new physican would arrive the following morning.

As Ruy considered Elaine's successor, his thoughts were interrupted by Vadinho's heartfelt wail. "No, no, doc, don't go, don't go! I'll be good, I promise!"

Ruy twisted around. Kate and Dan Brock jumped visibly, gawking in surprise at the youth who was tugging at Elaine's arms. Her determined expression softened as she stroked the smooth dark cheek streaked with tears. "Vadinho," she admonished bleakly, her eyes desolate, "please don't cry. I told you, it's just time for me to leave. I'm not going away because of anything you did."

"Yes, you are," he choked. "Everything was fine. You liked us here. You liked the boss. When we opened our presents on Christmas Eve, it was—it was almost like being a family." His voice cracked with emotion. "Th-then I ruined everything. You told me not to help Luis build that rocket and I did anyway and he got hurt and now you—you're l-leaving!" His words melted into racking sobs.

Dropping her handbag onto the dirt at her feet, Elaine wrapped her arms around the weeping boy and cradled him against her. His casts made the embrace awkward, but she managed to guide his head to her shoulder. "Vadinho, Vadinho," she crooned, closing her eyes and rocking back and forth until his moans faded to moist sniffles, "I promise you it's not your fault I have to go. You're the one thing that could keep me here."

Ruy watched with awe while Elaine comforted the boy, her soft white arms wound through his thin brown ones. It had been hateful and unjust of him to accuse her of being a snob, he knew. Perhaps he'd simply been jealous. In his entire life, nobody had ever shown him the intense tenderness with which Elaine held the child. She radiated an almost visible aura of love and gentleness and warmth, enveloping all who looked on.

Almost all. As Ruy gazed at Elaine and Vadinho, his eyes flicked past them to the couple standing on the other side. Kate was watching her sister a little ambivalently, yet she appeared benign and sympathetic; she was a mother acknowledging another woman's maternal instincts. But behind Kate loomed her husband, Dan, and Ruy spotted something in his eyes as he gazed at Vadinho that brought back memories of his own miserable youth. The look was quickly veiled the instant Dan realized he was being watched, but Ruy saw enough to recognize the expression. Dan was regarding Vadinho with the same air of distaste, disdain and dismissal that had met the ragged waif Antonio whenever he'd dared to approach his betters.

Clenching his jaw, Ruy asked himself how he could ever have been deluded enough to think the world had truly changed.

DAN SAID, "Elaine, you have lost your mind."

Kate squeaked indignantly, but Elaine shushed her. She gazed at her brother-in-law across the expanse of the linen-covered table, relaxing in her chair while the dessert plates were cleared away. They were dining at Le Saint Honore, the gourmet French restaurant atop the Hotel Meridien, where she and Ruy had stayed during their weekend in Rio. The panoramic view of Copacabana from the thirty-seventh floor was as spectacular as Elaine remembered. She found it ironically amusing, and typical, that the site of the most romantic two days of her life had been chosen by Dan not for its beauty, elegance, or sheer class but because the hotel boasted a business center with telex and secretarial services.

Elaine had not expected to stay at the hotel in Rio with Kate and Dan. She had planned to book a seat on the next plane to the United States; the open-ended ticket Ruy had given her for her flight to Brazil required only that she confirm her departure date with the airline. Unfortunately, she had not counted on the holiday crush. The clerk at the airline reservation desk was gracious but adamant that they could not make room for her before the second of January; even the standby passenger lists for each flight were already filled. However, he had added, if Dr. Welles had to be grounded for several days, then she could not ask for a more enjoyable place in which to spend those days: the New Year celebrations in Rio were a spectacle unmatched anywhere else in the world.

Elaine had left his desk daunted, wondering if she was going to encounter the same difficulties booking hotel accommodations. She could think of few prospects less appealing than sleeping on a roll-away bed in Kate and Dan's room. To her relief, the Meridien did have one single still available. It was tiny, and faced away from the beach, but it was blessedly private. As Elaine had stretched out on the narrow bed to relax, she had conceded that once in a very great while there were advantages to traveling alone in a world of couples.

The waiter set out their postprandial coffee in tiny porcelain cups and presented the check for the meal to Dan, who absently scrawled his room number across the bottom of the bill and pocketed the receipt. Elaine picked up her cup and inhaled deeply, savoring the rich aroma of the steaming brew. When she tasted the coffee gingerly, trying not to burn her tongue, she was pleased to discover the dark liquid was unsweetened, unlike the syrupy *cafe-zinhos* she'd drunk in São Paulo with Sonia Oliveira. She sighed wistfully. Less than two months had passed since her arrival in Brazil. It seemed like two years.

As soon as the waiter departed, Elaine pressed, "Okay, Dan, would you care to elaborate on what you said a moment ago? I'm curious to know exactly why you think I'm mad to want to adopt Vadinho."

Her brother-in-law's hazel eyes narrowed as he stared back at her. With his knuckles he brushed a lock of brown hair forward so that it covered the receding scalp line at his temple. "It doesn't take any great insight to realize that Burton would have a cow if he knew you were even considering the idea."

"I can't imagine why," Elaine said blandly. "Father always did want us girls to give him grandsons."

Dan's wide mouth twisted with impatience. "Natural grandsons, he meant. Boys with Burton's blood in them—like Danny. Surely you don't think your dad would acknowledge a scrawny little black stray from the Rio slums as a Welles, do you?"

She felt her temper rising. Struggling to maintain her equanimity, she observed, "I can't see that Vadinho's color would make any difference to Father. The man may be a lot of things, but I've never considered him a racist."

"Meeting people in business or social settings is not the same as welcoming them into the family."

Entering the conversation for the first time, Kate ventured timidly, "You know, Elaine, I'm afraid Dan may have a point."

Elaine stared at her sister. "Since when did you become a bigot?"

Kate recoiled, affronted. "Oh, Elaine," she gasped, "that's not fair! I'm not saying there's anything wrong with you helping that boy or even adopting him, if that's what you want. He seems like a sweet kid, and you'd be a great mother. But I just think you should remember that there are people in this world who will never approve, no matter what you do. You have to ask yourself whether it would be fair to Vadinho to expose him to the kind of unpleasantness you two might have to face."

Exhaling with a shudder, Elaine said, "When Vadinho was only ten years old, his natural parents threw him out into the streets to fend for himself. Ever since then he's had to beg, steal and hustle any way he could, just to survive. How would his life possibly become any more unpleasant than it's already been?''

She reached across the table to pat her sister's hand. ''I'm sorry I called you a bigot, Katie. The crack was hateful and completely out of line. Please forgive me. It's just—oh, hell, I can't begin to describe what it does to me to be with Vadinho. He's a very special young man. He's extremely intelligent and industrious and good-natured despite all the things he's been through. He's eager to learn, and so pathetically grateful for the least little kindness anyone shows him, that it makes me want to cry. I'd like to send him to school so he can start really using that brain of his. I'd like to give him a home life with love and stability and discipline. Is that crazy? We've always had so much. My God, Dan didn't even look at the check just now, and I'm sure it amounted to more than a lot of Brazilian families earn in a month. Why shouldn't I share the wealth if I want to?''

Before her sister could reply, Dan cut in, ''You know, Elaine, I'm not quite the redneck you'd like to make me out to be. I don't mind if you want to help some underprivileged youngster get a good education. That's very noble of you. But I agree with Kate: it wouldn't be fair to the kid to bring him back to Denver and treat him like one of the family, maybe give him the idea that he'd have a right to some of the money that will come to Burton's real grandson eventually—''

Elaine blinked in confusion. ''Who said anything about Danny's inheritance?''

''One has to consider all the ramifications,'' Dan pointed out. ''I'd be a hell of a poor father if I didn't look out for my son's interests.''

Huffing impatiently, Elaine declared, "Well, you needn't worry, Dan, I have no designs on your son's birthright—or your daughter's, either, in case you've forgotten about Melissa. I do think it's a little early to talk about legacies, because at this point I have no idea whether I'll be able to adopt Vadinho. I don't know what the laws are. But it looks as if I'm going to be stranded in Rio for several days, and I intend to use the time to find them out. Maybe I can locate someone at the American consulate to advise me. In any event, if I am successful, Vadinho will have no claim on the rest of you. He'll be my heir. Whatever he gets he'll get from me."

Instead of placating Dan, Elaine's conciliatory words only seemed to infuriate him. "You think that's better?" he demanded. "That's Corminco money we're talking about, family money. What right do you have to pass it to someone who isn't even—"

"Now, Dan," Kate began, laying placating fingers on her husband's arm. He shook her off.

"Shut up, Kate," he barked. "I've been thinking about this for a long time, and I know I'm right. You ought to be able to see it yourself. It's been obvious for years that your precious sisters are both so engrossed in their wonderful careers that they can't be bothered to have babies like normal women. Since they've left it up to you to do their duty to the family, then they owe it to you to leave their money to your children!"

Cold rage washed through Elaine. Until that moment she had not realized exactly how much she despised Kate's husband. In tight, caustic tones she noted, "I just love the way you keep harping about 'the family,' Dan. You make us sound like the Mafia. Besides, the last time I looked, your name was Brock, not Welles."

Dan's hands gripped the edge of the table. "I'm a better Welles than you've ever been!" he declared vehemently.

"Yeah, sure, if by that you mean you've remade yourself in Father's image—"

Kate whimpered, "Oh, please, both of you, can't you save this for some other time? You're embarrassing me."

Breaking off, Elaine gazed remorsefully at her sister. Kate's petite, pretty features were flushed with mortification. Her mouth quivered as her eyes darted nervously toward nearby tables. Seeing her sister's distress, Elaine sighed. "I'm sorry, Kate. You'll have to chalk up my bad manners to extreme exhaustion. Or maybe living in the backwoods has made me forget how to behave among civilized people. In either case, I think I'd better excuse myself for the night. Thank you for a lovely dinner." As she reached for her handbag, a waiter magically appeared behind her to draw back her chair. Murmuring her appreciation, Elaine slipped quietly out of the restaurant.

SITTING OUT ON HER BALCONY, Elaine gazed at the dark mountains overlooking Rio. Above the lights that twinkled halfway up the hills, most of the peaks were only shapeless black hulks obscuring the stars. The exception was Corcovado. Green floodlights shone on the mist that veiled the seven-hundred-ton statue of Christ the Redeemer at the tip of the mountain, so that the figure seemed to radiate unearthly glory. Even to a cynic like Elaine, the effect was awe inspiring and strangely comforting. She sighed. She could use a little comfort right now.

Oh, God, she hurt. If only there were someone she could talk to, she thought, someone she could confide in—someone who would listen while she tried to explain why she felt as if her heart were being carved out with a dull scalpel. The pain was so great that for the first time ever she truly began to comprehend the despair that drove some people to end their own existence.

We don't need you here. How calmly, with what casual cruelty he had stood there in the rising light on Christmas morning and ripped her life apart. *We don't need you here.* The words beat mockingly at her ears. Of course she'd suspected all along that her presence in Serra Brilhante was not quite as indispensable as he'd made out. The ease with which he'd located a replacement had only proved her right. From the beginning she'd half known that his determination to get her to work in Brazil had had a deeper purpose, one he perhaps was unwilling to voice even to himself.

She stared at the statue on the mountaintop. If hubris—overweening pride—truly invited divine retribution, then she supposed she was long overdue for her punishment. She'd prided herself on her self-sufficiency most of her life—for twenty-two years, to be exact, ever since the people closest to her had failed her. Lying weak and bereft—and alone—in her posh private hospital room in Switzerland, abandoned by her lover, forsaken emotionally by her parents, she had vowed she would never again depend on anyone but herself. In some ways that vow, which she had kept religiously, had given direction to her life, fueled her success. Determination had fired her ambition, giving her the strength to succeed in a demanding career—but at the same time it had also prevented her from interacting with people in any but the most superficial ways. Because she was kind by nature—sympathetic and intuitive—she could go through the motions of loving and being loved, but she had never again truly surrendered her heart. Until now.

She supposed there was a fine, ironic justice to the fact that the man who had ultimately shattered her wall of self-sufficiency was in fact the same one who had caused her to build it in the first place.

She needed him. But he didn't need her. He'd told her so bluntly, and his rejection left her no choice but to go on as before, hiding her broken dreams behind an aloof, independent mask, parading before the world as a self-reliant woman who faced life on her own terms. The pity of it was that nobody except herself would ever know the difference.

"TRUCE?"

Elaine glanced up from the magazine she'd been leafing through listlessly. She was seated in a corner of the hotel lobby, in a conversation pit away from the swirl of holiday revelers, where she could read or people watch undisturbed. Celebrations had been in full swing for hours in the various clubs and restaurants throughout the hotel, and Elaine had amused herself for a while by trying to identify the nationalities of the people who had paraded by, dressed in saris, dashikis and djellabas as well as conventional black-tie. One or two men had glanced speculatively in her direction, but she'd quickly discouraged them. She had no desire to party with anyone. She just didn't want to greet the New Year alone in her hotel room.

"Truce?" Kate repeated hopefully, her amber eyes entreating.

Elaine sighed. "You and I aren't at war, Katie," she said, motioning to the chair next to her own. As Kate sank into the plump cushions, Elaine scanned her surroundings. "Where's Dan?"

Kate shrugged. "I think he's in the same place he's been for days—up at the business center dictating some notes."

"On New Year's Eve? Doesn't the man ever think about anything but Corminco?"

"Not that I can tell," Kate grumbled drearily.

Elaine studied her sister's morose expression with a pang. It took little deductive power to conclude that the second honeymoon Kate had longed for had been a flop. Elaine hoped her own bad temper had not contributed to its failure. "I can't tell you how sorry I am for having gotten into that argument with Dan the other day. I was very rude, and I put you in an awkward position. That's the main reason I've tried to keep out of your way since then. I thought you and Dan might get along better if I wasn't around to stir up trouble."

Kate ducked her head, and her smooth hair hid her expression. "I appreciate the diplomacy, but I'm afraid the trouble between Dan and me dates back a lot further than that argument. Besides, for the most part I thought you were right." She hunched her shoulders in confusion. "I don't know how to explain what's happening. Sometimes it feels as if I don't know my own husband anymore. He's a stranger to me. Sometimes it feels as if *I'm* a stranger to me! You know the old saw that goes, 'Be careful what you wish for; you may get it'? I've been thinking about that often, lately. I wanted Dan, and I got him—but what did I get, really?"

"Well," Elaine mused, "you got thirteen years of what at least in the beginning appeared to be a pretty solid marriage. You got two wonderful children."

Kate's face softened tenderly, and her quiet features glowed with loving radiance. Observing her sweet smile, Elaine wondered how many people, overwhelmed by Jennie's glamor and magnetic charm, had failed to notice just how beautiful Kate really was.

"Yes, I do have two wonderful children, don't I?" she whispered fondly. "Melissa and Danny are the only things Dan and I ever did exactly right." Breaking off, her smile faded. "I'm sorry, Elaine," she declared remorsefully. "Here I am moping about my problems, and I haven't even stopped to ask how it's been going with you. What have you been doing these past couple of days? Were you able to talk to anyone at the consulate about Vadinho? What did you find out?"

Elaine frowned. "Well, the first thing I found out was that the week between Christmas and New Year's Day is a lousy time to try to get anything done. Almost everybody's away on vacation, and the few staff members who do remain on duty have their hands full with the usual tourist crises, such as lost passports. They all told me to come back later in January. When I said I wouldn't be here in January, one of them finally referred me to a local child-placement agency. The woman I spoke to there said it would not be impossible for me to adopt a Brazilian national, but she warned me the procedure would be complicated and protracted and very, very expensive." Elaine's lip curled in distaste as she added, "The woman also looked me square in the eye and asked if I didn't think there was something a bit perverse about a middle-aged spinster being so obsessed with a teenage boy."

Kate winced. "So what do you plan to do now?"

"Go home, I guess. Maybe talk to some people at Immigration." She sighed. "I never expected anything concrete to be accomplished overnight, but I had so hoped that I'd at least be able to make a step in the right direction before leaving this country. As it stands, I'm afraid to even call Vadinho and tell him what I'm considering, because it might never work out.''

For several moments Kate was silent, then she suggested diffidently, ''It seems to me that the person you ought to be talking to is your friend Ruy. He strikes me as a man who knows all the angles. Once he decides to do something, I can't imagine he lets very much stand in his way.''

''That's very true,'' Elaine conceded.

''Then why don't you call him? Even though I have no idea what happened between the two of you to make you walk out on him the way you did, I have the feeling that if anybody is going to be able to help you, he's the one.''

''You're probably right, but the problem is I called him already,'' Elaine admitted, sounding defeated. ''I telephoned Serra Brilhante yesterday, and when the manager told me Ruy wasn't there, I tried A&O headquarters in São Paulo. But the offices there are closed for the week. Finally I got through to his partner's wife. Sonia said she has no idea where Ruy is, but she thinks there is some woman he goes to see about this time every year.''

''Some woman?'' Kate repeated. ''You mean like another lover?''

''I don't know what Sonia meant,'' Elaine said. ''The plain truth is I have no idea how many women there've been—or still are—in Ruy's life. When he wasn't with me, he could have been sleeping with half of Brazil. It's not a subject we ever discussed. All I do know is that he didn't get to be as good a lover as he is by reading the *Playboy* 'Advisor'!''

Kate blushed. Elaine knew her sister hated her tendency to color wildly whenever she was flustered, but personally Elaine found it to be one of Kate's most endearing traits. She could remember times in their childhood when she had deliberately teased Kate just to watch the hot-pink tide well to the roots of her hair.

Taking mercy on her, Elaine laughed lightly and declared, "Just listen to the two of us, will you? We sound like the women at those boring teas Mom used to host on Tuesday afternoons when we were girls. Even though they were supposed to discuss art or poetry or something equally high-minded, as I recall, the guests always seemed to end up bitching about the men in their lives."

Perking up, Kate agreed dryly, "Then it's too bad Jennie isn't here with us now. She could bitch about Andy."

Elaine nodded wistfully. "Yes, it would be nice if Jen was here, wouldn't it? It's been so long since the three of us were together just to enjoy each other's company. *Fun in Rio with the Welles Sisters*. It'd be almost like old times."

"Fun in Rio with anyone would be nice right now," Kate said poignantly, "but it's never going to be like old times again, and it's all my fault. Jennie will never forgive me for stealing Dan from her."

"But that was nearly half a lifetime ago!" Elaine protested. "You were both teenagers. Since then she's gone through twice as many lovers as you and me combined. You cannot convince me that after all these years and all those men, our baby sister is still cherishing her adolescent infatuation with the star football player!"

Kate said huffily, "Scoff if you will, but it's a fact that the only reason Jennie moved in with that movie star of hers is because he looks just like Dan."

Elaine eyed Kate askance. Further argument was pointless. Any woman who could equate Daniel Brock with the beauteous Andrew Proctor was clearly in no mood to be reasoned with.

To change the subject, Elaine covered her mouth with her hand and yawned windily. "I need to get up and stretch. I must have been sitting here for hours. Would you care for a drink? My treat."

"Sure," Kate said. "Anything long and cool sounds good right now. Maybe if I'm lucky they'll stick an orchid in the glass. I'd like to be able to tell my friends I did *something* exotic while I was in Rio!"

As the two women stood, Elaine automatically glanced inside her handbag for her wallet. She stilled. "Oh, dear," she murmured, pulling out a velvet-covered jewel box.

Kate stared. "My God, sis, is that what I think it is?"

Elaine opened the hinged case, revealing a delicate platinum bracelet set with sparkling sky-colored topazes. "I've had it in my suitcase the whole time I've been here! I meant to put it into the hotel vault. But I must have been distracted and I forgot about it."

Kate drawled, "I certainly hope you're not that forgetful in the delivery room. You might forget to catch the baby." She chuckled affectionately. "Come on, honey, let's go stash that trinket before something happens to it. I get the willies thinking about you walking around, just waiting for your purse to be snatched."

They wound their way through the lobby, aiming for the front desk. Elegantly dressed partygoers were still flooding into the hotel, headed for the Rond-Point jazz bar or Regine's, a branch of the New York nightclub. Stepping out of the path of one couple, Elaine almost collided with another. Two women who, like her and Kate, were moving against the flow of the crowd, swept past. As Elaine stepped aside, she mumbled her excuses, then she halted abruptly, gazing after them.

She recognized the younger of the women; she'd noticed her in the restaurant the night before. A tall, sloe-eyed beauty with the face and carriage of an Egyptian princess, she'd been wearing a Geoffrey Beene jumpsuit. Tonight the woman, like her companion, was robed in a long, loose dress of white cotton. Its gathered skirt just brushed her bare toes. Around her head more of the cloth had been wrapped into a turban-like headdress. In her arms she held a sheaf of white roses, while the older woman carried a shopping bag filled with candles and short wooden rods.

Elaine and Kate reached the front desk just as the two women exited from the hotel and strode across the Avenida Atlantica to the sands of Copacabana. As Elaine watched curiously, she suddenly realized the beach was packed with people, more people than she'd ever seen there. Many were dancing and swaying in time to drumbeats that wafted back across the promenade. "Take a look, Kate," she muttered, tapping her sister's arm. "I wonder what's going on?"

Wandering toward the door for a better view, Kate squinted through the glass. "Whatever it is, I don't think they have anything like it in Denver."

"Excuse me," a voice interrupted in heavily accented English. Glancing up in surprise, they saw the doorman approach, touching the bill of his braided cap. He murmured, "If the *senhoras* are curious about the ceremony on the beach, I can explain. Those people are worshipers of the great goddess Yemanjá, mother of the sea. Tonight is her festival."

Elaine and Kate gaped at each other, then toward the beach again. Elaine could see the wistful excitement in

Kate's eyes. Elaine addressed the doorman. "Pardon me, but would it be considered...inappropriate...if the two of us went across the street to watch?"

He surveyed them quickly and smiled his approval. "I am sure the *senhoras* would not dream of doing anything disrespectful. The goddess will not mind."

"Thank you," Elaine said quietly. She glanced at her sister. "Well? You wanted to do someting exotic."

Kate hesitated. "I don't know. I'd love to see everything that's going on, but I'm sure Dan won't approve of my wandering off."

Elaine snorted. "So what? Dan's not here, and he has no right to expect you to stay cooped up in the hotel while he works."

She could see the tension and frustration in Kate's face as she weighed her options. Her amber eyes clouded and she nibbled her lip. Lifting her lashes, she gazed longingly toward the dancers. Then all at once her expression cleared and she sagged with relief. "You're right," Kate pronounced, laughing, "Dan's not here. So to hell with Dan!"

Giggling like truant schoolgirls, the sisters left the hotel and joined the stream of people pouring across the mosaic sidewalk onto the moonlit sand.

CHAPTER FOURTEEN

THE WARM, SALTY BREEZE riffled across the beach, fluttering white banners and freshening the air that was heavy with the smell of smoke, the scent of roses, and the tang of thousands of close-pressed bodies. Flickering votive candles encircled improvised altars of mounded sand that dotted the beach. Some of the little shrines were covered with magic symbols inscribed directly into the sand; white tablecloths draped others. On every altar waving candlelight was reflected onto flowers, mirrors, jewelry, bottles of perfume and bottles of wine. Elaine noticed one or two small wooden cages of squawking chickens, making her wonder queasily if the night's festival would include blood sacrifices. But for the most part the offerings were gentle ones, the kind of presents a woman would enjoy. Her impression was confirmed when she saw the icons of Yemanjá, a beautiful, statuesque woman striding the waves in a gown of sea-foam blue, a crown of stars in her flowing black hair. As Elaine and Kate watched in awe, all around them the faithful of every age, color and social standing laid down their gifts and joined the chanting throngs singing tributes to the goddess.

"I wish I knew Portuguese," Kate whispered as they picked their way cautiously through the crowd, taking care not to blunder into the rings of worshipers. "Do you understand what they're saying?"

Elaine listened intently, straining for the words of the hymn. "'Mother Yemanjá...have pity and...and aid us. The woman'—" She broke off. "No, that's not right. *Mundo* means 'world.' That's it. The second line goes, 'The world is great, but you are greater.'"

Kate nodded appreciatively. "That's pretty. It sounds almost like something from a Mass."

"From what little I know of the spirit cults, I understand the Umbanda uses a lot of Catholic imagery. It dates back to the days when European settlers here tried to force their slaves to abandon their native religions in favor of Christianity."

"Enslave the body so you can save the soul, huh?" Kate noted ironically. "Shades of the Inquisition. No wonder a lot of people preferred to stick to the old ways."

The two women wandered further. Nobody appeared to notice or mind them. The celebrants, most of them dressed in white, were swaying to the tinkle of bells and the throb of tall, brightly painted drums, and were too absorbed in their ceremonies to pay attention to the pair of gawking sightseers.

Kate and Elaine halted to watch a woman laden with beads and charms—including crucifixes—move slowly along a row of supplicants. She stopped to blow cigar smoke on each one, then pressed the believer's hands between hers in what appeared to be some sort of cleansing ritual. Nearby a young man suddenly staggered as if he'd been shot. Trembling violently, he fell to the sand in a trance. When his friends lifted him up, he began moaning in an unnaturally guttural voice. From the reverential expressions of the onlookers, Elaine guessed that the man was a medium, and the voice was supposed to be that of some spirit speaking through him. All at once she

remembered that Ruy's patroness Dona Maria had been
an Umbanda priestess.

The thought of Ruy jarred Elaine. She glanced around
in bewilderment, suddenly struck by the strangeness, the
unreality of the activity going on around her. How would
a man as intelligent and sophisticated as Ruy have been
taken in by something so theatrical, so—so primitive?

Then she recalled that Ruy had never actually said he
subscribed to Dona Maria's beliefs, only that he re-
spected them. She looked at the revelers again, and her
cynicism faded. He was right. The faith and devotion of
the celebrants on the beach was too intense to deride.
Elaine did not understand everything that was going on
around her, but she could recognize sincerity when she
saw it. The people around her were not putting on some
show to entertain nosy tourists; they were performing
rites of worship as real and heartfelt as any she'd ever
participated in. She owed them the courtesy of tolerance.

Kate tapped Elaine's arm. "Let's go down to the water," she whispered excitedly. "I think something is going
to happen there at midnight. People have started wandering that way, and they keep checking their watches."

Smiling at her sister's enthusiasm, Elaine suggested,
"Maybe we'll all join hands and sing 'Auld Lang Syne'
in Portuguese."

Kate made a face and dragged Elaine through the
crowd. Something *was* about to happen, Elaine could tell
as she and Kate moved toward the Atlantic. In the
moonlight she could see the surf glow phosphorescent
green as the waves crested and broke, but their soothing
thunder was drowned by the pulse of the drums as they
beat ever louder, more insistent. Gazing in both directions, she realized with amazement that the crowd she

was part of stretched for miles. From the base of Sugar Loaf, southeast along the gentle crescent of Copacabana, and around the point of Ipanema, bonfires and candles turned the dark shore into a necklace of light sparkling like black diamonds.

At intervals along the water's edge small groups of people knelt in clusters, engrossed in mysterious activity. Elaine and Kate crept closer until they were almost within touching distance of two women in white headdresses who were bent over a pile of wooden rods, and were carefully lashing them together with cords. When Elaine noticed a shopping bag and a sheaf of roses lying on the sand beside them, she identified the women from the hotel. After a moment she realized that what they were doing was assembling a tiny raft.

She must have made a surprised sound, because the younger woman glanced up, her fashion-model face lighting in recognition. "Hello. May I help you?" she asked in cultured English.

"Please forgive us for intruding," Elaine replied. "We didn't mean to disturb you. We only wanted to figure out what is going on."

The woman smiled. "You haven't disturbed us. My mother and I are almost ready." While she spoke, her hands continued working, securing the last cord that bound the raft. She began to arrange the roses in a spray across the platform, while her mother carefully placed candles in a circle around the flowers. "The explanation of what we are doing is very simple, actually. My father is with our diplomatic mission in London. The day after Christmas he had emergency bypass surgery on his heart. The doctors say his prognosis is good, but naturally everyone in our family is very worried. So my mother and

I decided to fly home and ask Yemanjá to grant him a speedy recovery."

Although she realized that by now she ought to be accustomed to Brazil's startling blend of cultures, Elaine still felt disoriented by the woman's casual intermingling of the diplomatic corps, modern medical technology and sea goddesses. "I-I'm sorry to hear about your father," she stammered uncomfortably.

Kate appeared to have no such difficulty. "I'm sure the goddess will listen to your prayers," she assured gently.

"Thank you. I suppose we'll know soon enough, won't we?" the woman said, sighing and glancing at her wristwatch. When she noticed the lingering confusion in Kate and Elaine's faces, she explained, "At the stroke of twelve Mother and I—and all these thousands of other people here on the beach—will carry our offerings into the water and launch them into the waves. The gifts that are carried out to sea will have won the Great One's favor and her promise to grant the petitioner's wish. But if an offering is washed back onto the beach...." Her voice faded, and she gazed with concern at her own mother's bent head.

Kate said encouragingly, "I'm sure Yemanjá will love those beautiful roses. Anyone would."

"You're very kind to say so," the woman murmured. Impulsively she picked up one of the flowers and offered it to Kate. "Here. Perhaps you have a request you'd like to make yourself."

"Thank you," Kate whispered humbly. "I hope you receive everything you wish for." Nudging Elaine with her elbow, she urged her away, and they left the grieving women to their meditations.

When Elaine and Kate discovered a pocket of relative quiet apart from the dancers and drummers, whose celebration was growing louder and more frenetic with every passing second, they stopped. Elaine watched Kate absently stroke her cheek with the fragrant white rose while she gazed in pensive silence toward the ocean. There was a peculiar speculative gleam in her amber eyes that Elaine did not think she'd ever seen before. She cleared her throat. "Kate, are you really planning on throwing that flower out into the water?"

Her sister turned to confront her defiantly. "I may—and you don't need to look at me as if you think I've taken leave of my senses."

"I don't think any such thing. It's just that, like most doctors, I'm a skeptic by nature."

"I know you are—and I find that very sad," Kate snapped. "I've often thought your life would be a lot happier if you didn't always insist on diagnosing everything to death. Why can't you trust your instincts occasionally?"

"Because the few times in my life that I have trusted my instincts, the results have been disastrous, that's why."

"So now you'd rather analyze every little particle of emotion until there's no feeling left, is that it?" Kate shook her head impatiently. "Look around you, Elaine, look at all these people. I don't claim to understand their beliefs any better than you do, but I can feel the excitement being generated here, all these thousands and thousands of minds releasing an unimaginable burst of psychic energy. Who's to say that energy doesn't have the power to heal a man's heart—or an ailing marriage?"

Or a love affair that's too weak to live and too stubborn to die, Elaine thought glumly. She sighed. "I'm sorry, Kate. I wish I could be as open-minded as you are, but I've just never been able to work up much belief in miracle cures."

Kate's eyes narrowed as she regarded her sister consideringly. She said, "I think the real problem, Elaine, is that you've never been able to work up much belief in yourself." Then she turned away to watch the festival.

The minutes ticked by. As midnight approached, more and more people pressed toward the water's edge, until Kate and Elaine's little area of privacy disappeared and they found themselves hemmed in on all sides by bodies straining like racers at the start of a marathon. The air was suffocating, filled with the odors of perfume, *cachaça* and sweat. Children fretted and women sobbed nervously. Tension grew.

Then all at once a huge explosion rent the air. Jerking around in alarm, Elaine saw dozens of rockets launch from the roof of the Hotel Meridien, turning the tall building into a giant Roman candle that sprayed showers of red, gold and green across the sky in a spectacular display that illuminated the city below. From every quarter of Rio sirens howled and bells clanged. On the beaches tens of thousands of throats shrieked their release, and with one mind the whole vast multitude surged forward and plunged into the surf.

Elaine could not hold back. The pressure of the bodies behind her forced her to stumble ahead or risk being trampled. She and her sister were gradually separated as more and more people dashed toward the water, and Elaine saw Kate's petite figure being swallowed by the crowd. For one terrifying moment Elaine thought Kate had been knocked down, but then she spotted a pale hand holding a single rose aloft, and she knew she was safe.

As quickly and dramatically as the mass of people had formed, it began to thin. The faithful in the front of the crowd waded waist-deep into the rollers to fling their treasures over the water. As soon as they were satisfied the offerings had been accepted, they relaxed and backed away, making room for those behind them. The surface of the waves quickly became strewn with flowers, ribbons, bobbing wine bottles. Farther out, makeshift boats alight with candles floated on the ebb until they were capsized by incoming breakers. Elaine hoped the raft constructed by the two women from the hotel made it out to sea.

She found Kate vacillating at the edge of the water, her shoes in one hand, the rose in the other. Kate glanced entreatingly at Elaine. "You're always so sensible. Am I being silly?"

Elaine saw the plea for reassurance in her sister's eyes. She saw the people all around her emerging drenched from the waves, their faces aglow with happiness at the confirmation of their faith. Taking a deep breath, Elaine said, "Trust your feelings, Kate. Go for it."

"You come with me."

Elaine hesitated only a moment. "Okay," she agreed, and she slipped off her pumps.

She waded alongside her sister into the water, which was colder than she expected, and tried not to wince at the gritty unpleasant feel of sand sticking to her nylons. She was doing this for Kate, she reminded herself as saltwater lapped onto the hem of her skirt. When a wavelet splashed against her knees, soaking her to the hips, she griped, "How far out do you plan to go?"

"This is far enough." Kate's voice sounded dreamy; her gaze was focused on some point above the dark horizon. Pressing the silky white petals to her lips, she

whispered, "Mother Yemanjá, help me stand up to
Dan." Then she tossed the flower into the surf.

Elaine could not fathom the presentiment that came
over her as she watched Kate's rose drift on top of the
water, slowly revolving in the depression between waves
as if waiting for something. Elaine was not a mystic.
There was no logic whatever in thinking the sea wanted
a sacrifice from her, too, before it would accept her sister's offering, but the sense of delay, of time being sus-
pended was unmistakable. She tried to shrug off her
foreboding. The feeling persisted. Hesitantly she opened
her handbag. There was a perfume atomizer at the bottom of it. Maybe goddesses liked Giorgio.

Then her fingers closed around the slim velvet-covered
jewel case, and suddenly she knew. She knew why she
had brought a bracelet she never wore to Brazil in the first
place, and she knew why she had carried it in her purse
for days, continually forgetting to stow it in the hotel
vault. If there had ever been a sign in her cynical, ra-
tional life, this was it.

She refused to allow herself time to reconsider. Beg-
ging silently, *Please let him love me for myself,* Elaine
snatched the box from her handbag and poised to throw
it.

Kate's eyes widened in horror. "For God's sake, no!"
she squealed, clutching Elaine's arm. "Don't be crazy!"

Kate spoiled her aim. The pitch that should have sent
the bracelet spinning out over the waves went awry, and
the case flew sideways, landing with a splash in the
backwash of the wave nearest the beach, where it pitched
and yawed like a tiny ark. Elaine glanced toward Kate's
rose. The flower was gone, pulled out to sea. As the sisters watched, Elaine's bracelet washed back onto the
sand.

"Oh, Elaine, I'm so sorry." Kate started to wade toward the jewelry box.

Elaine shook her head. "Leave it alone," she commanded thickly. "I never want to see that damned bracelet again."

"Are you sure? You really ought to—"

Her sympathetic words were interrupted by a hoarse shout. "Kate—*Kate!* Goddammit, where are you?" The two women turned toward the source of the noise. Dan was sprinting clumsily across the beach as fast as his black leather wingtips would carry him in the loose sand. Strolling behind him, his hands deep in the pockets of his white slacks, came Ruy.

Dan reached the shoreline first. Gasping for air, his broad face flushed and furious, he railed, "Kate, you stupid bitch, what the hell do you mean by an idiot stunt like this, running off in the middle of the night with a bunch of whacked-out voodoo freaks? If the doorman hadn't remembered seeing you, I would have called the cops by now. How dare you worry me sick? And just look at you. You're soaked! Have you lost your mind? I swear, sometimes you act as if you don't have any more sense than Melissa!"

"Now, listen here, Daniel Brock—" Elaine watched in amazement as Kate confronted her husband. Instead of shrinking from his violent anger, she rounded on him indignantly, her eyes flashing. "Don't you *dare* talk down to me as if I were a child! I'm a grown woman perfectly capable of taking care of myself—which is what I intend to do from now on. And if you don't like it, you can go to hell." Tilting her chin resolutely, Kate squared her shoulders and stalked past Dan, heading up the beach toward the hotel. Her husband gaped at her retreating back for several stunned seconds, then he ran after her.

Elaine turned away. Ruy was standing a few feet from her, regarding her enigmatically. "It was a surprise to bump into your brother-in-law," he murmured. "I expected the three of you to be in Colorado by now."

"There weren't any flights available until the second," Elaine explained. She glanced at him, noting the loose shirt of frilled white cotton opened at the throat to reveal the *figa*. The local costume suited him. As she admired the way the shirt draped his strong torso, setting off his dark tan, Elaine realized she'd never seen him dressed so casually before. Whenever they were together, Ruy had either been attired formally, or else naked in her arms.

She let her gaze slide hungrily down the length of him. His feet were bare, and the cuffs of his trousers were stained with saltwater and wet sand. "What are you doing here?" she asked unnecessarily.

He surveyed the sodden skirt plastered to her legs. "The same thing you are, apparently. I come here every New Year's to take part in the ceremony, as I promised Dona Maria I would all those years ago. I make offerings in her honor." As he spoke, he glanced past Elaine, and suddenly his brows came sharply together. Scowling, he stalked past her and sank onto one knee in the sand where the velvet-covered box had come to rest. He snapped open the hinged case and stared at the twinkling jewels inside. Dropping the bracelet as if it were unclean, he rose slowly to his feet again. He was shaking.

In a voice as grainy as the beach they were standing on, Ruy declared, "My old friend would *not* appreciate you mocking her beliefs by making a sham sacrifice!"

Elaine looked confused. "What do you mean, a sham? Are you telling me the stones are fakes?"

He shook his head impatiently. "The topazes I gave you are real enough—but you place no value on them, no more than you value any of the other luxuries you and your family take for granted. An offering is supposed to be something precious. Yours is meaningless."

She blinked. If she had entertained any lingering hopes that Ruy might yet love her, he had just quashed them. No matter what she did, no matter how hard she tried to understand the man and his background and the culture that had shaped him, he would never see her as herself, she realized, but only as a representative of the class he both envied and despised. Dully she said, "You're right, of course. It was foolish of me to imagine I could have duped a goddess. Obviously Yemanjá saw through me, since she rejected my gift and my petition."

Ruy relaxed slightly. "As long as you understand. Out of curiosity, just what petition did you make?"

Improvising quickly, Elaine said, "I asked for help in my efforts to take Vadinho back to the United States with me. I want to send him to school there, but so far all I've gotten is the runaround from everybody I've talked to."

Her answer seemed to surprise Ruy. Mulling it, he said seriously, "In that case, it's better that your request did fail. I know you mean well, Elaine, but believe me, taking the boy to live among rich Americans would only confuse him and make him discontent, wanting things he can never have."

"But I intend to see that he does get those things he wants," Elaine insisted. "If we can ever manage to cut through all the red tape, I hope eventually to be able to adopt Vadinho."

"And turn him into an ersatz Welles?" Ruy growled, his eyes flashing. "Impossible! Vadinho is not some clay

doll you can mold to suit your own vanity. He's a Brazilian, and you have no right to take his identity from him."

The force of Ruy's attack flabbergasted Elaine. "I
have no intention of taking anything from him," she
protested. "I want to give him things like love and security, things that have been lacking in his life so far." She
paused, noting out of the corner of her eye the shadowy
forms beginning to appear on the beach now that the
crowds had dispersed, small ragged figures who darted
along the water's edge like sandpipers as they furtively
scrabbled for food or trinkets left by the waves. Elaine
said, "I want to give Vadinho the kinds of things most
children around here seem to lack."

Ruy sighed angrily. "I never said this country was
perfect, Elaine," he declared coldly, "but it has been
good to me, and I will see that it is good to Vadinho, as
well. The boy won't be neglected once you've gone home
to America. I'll make sure he gets an education in a
school where he can grow up among his own kind, and
when the time comes, I'll help him make his start in
business. In other words, I'll give him the things your
family refused to give me. But if you want a child you can
play Lady Bountiful for—someone to appease your
frustrated maternal instincts and ensure the continua-
tion of the almighty Welles clan—then I suggest you stop
pretending you're some sort of dried-up spinster—which
I know damn well you're not—and have a baby of your
own before it's too late!"

Elaine bit her lip so hard she could taste the coppery
tang of blood in her mouth. "It's already too late," she
mumbled.

Ruy scowled. Leaning closer, he demanded, "What did
you say?"

She spat, "I said it's been too late for twenty-two years!" When Ruy's eyes widened, she confessed hoarsely, "When you left me in Switzerland, I was pregnant. I would have told you, only you didn't stick around long enough to find out. From the beginning you've been absolutely convinced that I'm a spoiled little rich girl without a care in the world, who has only to snap her fingers to get her every wish granted. Well, snapping my fingers didn't bring you back when I needed you desperately. And snapping my fingers didn't give me someone I could confide in when I was so sick and scared I wanted to die. Then when I *did* almost die, all my family's money couldn't save the baby. Wham, bam, and they were all gone forever—your baby, my baby and all the babies I would have someday wanted to give a husband. You've always been so sure you knew everything about me, Ruy, but you never knew that you stole something from me a lot more precious than my great-grandmother's gold bangle."

When she paused for air, her lashes heavy with tears, Ruy gulped fishily. "Why are you telling me this now?" he choked.

Elaine gazed up at the face she loved, the face she had never stopped loving. Life would be so much easier if only she could hate him, she thought fleetingly. Taking a deep, cleansing breath of salt air, she declared, "You're over forty now, my darling. I think it's high time you quit seeing yourself as some sort of peasant hero out to avenge the depredations of the overprivileged, and faced a fact that I've had to live with since I was fifteen—*nobody, nowhere, has ever been rich enough to have it all!*"

Without waiting for him to respond, Elaine pivoted on her heel and walked away, striding resolutely across the beach as fast as her stockinged feet would carry her over

the soft sand. As she headed for the hotel, she disregarded the lurid wolf whistles and shouts of *"Feliz ano
novo!"* directed her way by a group of men celebrating
boozily around a bonfire. She paused on the mosaic
sidewalk only long enough to slip her pumps back onto
her gritty feet, and she ignored the indignant honking of
a car horn as she jaywalked across the Avenida Atlantica. She could not rest until she was safely inside the
Meridien again, with the doors closed firmly behind her,
shutting out forever the shrill, jubilant squeals of the
beggar child who had just discovered the discarded
bracelet and the sound of Ruy calling her name.

CHAPTER FIFTEEN

ELAINE'S HANDS SLAMMED down on the keyboard, and the jangling discord echoed mockingly throughout her flat. She stared in frustration at the sheet music before her. The piece was a samba, one of several she'd purchased in Rio the weekend she and Ruy had been there. But no matter how carefully she played the notes, she could not make the music sound as it had in Brazil. She supposed she lacked the flair for Latin syncopation. Or else, she considered, a single instrument simply could not reproduce the seductive, infectious rhythm of big, hollow drums pulsing in time to the haunting melody of guitars and saxophones.

Or perhaps it was the setting that was wrong, Elaine mused, glancing at the snow mounded on the windowsill. To appreciate a samba properly, she decided, one had to be in a dingy cabaret where the smoky, rum-scented air was stirred only occasionally by a breath of sultry tropical breeze. She and Kate and Dan had landed in Denver just as a blizzard of historic proportions had begun; within two hours of their touchdown, Stapleton Airport had ceased operations completely. The taxi driver ferrying Elaine back to her condominium had griped the whole way about what the tire chains were doing to his new set of radials.

Elaine closed the piano, stood up and tucked the sheet music into the bench. Then she tossed another log on the fire. It was the middle of the afternoon—time to think about something for lunch. At least the onset of the storm had waited long enough for her housekeeper to air out the flat and restock the kitchen cupboards. Originally Elaine had intended to return to Denver unannounced, but on impulse, just before leaving Brazil, she had wired Mrs. Tanner to say she was on her way home. She was now very grateful for the spontaneous action, since the record snows had rendered the roads almost impassable. Elaine would not have relished having to brave the needle-sharp wind and icy pavement just for a carton of milk.

Of course, she conceded, the storm did give her a perfect excuse to hibernate beside her fireplace, snug and cut off from the outside world. For three days now she had not telephoned anyone. Her office staff was not expecting her before February at the earliest, and her friends were equally snowbound in their own homes. There was no reason to contact any of them just yet and face their well-meant but painful questions about her stay in the Southern Hemisphere—questions to which she wasn't sure she'd ever know the answers.

Elaine was removing the foil wrapper from a portion of frozen lasagna, in preparation for cooking it in the microwave, when her doorbell rang. She set aside her lunch and padded through the apartment to the front door, puzzling over the identity of the caller. Mrs. Tanner wasn't due for another couple of days, and apart from her immediate family, nobody else knew she was home. When she peered through the peephole, her confusion increased. Her expression was leery as she opened the door to the tall, dark-haired woman shaking snow from the hood of her mink-lined cape. "Hello, Mom," she greeted in guarded tones. "What brings you here?"

Carolyn gazed down at her oldest daughter. Her exquisite face looked tired and pale, and for the first time Elaine could detect lines scoring and aging her petal-soft skin. Beneath the perfectly applied lipstick her cupid's-bow mouth appeared puckered and dry. As Carolyn smoothed back her hair from her temples, Elaine espied with amazement a gleam of silver at the roots of the sable strands. She wondered how long her mother had been dyeing her hair.

"It's been almost three months since we've seen each other, Elaine," Carolyn said regretfully. "Won't you at least invite me in?"

"Of—of course," Elaine stammered, belatedly recalling her manners and beckoning her mother inside. They hugged. Elaine grimaced when her skin touched the ice crystals clinging to the chilly fabric of the cape. "This thing is soaked. I'd better hang it up somewhere to dry. How long have you been outside, anyway?"

"Oh, not long, dear," Carolyn replied unconvincingly as she shrugged off the wrap. "I was doing a little shopping, and I decided to drop by. I walked a couple of blocks."

Elaine regarded her mother steadily. "Mom, even a die-hard shopper like you is going to think twice about venturing out into a hundred-year snow. Besides, the only store within half a mile of here is Seven-Eleven. I hardly think you drove all the way across town to pick up a loaf of bread."

Carolyn slumped slightly. "Very well, I've been standing outside for the past twenty minutes, trying to decide whether I should venture up here or not. I wasn't sure I'd be welcome."

"My God, why would you think a thing like that?" Elaine exclaimed.

"Because you've been home for days and you haven't come to see me, that's why!"

"But I called you," Elaine reminded her. "I told you I needed to rest but that I'd come over as soon as the weather cleared a little. It hasn't. You shouldn't be out in it, either."

"I wanted to see you. I've missed you."

Elaine sighed. "I've missed you, too, Mom." She glanced at the cape she was still holding. "Why don't you warm up by the fire while I hang this? Then I'll fix some coffee and we'll talk."

When Elaine returned, Carolyn was admiring the Wedgwood ornaments displayed on the mantel. "I think you've added some pieces to your collection since I was last here," she noted. "This little box—is it new?"

"I bought it when I went to New York last June to see Jennie."

Carolyn looked startled. "Has it been that long since I've been here?"

"Probably. You always expect me to visit you in Cherry Hills," Elaine said. "Speaking of Jennie, did you see her at Christmas?"

"Unfortunately, no. With Kate and Dan gone, I decided I'd better stay here with the children." Carolyn's dark eyes narrowed. "I'm very concerned about Kate, you know. Ever since she and Dan returned from Brazil, she's been behaving oddly. I'm not referring to her sudden brainstorm to go back to college, either. It's just . . . I'm afraid she may actually be considering a divorce."

"It may not come to that, Mom," Elaine reassured her. "I know Kate wants to make a go of the marriage, for her and Dan's sake and also for the sake of the twins.

But it's going to take some effort on her husband's part, as well.''

"Your father thinks everything would be fine if Kate would just have another baby."

Elaine smiled sardonically. "Well, that would take some effort on Dan's part, too, wouldn't it?"

Carolyn's fine brows came together. "What do you mean?"

"Nothing," Elaine dismissed hurriedly. Her parents were obviously unaware of the extent of the Brocks' estrangement, and she had no intention of being the person to enlighten them. After a pause she suggested gently, "As much as we all worry about Kate, I really believe the best thing we can do for her is not interfere. Let her and her husband work out their differences on their own."

"That's easier said than done with us all living in one house," Carolyn noted. Her mouth curved with a touch of self-mockery. "I know I protested when you and Jennie moved out, but sometimes I think you both did the wisest thing. Poor Kate. When she and Dan married, they were just kids, and it didn't make any sense for them to have to squeeze into some tiny apartment when we had all that room going to waste. But I should have warned her. God knows *I* know what it's like to be a newlywed in a house full of relatives! When Burton carried me across the threshold, not only was Maggie waiting for us on the other side of the door, but also Burton's brother, Joe III, and their father, Joseph, Jr. There was no such thing as privacy, and if we had any sort of disagreement, everyone immediately took sides. I always figured Burton's mother died young just so she could have a nice, quiet grave all to herself."

Elaine glanced sharply at her mother. She couldn't recall the last time Carolyn had confided in her about the past. She suddenly wished her mother would do it more often. There was something endearing about the picture of the grande dame of Denver society as an insecure young bride with in-law problems.

After a moment, when Carolyn did not continue speaking, Elaine turned toward the kitchen and suggested, "Now, why don't I go brew us some coffee?"

When Carolyn noticed the thawing lasagna, she insisted that Elaine finish her lunch. Conversation between the two women remained desultory until they sat at the cherry wood breakfast table, sipping coffee and staring out at the snow-covered plains that were gray and bleak beneath a leaden sky. Then Carolyn said, "Kate tells me you weren't entirely happy yourself in South America."

Elaine's knuckles whitened around the cup. "Kate's wrong," she responded in clipped tones. "I found Brazil a fascinating country. There was something new every moment. I was never bored."

"She didn't say you were bored, she said you were unhappy," Carolyn corrected. "'Unhappy,' as in, 'because of a man.' I presume she was referring to the charismatic Senhor Areias."

Elaine muttered, "I'd think Kate would be too preoccupied with her own problems at the moment to gossip about mine."

"Kate worries about you as much as you worry about her. As much as I worry about all my daughters." When Elaine did not speak, Carolyn cried, "Please, darling, don't shut me out! I love you and I want to help you, but for as long as I can remember, there's been this wall between us. We talk, we smile, and from a distance we get along beautifully, but every time I try to move closer to you, you slam the door in my face."

With great care Elaine set down her coffee cup. She gazed deliberately at her mother. "And you don't know why?"

Under her daughter's scrutiny, Carolyn's face grew ashen. Staring fixedly at her reflection in the glossy tabletop, she whispered, "Of course I know. All these years I've seen you become more brittle and cynical with each birthday, watched you freeze off any man who really cared about you—including that nice young surgeon we all liked so much. I've always known what was behind it. I've always known it was all my fault."

The confession caught Elaine off guard. "I've never thought it was all your fault, Mom. Father bears a lot of culpability himself, you know."

Carolyn shook her head. "You don't understand. Burton is... Burton. You might sympathize with him more if you'd known his father, Joseph, Jr., but I can't say I'm sorry you missed the opportunity. The two years I lived in the same house as that man were the most miserable ones of my life. He was a self-indulgent, narrow-minded bully. He was born a month after his own father was killed, and he grew up thinking he was some kind of demigod. The only person who maintained any kind of control over him was Maggie—and he hated her for it. But she was his mother, so he took out his resentment on other women. His own marriage must have been hellish."

Elaine pressed, "And that's why Father is such a chauvinist?"

"More or less," Carolyn said. "Unlike Joseph, Jr., Burton doesn't hate women. He just doesn't think we're very smart. He's thoroughly convinced we'll all be a lot happier with some nice strong man to control and guide us along the paths preordained by our physiology. And to my lasting shame, I've let him go on believing that.''

Propping her elbows on the table, Carolyn slouched uncharacteristically, her chin on her folded hands. "If I'd made enough of a fuss, I could have stopped him from sending you away to Switzerland. I didn't like the idea of you being so far from the rest of us, but, well, it was the sixties, and we had other friends whose teenagers were beginning to turn into flower children and running off to join communes or, worse, motorcycle gangs. In fact, my Tuesday group finally disbanded when one of the members unwittingly brought some brownies her daughter had laced with hashish. Fortunately they tasted funny, and nobody ate more than a bite. But all around us intelligent, well-bred children just like you seemed to be going crazy, and after a while Switzerland began to sound like a haven, someplace you'd be safe from all these bizarre, frightening influences.''

Elaine stared. "I always thought you sent me to Europe because you wanted to get rid of me.''

"We sent you there to protect you,'' Carolyn said sadly, "and instead, you almost died.'' She covered her face with her hands. "I've never been sure which I feel more guilty about: exposing you to danger, or the fact that when you needed my help, you were afraid to ask for it. All I do know is that I failed you completely. There have been times when the least little reminder was more than I could bear.''

"Is that the reason why you gave away my christening gown?'' Elaine asked, shaken by her mother's pain. "That—that really hurt me.''

Carolyn nodded miserably. "I'm sorry, darling. It was another stupid, selfish thing I did. I had no right to give away something that was yours to treasure, but when I came across it that day, I couldn't stand to look at it. I just threw it in the box with all the other things I was collecting for the Junior League rummage sale. I never stopped to consider that if you married someone with children, you could still have grandchildren you'd like to pass the gown to. Or you could adopt a baby yourself.''

Elaine sighed. All these years and she hadn't known her mother half as well as she'd thought she did. She'd never even guessed at the burden the woman carried inside her. She'd thought the anguish was all her own. A tiny, hateful part of her was almost glad she had not suffered alone, and yet, after so much time, did it make any sense for either of them to suffer further for something that was simply a fact of life?

She patted Carolyn's shoulder consolingly. "You don't need to worry about anything, Mom, certainly not the christening gown. At this point in my life I think it's pretty unlikely that I'll ever marry anybody, stepchildren or no. And if by chance I do adopt someone, I can guarantee right now that the gown wouldn't fit him.''

DAYS ON THE TELEPHONE convinced Elaine that her plan to adopt Vadinho was a pipe dream.

Harrassed civil servants at the Colorado Department of Social Services, understaffed because of the record snow, suggested she contact the Foreign Adoption Center in Boulder if all she wanted was information. When she telephoned the Center long-distance, workers there, operating under the same handicaps as the people in Denver, referred her to a local attorney. She finally tracked down the man in his office, but she had to use her father's name to convince the attorney to make time in his schedule to see her. By the time she found herself seated in his stuffy, overheated office, Brazil seemed illusive and very, very far away.

"You're thirty-seven years old and you've never been married. Is that correct, Dr. Welles?" the lawyer inquired, making notes on a long yellow pad. When Elaine nodded, he continued, "May I ask why you've remained single all this time?"

Elaine stiffened. "That's none of your business."

He smiled dryly. "I'm sorry if you think I'm being nosy, but personal questions of that sort are exactly the sort of thing you're going to have to put up with if you seriously expect to adopt a child. The domestic appraisal that's required by law will necessitate our prying into every aspect of your life. You will have to explain why you've never married, why you wish to adopt a child without getting married and why you think you can raise that child alone. You'll be asked about your emotional stability, your finances and your most intimate relationships. If you're unwilling to open your private life to such examination, you might as well forget the whole idea now."

Elaine sighed. "Very well. I've never married because I've been busy with my career and never met the right man. I don't smoke or do drugs, I drink rarely, and I've never had a nervous breakdown. I make a lot more money than I can possibly spend. In Brazil I met a child who needs love and attention, and I think I'm the person to give those things to him. Anything else?"

The attorney was writing rapidly. "This boy in Brazil: I presume he's eligible for adoption? I mean, he has no known parents?"

"They abandoned him on the streets three years ago," Elaine said grimly.

The attorney scowled. "But did they ever formally rescind custody of the boy?"

Elaine stared. "I . . . I don't know. Surely the fact that they deserted him would long ago have cost them any legal hold they had over Vadinho. He hasn't seen them since he was ten!"

Lifting his head abruptly, the attorney probed, "This child is what—thirteen years old now? Oh, dear, that could present a serious problem."

"What do you mean?" Elaine asked warily.

The man sighed and leaned back in his chair. "Dr. Welles, as you must have figured out by now, arranging a foreign adoption is a very tedious, drawn-out process, partly because everything must be done in duplicate, first in the child's country of origin, then in the United States. Just the initial step of obtaining a study will take months. But even assuming everything goes swimmingly and Brazil grants you custody of this boy, in order for him to immigrate here at once, bypassing the quota system, you will have to obtain a preferential visa for him—and such visas are issued only to children under the age of fourteen."

Elaine felt herself grow cold. "What happens if we can't get the paperwork done before his next birthday?"

The attorney shrugged helplessly. "If the boy is not eligible for a preferential visa, then you could, I suppose, wait out the quota system—a matter of years, unfortunately. If you were willing to live with him in Brazil for two years after adopting him there, then you could bring him with you when you return home. You might try to get him into this country with some other kind of special visa—on medical grounds, perhaps, or as a visitor. And of course, if all else fails, you can always apply for a special Act of Congress, although that will take at least a year, too...."

Elaine shivered. Tears of temper and frustration stung her eyes. "I don't believe this," she grated. "Vadinho is a harmless little boy all alone in the world. He desperately needs someone to care for him, to give him a home. I'm ready and eager to give him that home. What kind of sense does it make, what compassion or justice is there in keeping us apart for years because of legal loopholes and bureaucratic red tape?"

Shaking his head sympathetically, the lawyer said, "I'm sorry, Dr. Welles, truly I am. I wish I could be more encouraging. In all fairness, I suppose I ought to point out that we live in a big world with lots of homeless children and prospective parents, and the laws have been written to benefit as many people as possible. Not that that's much comfort to you, I'm sure. But if you like, I'd be willing to represent you in any action you wish to initiate. We can always hope for a miracle."

"I'm afraid a miracle is exactly what it's going to take," Elaine sighed, and she reached into her handbag for her checkbook.

IF THE SESSION with the lawyer was difficult, Elaine's reunion with her father was even more so.

Seated in her favorite leather armchair beside the grand piano in her parents' library, Elaine nursed her liqueur and gazed warily at Burton. The house was dark and quiet. Outside, the sky was clear for the first time in a week, and the rest of the family had driven north to Loveland for a day's skiing. When Elaine answered her father's invitation and discovered everyone else gone, she knew she was in for an interrogation.

He began his probe obliquely. Gazing across the room at her, his sapphire eyes slits above his jowly cheeks, Burton commented, "I was a bit surprised when you came home from Brazil so soon."

Elaine said, "There was never any set time for my stay. It just turned out they didn't need me quite as long as originally expected."

"But the people at Serra Brilhante were satisfied with your work?"

"Oh, yes. Apart from some difficulties at first with the language—and I was picking up Portuguese pretty quickly—there were no problems."

"That's good," Burton declared. "As I believe I mentioned in that letter I wrote you, I considered you Corminco's representative down there. I'm glad to hear you made a favorable impression."

Dryly Elaine said, "You needn't have worried, Father. I managed to uphold the family honor."

Burton paused. "You know, Elaine, if you had remained on-site longer, I would have asked you to take a more active role on Corminco's behalf."

"How do you mean?"

"I wanted you to keep an eye on A&O's activities, especially the way they handle the minerals mined at Serra Brilhante." He hesitated as if shaping his words. "This is not the kind of news I would ordinarily trouble your mother or any of you girls with, but, well, you're pretty sensible, and I think you can deal with it. There is reason to believe that some of the gemstones we've received have been doctored."

Elaine frowned, remembering that Dan had flown to Brazil because of a dispute over the quality of the stones. Because she knew that grading jewels was a fairly subjective art, she'd assumed he was referring to some routine difference of opinion between A&O's appraiser and Corminco's. "What do you mean, 'doctored'? You mean they've been treated with lasers, radiation?"

"You know about this sort of thing?" Burton asked in surprise.

"I've heard a little," Elaine admitted cautiously. "But what makes you think there's something wrong with the stones?"

Burton said, "That's just it, we don't know for a fact that there is anything wrong. The head of the brokerage house I use came to me privately and said he was suspicious of a few of the largest items in the first lot we sent him. He conceded all he really had to go on was a gut instinct derived from forty years in the jewelry trade, but something just didn't feel right to him."

Recalling the radioactivity in the gemstones she'd seen in São Paulo, Elaine asked, "But aren't there ways of analyzing the stones to be sure they're natural?"

Burton shrugged. "Yes and no. Properly done, many treatments are completely undetectable. Others will show up in the right kind of chemical test, but you have to destroy the stone in order to perform them! But in any case, we don't dare conduct the tests."

"Why on earth not?" Elaine demanded.

Her father looked uncomfortable. "The problem is, the mere fact that a test has been conducted could be disastrous, no matter what the results were. That's why the man who complained was so discreet about it. In the gem trade, reputation is everything. If Corminco comes under suspicion the very first time we offer stones for sale—hell, we might as well bring all our equipment home from Brazil and go back to building condos."

The longer Burton spoke, the more alarmed and confused Elaine became. From the beginning she'd known there was more to Ruy's reappearance in her life than a desire to resume an old affair. She knew he harbored a grudge against her family that bordered on the neurotic. But even though Ruy had admitted openly that it would not be difficult to take advantage of Burton's inexperience with precious stones, Elaine could not imagine him committing deliberate fraud. There was something too devious, too underhanded about the idea; it seemed out of character for him. Ruy was a man who might fight dirty, but he'd always fight face-to-face; a man who could kill in a duel but never with poison.

With outward casualness Elaine observed, "I thought Dan and Ruy had worked out everything in Brazil. I distinctly recall Ruy giving his word that the 'situation' had been resolved."

Burton harrumphed. "What did you expect him to say—that A&O plans to go on cheating us? Of course it's all resolved, for the moment."

"Have there been more doctored stones?"

"Not as far as we can tell," Burton admitted, "although that's probably not saying much, since we've only received one more packet since you and your sister and Dan were down there. But that's why I wish you were still at Serra Brilhante, to keep an eye on things."

"But what good could I do? I know nothing about mineralogy."

"You know a little something about men, don't you?" Burton retorted impatiently. "If you'd use those dormant feminine wiles of yours, I'll bet you could worm the truth from Areias. In fact, considering how attracted the man seems to be, if you play your cards right, you might even be able to wangle a proposal."

Although Elaine knew she ought to be inured to her father's disdain by now, his insensitivity angered her.

"For your information, Father," she stated coldly, "I have never had to use my 'wiles' to 'wangle' a proposal from any man—including Ruy Areias."

Burton stared. "Are you saying he actually asked you to marry him?"

"That's right."

"But what happened? Why didn't you say anything? I mean—my God, you didn't tell him *no*, did you?"

Enjoying his shock, Elaine remarked, "I believe my exact response was that I'd have to think it over."

"But what is there for you to think about? The man is a great catch!"

"For me—or for Corminco?" Elaine queried acutely.

Burton started. "Well, for—for both, I suppose," he conceded. "Areias is a shrewd businessman, and Lord knows your marriage would guarantee good relations between his company and mine—but damn it, Elaine, I'm not some Medici prince trying to cement a trade agreement with a wedding! Areias may be my business associate and rich, to boot, but the man is also good-looking, intelligent, charming and very attracted to you. What more do you want?"

What more do I want? Elaine asked herself drearily. *What more have I always wanted? Not much—just the one thing I've always been denied. Just love.*

When she did not answer him, the blustering tone faded from Burton's voice. "My dear, it's not that—that old problem that's making you hesitate, is it?" he asked, sounding peculiarly diffident. "You shouldn't worry about it anymore, you know. I figured out a long time ago that the reason you wouldn't marry that other doctor was because he wanted a family, but at your age I think it's pretty unlikely Areias would expect you to give him children."

Elaine gasped, scarcely able to believe what she was hearing. For the first time ever, her father was speaking about the forbidden subject. For over two decades he had avoided the topic so completely that Elaine had often wondered if he had not truly succeeded in expunging the knowledge from his mind. And now he was making a direct, voluntary reference to her sterility.

She said, "I thought you'd forgotten."

Burton's eyes widened. "What?"

"All these years, and you never once mentioned what happened to me in Switzerland. I finally decided you must have made yourself forget."

Burton's amazement mirrored Elaine's own. "Dear Lord, if you only knew how often I've wished I *could* forget!"

"What do you mean?"

Her father averted his eyes, his weathered cheeks oddly flushed. "Is it really necessary to talk about this?" he asked brusquely. "What difference could it make now, after all this time?"

Elaine insisted, "It makes a great deal of difference. Surely you must realize that losing that baby has affected my whole life, clear up to the present. Please, Father. We've spent over twenty years avoiding the subject. Can't we, just this once, be honest with each other? I need to know how you feel about what happened to me."

Scrubbing his face with his hands, Burton blurted, "How did I feel? How the hell do you think I felt? To my dying day I'm going to be haunted by the memory of the way you looked when your mother and I first saw you in that hospital. You were so thin and frail and white, with big purple shadows around your eyes, and there were all these tubes....I cried."

"I don't remember you crying," Elaine said incredulously. "All I remember is you frowning down at me like God eyeballing some miserable worm of a sinner. I was so ashamed. I wanted desperately for you to hug me or at least say something comforting, and instead I half expected that at any second you'd call down lightning to strike me for failing you."

Burton sighed. "Oh, darling, you've got to believe me. I didn't think you'd failed me. I realize I should have said something, but I'm no damn good at expressing my feelings, never have been. I wanted to cradle you in my arms, but you were so—so fragile looking. I was afraid if I so much as touched your hand, you'd...slip away from us." He shook his head as if warding off the vision. "That recollection is what I couldn't deal with, not the fact that you'd never have children, although the Lord knows I hated that, too."

Elaine took a deep breath, thinking of all the years wasted, all the misunderstandings. "I wish you'd said all this before," she declared wistfully. "There were a lot of times I could have used someone to talk to, especially when all my school friends started gushing about weddings and baby showers. I had a lot of questions I needed to ask."

As she spoke, a voice echoed in her memory, a voice tinged with fatigue and spiritual weariness. *Ask your father,* Ruy suggested, and his words had sounded oddly chilling on a tropical Christmas morning.

Rubbing his jaw uncomfortably, Burton observed, "I guess becoming an obstetrician was a way to find out the answers to all those questions?"

"Not all of them," Elaine said quietly. "There are things they can't teach you in medical school." She paused. "Things like—what did you do about Antonio?"

Burton jerked upright in his chair. "What did you say?"

Elaine's gaze remained steady. "You heard me, Father. I'm talking about Antonio, the boy who made me pregnant. I know you knew who he was, because while I was still in the hospital, you and the director of the school badgered me until I told you. What I don't know is what you did with the information. But I don't for a minute believe you just let the matter drop."

Under his daughter's intense scrutiny, Burton's face grew chalky, his eyes haunted. His hands began to clench and unclench on the arms of his chair. Clearing his throat raspily, he said, "I . . . put out a contract on the boy."

"You what?" Elaine choked, horrified despite the fact that she now realized she'd half anticipated what her father was saying.

Burton chuckled humorlessly. "I put out a contract on the kid. Isn't that what they call it in the movies when you hire a murderer? Just imagine, your old man carrying on like Humphrey Bogart—or maybe the Three Stooges. It was the only time in my life I ever tried anything overtly criminal, and I didn't know what the hell I was doing. While your mother was with you in the hospital, I started cruising the seamiest dives in Bern until I spotted a couple of thugs, expatriate Americans, who looked like they'd do anything for a price. I offered them five thousand dollars apiece to track down the kid and kill him. They took the money, and I never heard from them again, so I have no idea whether or not they did what I paid them for. But either way, I still find it impossible to feel guilty."

More fragments of conversation drifted through Elaine's mind: *miserable...wretched...returning to Europe was impossible...I was scared witless...."* No wonder he hated the Welles family.

Elaine jumped to her feet. Her voice quavered as she demanded, "How could you? He was only a teenager, little more than a child!"

"*You* were a child," Burton retorted. "You were my baby and I loved you and that guttersnipe hurt you. I couldn't let him get away with it."

Elaine knew she ought to feel thrilled because her father had just told her he loved her. She'd spent a lifetime waiting to hear those words. Instead, all she could do was ask drearily, "Tell me, are you familiar with the expression, 'Hoist with his own petard'?"

Burton looked puzzled. "Of course, I am," he said testily. "*Hamlet*, act three, scene four. I do occasionally read something besides mining journals, you know. What on earth are you rambling on about?"

As she loomed over Burton, Elaine's smile was wan. "It's simple, Father. Antonio did 'get away with it.' Your hired assassins missed him. He escaped to South America and changed his name. Now he's your partner."

Burton stared up at her, stupefied. He tried to speak, but his lips moved mutely. Strangled noises issued from his throat. At last he gasped, "You mean I've been set up from the first?"

"So it would appear."

Suddenly Burton looked very old, very feeble. "But I—I've gambled everything on the Brazilian venture: the family's assets, my—my reputation. I wanted—I had this dream...."

Elaine had not been certain exactly how much of a threat Ruy actually presented, but her father's obvious fear convinced her the danger was considerable, and very real. For a moment she tried to imagine family life without the comfortable cushion of Corminco's assets. She was sure she and Jennie could manage all right, but what about Kate and the children, what about her mother? She gazed down at Burton, who sat hunched in the chair, his face in his hands. What about her father? Could Burton Welles survive without Corminco? Could he endure the ignominy of being exposed to the world not as some infallible, monolithic being, but as she was seeing him now: as a tired, aging man with very human failings?

She patted his shoulder consolingly, knowing his moment of weakness would pass. Welleses were too resilient to keep down long, and soon Burton was sure to be his old authoritarian self again, trying to run his business and his family with the same iron hand. Most of his family, that was. Elaine had seen through him; she'd never have to prove herself to her father again.

Leaning down, she wrapped her arms around Burton and pressed her lips against his weathered cheek. "Cheer up, Daddy," she whispered bracingly, "it's going to be all right. Even if Ruy proves to be no more merciful to us Welleses than we've been to him, the family will stick together. After all, we're not Maggie's offspring for nothing."

CHAPTER SIXTEEN

"EASY NOW," Elaine crooned, her eyes focused on the first glimpse of wet, blue-black hair. "Don't hurry. You've waited nine months for this, a few more seconds won't hurt. I'll tell you when to push. The baby's crowning and you're doing great. Gently, gently...." Her voice was low, soothing, almost a lullaby.

"I can see it!" the mother sobbed, exhausted but elated, clutching at her husband's hand. "Look, darling, in the mirror, do you see?" Another contraction began. "Oh, God—"

"Shhh," Elaine said reassuringly, "just relax. Everything's perfect. Okay, Daddy, time to help her. That's wonderful. Deep, cleansing breaths now. Here comes the head—" Step by step, with loving care, Elaine paced the young couple through the birth, until at last she was able to hold up the baby, his copper skin pale with the creamy vernix that had protected him in the womb. Smiling, she said, "Congratulations. You have a beautiful little boy."

When she returned to the locker room, her eyes were misty, her feet light despite her fatigue. The miracle never failed. Each delivery, no matter how difficult, moved and awed her, revitalized her spirit, restored her faith. Elaine could not imagine what her life would be like without that daily renewal. Sometimes she thought it was the only thing that gave her the strength to go on.

She stripped the protective cap off her hair and removed the sloppy paper booties that made her feet look like paws, discarding them in the waste receptacle. Then she sank onto one of the molded plastic chairs scattered about the room. After every birth she needed a brief period of decompression, a few moments to permit her overstimulated emotions to cool down before she was able to cope with mundane concerns like traffic or laundry. This morning she had rounds to conduct before she left the hospital, and once those were completed, there were earth-shattering decisions to make, such as whether the carton of weepy yogurt in the back of her refrigerator was fit to eat, or if she should go to the supermarket.

Pulling her handbag from her locker, Elaine fished inside for a hairbrush. Her fingers landed on a wrinkled envelope plastered with airmail postage and rubber-stamp marks reading *Por Avião*. She slipped out the onionskin sheets to reread them: "Deer doc, this is my first leter ever and in English to, are you impresed? The boss gave me the sta—" the rest of the word was blotted out "—the paper to rite on. I sure do miss you...."

"I miss you, too, Vadinho," Elaine murmured with a nostalgic smile as she waded once again through the boy's scrawled, barely literate note. The cast was off his arm, and he was starting to grow so much he'd soon have to get a new one on his leg. Vadinho wished it could be off completely before school started at the end of February, but the new doctor told him leg bones took longer to heal. Luis was home from the hospital. His scars looked really bad, but the boss said there were plastic surgeons in the big cities who could fix him up good as new. And speaking of the boss, had the doc heard that the other boss, the one nobody liked much, had been arrested?

That last remark puzzled Elaine. After her first few days back in Denver, she had deliberately kept herself too active to think. She had simply waited for the ax to fall. But despite her father's fears, so far nothing had happened to indicate that Ruy intended to use his power to harm the Welleses. The packets of gemstones continued to arrive at regular intervals from Brazil, and those already on the market were commanding premium prices. Burton confided with relief to Elaine that the head of the brokerage house had decided his gut instincts must have been at fault about the so-called questionable stones in the first shipment; it looked as if Corminco was going to receive an excellent return on its foreign investment.

But if there was nothing wrong with the stones, Elaine asked herself in confusion, then why had João been arrested? And if the man was guilty of attempted fraud, how had Ruy avoided being indicted, as well?

Changing from her scrubs to a skirt and blouse, Elaine donned her white coat and began her rounds. She'd been busy ever since coming back to work, her patient load heavier than usual. Her leave of absence had caused less disruption in her practice than she'd expected, but she felt honor-bound to relieve her colleagues who had filled in while she was away. At the moment she was handling maternity cases for a general practitioner vacationing in the Bahamas. Between his patients and hers, she hadn't had a day off in nearly two weeks. After she checked the progress of several new mothers, signed the discharge papers for one, and reassured another, whose preemie was going to have to remain behind in the nursery after she left the hospital, Elaine stopped at the nurses' station.

"What a morning! I don't suppose I could talk you kind, generous ladies out of some of that coffee, could I?" she asked hopefully, glancing toward the steaming pot behind the counter. An aide who'd been sorting patient folders giggled and handed her a Styrofoam cup. As Elaine sipped the scalding brew, she realized the women were staring at her with wide, expectant grins. Perplexed, she noted, "You all certainly seem to be in good moods. What's going on? Did one of those lottery tickets you chip in on turn out to be a big winner?" The aide giggled again.

Relaxing against the counter, Elaine noticed for the first time the flower cart at the other end of the station, where pastel carnations in lamb-shaped china vases or potted chrysanthemums with pink and blue ribbons waited to be delivered. Towering over the more sedate floral offerings was an enormous silver basket filled with dozens of long-stemmed roses whose petals—white on the outside, velvety dark red on the inside—exuded a heady perfume that was almost dizzying. "Good grief," Elaine exclaimed, impressed, "which lucky mother rated those beauties? Mrs. DeNiro with the triplets?"

"Guess again, doctor," the head nurse said with a chuckle.

Elaine stared. "For me?" she gasped. When the woman nodded, Elaine set down her cup and rounded the counter to the cart. She scanned the bouquet with a faint frown. "Is there a card?" she asked. "Which florist delivered these?"

"They were carried by hand."

"By hand? But who—" She broke off. In the dark green recesses of the spray, among the thornless stems, she caught a glimpse of something shiny. Gingerly she reached for it. When her fingers closed around the gleaming metal, she grew very still.

She had not seen the hammered gold circlet in over twenty years, but she still remembered every arabesque, every finely engraved curlicue that the jeweler in Switzerland had not quite been able to duplicate; she knew the rich luster the copy had never equaled, a patina created by eight decades of wear, first on her great-grandmother's arm, then her own—

"Doctor, are you all right?" one of the nurses asked with concern. "You've gone all white."

"Where is he?" Elaine rasped.

"Who? The guy who looks a little like Ricardo Montalban? I think he's taking a peek at the babies."

Elaine ran.

He stood alone at the nursery window, gazing through the soundproof glass. A wistful yearning shimmered in his lion-dark eyes as he peered down at the rows of newborns in their clear plastic isolettes. The attendant on duty in the nursery gestured to the name tags identifying the occupants of each little crib, asking if there was a particular one he wished her to wheel to the window. When Ruy pressed his lips together and shook his head, Elaine could tell the nurse was mystified.

When the nurse spotted Elaine, her face lighted in recognition. Elaine pointed to the baby she'd assisted into the world earlier in the day, and the woman carried him up to the window. A doll-sized blue cap rested jauntily on his black hair, and in the middle of his small, perfect face, still puckered with newness, a tiny blade of a nose already proclaimed his Native American ancestry.

"A fine boy," Ruy judged quietly, not looking at Elaine.

She said, "I delivered him this morning."

"You must feel very proud."

"I feel humble," Elaine corrected, "humble and deeply moved. Every one of them is such a miracle, so much alike and yet so individual. After all these years, I am still awed."

They stood side by side, not touching, not speaking, until the attendant returned the baby to his crib and drew the blinds across the nursery window. Then Elaine said, "Thank you for the roses, Ruy. They're unusual and very beautiful."

"When I saw them, I was intrigued by the cool white exterior enclosing a core of passionate red," he claimed. "It made me think of you."

"That's very poetic."

"Most Brazilians are poets at heart."

Elaine took a deep breath. "I've always admired your way with words. Even when you were a boy you seemed to have an explanation for everything." She held the bangle in her outstretched palm. "How do you explain this?"

He stared at the gold gleaming in her hand. "I kept the bracelet. I took it from you in a fit of pique, and at first I suppose I intended to pawn it. But I discovered that even when I went hungry, even when I was desperately searching for a way to escape your father's goons, I couldn't bring myself to part with it." He sighed. "It was the only bit of you I had."

"And you've treasured it all these years?" Elaine's expression was ironic. "Somehow I'd find you a lot more convincing if I wasn't sure you'd plotted to destroy my family."

"Excuse me—" A patient in a ruffled bathrobe was trying to pass them, clinging to the handrail along the wall; she moved gingerly, as if unsure of her balance. Ruy and Elaine stepped into the middle of the corridor just as an orderly pushing a gurney wheeled by.

Ruy glanced around. "Is there someplace we can talk? There is much I must tell you."

Elaine hesitated. "We could go down to the cafeteria, I suppose. If I'm needed for anything, they can beep me."

In the basement lunchroom, Elaine sat beside Ruy at a cramped Formica table and poked dubiously at her limp salad. "Hospital food," she grimaced. Then she looked at him and waited.

He sighed. "Do you want me to say I never thought of trying to wreak some kind of vengeance on your family? I'm sorry. I can't. Yes, I did plot against you. As I told you that time in Brazil, it would have been easy. Years ago João had told me about his idea of substituting inferior, doctored gems for more valuable ones and pocketing the profits. Done correctly, the scheme would have been difficult for anyone to detect. Given your father's inexperience with precious stones, it was almost foolproof."

His mouth quirked as he gazed at Elaine. "But if you think I've spent the past two decades scheming how to revenge myself on your family, you're wrong. I was much too busy building my own career, my own fortune. I never forgot what your father had done to me, just as I never forgot you, but I didn't dwell on those memories any more than you lay around pining for me like the Lady of Shallott. I had better things to do with my life."

"Then what made you decide to come after the Welleses after all this time?" Elaine asked reasonably.

Ruy's fingers flicked his chin. "It's difficult to explain. No matter how successful I was in my business, the older I became, the emptier my existence seemed—a classic example of mid-life crisis, I suppose. Rather than analyze what was nagging me personally, I tried to give myself direction by expanding A&O. The time seemed ripe to seek foreign investors. The dollar was strong, and a consortium with some U.S. firm sounded ideal. So I had my contacts in the States put out feelers. When one of them produced the name Corminco, suddenly everything fell into place."

"You decided it was all those unresolved conflicts from your youth that were bothering you?" Elaine suggested acutely.

Ruy nodded. "I'll grant you the connection between those memories and my current discontent was tenuous at best, and yet, such thoughts can be rather like a sore tooth—once you become aware of it, you can't stop prodding to see if it still hurts."

"And the more you poke, the more it does hurt," Elaine said.

"Exactly."

Pursing her lips, Elaine pondered, "So you're telling me you convinced yourself that ruining Corminco would be just the jolt you needed to jar you out of your male menopause?"

He laughed. "That's one way of looking at it, I suppose. Of course, making contact with your father's company also gave me an excuse to see you again, see for myself the kind of man you considered 'good enough' to marry you. It never occurred to me that you might have remained single."

"What did you think when you found out I wasn't married?"

Ruy regarded her evenly. "I thought that seducing you again might add a certain fillip to my revenge."

Elaine considered the way he had pursued her from the beginning, his persistent, not-very-subtle efforts—efforts that worked. Even now she admitted it was only sheer luck that had prevented her from inviting him into her bed on their very first date. She declared, "Heavens, I suppose it's too bad I wasn't married, after all. Everything would have turned out differently if only I'd had a husband to protect me."

Ruy grated, "Don't count on it, *querida*."

She stared at him. His eyes were heavy with remembered passion. "You—you certainly have a lot of confidence in your appeal," she observed shakily.

"But not without reason, surely?"

His expression was enough to make her whole body clench with hunger. "No, not without reason," she agreed huskily.

After a moment she forced herself to look away. "If you and João Oliveira cooked up a foolproof scheme to destroy Corminco," she summarized, "why didn't you go through with it?"

"I couldn't," Ruy said. "In the end, the choice was as simple as that. I had wanted to wait before implementing the plan, to savor my revenge. I wanted to see your face when you were confronted by the man you'd said wasn't good enough for you, the one your father had tried to kill for daring to love you—"

"And when you did see me, you suddenly knew that you couldn't deliberately hurt me?" Elaine's expression was skeptical.

"You don't believe me, do you?" Ruy muttered.

"I'd like to. What you've said sounds terribly romantic, almost as romantic as those roses you just gave me—but unfortunately, I've always been instinctively suspicious of miracle transformations. My field is birth, not rebirth."

Ruy grimaced ironically. "Well, my love, in this case your instincts are correct. I wish with all my heart that I could say I took one look at you and my desire for revenge dissolved, but I can't. It wasn't until after we became lovers again that I abandoned my crackpot schemes of what I'd do once you were alone and at my mercy...."

"How kinky," Elaine observed dryly. "Just what had you had in mind?"

"I suppose I planned to make love to you until you were so besotted with me you'd do anything I asked—including betray your own family."

Elaine's mouth tightened. "I would never betray my family," she said flatly.

Ruy nodded. "I know that. I suppose I knew it then. In fact, in retrospect, I think your loyalty is one of the characteristics I find most appealing about you. If you care about someone, nothing will stop you from supporting them, even when it's to your disadvantage to do so. I've seen you walk out of a party without a second thought to help a patient who needed you. I've seen you give in to your parents' pleas to disrupt your life and, much against your will, go to South America. I've seen you open your heart to a homeless child who had absolutely no claim on you beyond that of common charity—only there's nothing common at all about your charity. When you love, you love completely, unselfishly.''

He hesitated. ''It took me a while to understand why it was that when you saw me for the first time at that banquet last September, you didn't recognize me—and I'm not talking about superficial reasons like gray hair or capped teeth. The real differences are much more profound. We aren't the same people we were in Switzerland, Elaine. What happened between that scheming, avaricious boy and that snobbish little girl happened to other people.'' Pausing again, Ruy gazed expectantly at Elaine.

She poked at her lukewarm salad. ''I hear what you're saying, Ruy,'' she began carefully, ''and in many ways I agree with you. Yes, we've both grown up since those months in Europe. We're not children anymore. But the past can't be dismissed so easily, especially when it impinges on the present. There are still things that need to be explained. You claim that the 'scheming' Antonio is long gone, but I know that something shady has certainly occurred in the present. At least a few of the first batch of stones you sent Corminco were questionable, and there were quite a few unexplained accidents at Serra Brilhante. And now I hear your partner has been arrested. Are you denying you played a part in these goings-on?''

''No,'' Ruy admitted drearily, ''I'm not denying my part. I can't. In some ways I consider myself directly responsible.''

''What do you mean?''

''If I hadn't encouraged João in the first place, he probably never would have found the nerve to try to carry out our dirty little plot. The man is a coward at heart. Unfortunately, he's also greedy, and he was unwilling to pass up a chance to make a quick fortune just because I changed my mind. With the assistance of his henchman, the mine foreman, he began pocketing the cream of the mine's output for himself and replacing the gems with doctored ones. Apparently they staged some of the accidents to divert the miners' suspicions when the finest stones always seemed to disappear.''

''Is that why the foreman was so upset that one time I went near the mine?'' Elaine asked.

''Most likely,'' Ruy agreed. ''João did not want to take any chances that you would see things you weren't supposed to—just as he also tried to keep you away from that gem exhibition in São Paulo. He knew one of the exhibits dealt with irradiation and other methods of enhancement.'' Ruy smiled grimly. ''In case you are unaware of it, you intimidated and terrified João. The man simply does not know how to deal with a woman who is intelligent and assertive and stubborn. He did not want you at Serra Brilhante at all, yet because you are a Welles, he could hardly prevent you from going there. The best he could do was try to keep you from talking to anyone. That's why he brought the nurse Magdalena to the site, to serve as a buffer between you and the women who might complain about their husbands' injuries.''

''And that's why he told me to mind my own business when I tried to relay those complaints to him,'' Elaine exclaimed.

''Exactly.''

Elaine shook her head in confusion. ''I still don't understand. João may not have wanted me around, but surely I was only a minor threat compared to the one you

presented. You *knew* what he was up to. João Oliveira
might not be the most imaginative man in the world, but
why wasn't he afraid of the way you'd react once you saw
that he'd proceeded with his scheme after you warned
him not to do it?"

"Because he thought he could handle me," Ruy said.
"Over the years I managed to amass a number of obligations, favors I owed João in return for favors he'd done
me. He thought that if I found out he was defrauding
Corminco, the weight of those obligations would prevent me from exposing him."

"But he was wrong, wasn't he?"

"Yes and no," Ruy said. "When your brother-in-law
came to Serra Brilhante to complain about the first shipment, I kept quiet. I pretended some mistake had been
made and I promised Brock it would never happen again.
After you all had left Brazil, I went to João and warned
him the incident had better never be repeated. At first he
blustered and denied my accusations, then he said he'd
implicate me if I tried to expose him. I told him he could
try."

"But you did turn him in?"

"I had no choice. After the way you complained about
the lack of safety precautions in the mines, I did some
investigating on my own, and I was appalled at what I
found. As I told you in Brazil, Serra Brilhante mines have
a good safety record—or rather, they *had* a good safety
record. Conditions have changed. João's confederate,
the foreman, was deliberately encouraging slackness as a
way of orchestrating the accidents that covered the thefts.
When I found proof, there was simply no other option
left for me except to turn João over to the authorities,
even at the risk of implicating myself. Fortunately for me,

the foreman turned state's evidence in order to save himself, and his confession exonerated me. But even if he'd remained silent, I could not have allowed the 'accidents' to continue. I cannot permit innocent people to be hurt—'' he paused "—the way I hurt you.''

The pain in Ruy's voice jarred Elaine. "But you never hurt me,'' she countered, knowing suddenly that it was true. She reached across the table and grasped his hand. Stroking his palm with her thumb, she could feel the heavy calluses, lingering reminders of the hard life he'd lived. Neither one of them had had it very easy, she admitted. They both bore scars.

Earnestly she told him, "Antonio hurt Elena, just as Elena hurt Antonio. But you said it yourself—what happened to those two unhappy children can't affect us anymore.''

Ruy closed his eyes and shuddered. "There is one way it still affects us, Elaine. I never knew about the baby. In my typically self-centered teenage way, it never occurred to me that there might be consequences of our lovemaking. I had no idea why your father sent someone gunning for me. Now that I know, I'm not sure I even blame him.... But how can you forgive me? I saw your face as you gazed at the infants in the nursery upstairs. You love them. You would have been a wonderful mother. I may be able to return the bracelet I stole, but there is no way I can make up for robbing you of the children you should have had.''

Elaine smiled tenderly. "You gave me more than you took,'' she corrected. "Without my illness, I know I never would have become a doctor. But because of the way things turned out, now instead of bearing one or two children, I've brought scores into the world, and in a very special way they're all mine."

Ruy exhaled gustily. "It's very possible that if your father's threats hadn't driven me out of Europe, I would have ended up...I don't know how. Perhaps burned out or dead before I was twenty-five, like others I knew in those days."

For a long while they sat silent, their hands clasped in a tight, unbreakable bond. At last Elaine asked, "So what do we do now?"

"You never gave me an answer to my proposal," Ruy reminded her. "I know your life here in Denver is important to you, and I know that there are things about my country that you have difficulty accepting—but perhaps that's all the more reason for you to remember that there are people there who need you, too."

"People?" Elaine queried wryly. "The last I heard, you seemed to be managing quite well without me at Serra Brilhante."

"I'm not managing well without you anywhere," Ruy snorted. "Neither is Vadinho. Most of the time he mopes around the clinic like a little brown shadow, getting in the way of Consuelo and that Bahian doctor I hired. They've finally begun training him to work as a nurse's aide, just so he'll be useful for something."

"Maybe when he's older you should send him to medical school," Elaine suggested.

"I'm sure he'd approve of that idea," Ruy agreed. "He's eager for an education. But as much as he likes to go to school, he'd like to be part of a family even better."

"You mean if I marry you, we can adopt him?" Elaine asked.

"Him and as many others as you want," Ruy agreed. "There are far too many abandoned children in my country. We could make a home for some of them."

Elaine's eyes glowed. "Yes—a home full of love." She blinked hard. "God, I think I'm going to cry...." Lifting her free hand to brush away the moisture beading on her lashes, she realized with surprise that she was still clutching Maggie's bracelet. She stared at the gold bangle, suddenly remembering all the hope—and pain—it symbolized. She felt herself grow pale. "Oh, Ruy," she whispered hoarsely, "I love you and I want to marry you, but isn't it crazy to think we can start all over at this point in our lives?"

"No!" he insisted, his voice gruff. "We belong together. We always have." He took the bracelet from her and slipped it firmly onto her wrist. "There," he said, observing the results with satisfaction, "a perfect fit— just like us." When he sensed Elaine's lingering doubts, he gazed pleadingly at her. "Darling, please, we're not crazy. Trust me. Give me that loyalty you bestow so freely on others, and I swear you'll never regret it. I love you. I loved you when I was a boy, but I didn't know what to do with that love. But I promise we'll make it this time. Nobody is ever too old for a new beginning."

After a tiny hesitation, Elaine nodded. "Yes, we will make it this time, won't we?" she breathed.

Ruy's fingers tightened encouragingly around hers. Lifting her hand to his face, he pressed his lips into her palm. His mustache brushed silkily across her skin, making Elaine shiver with renewed hunger as she gazed at his bowed head. But she knew now that there was something more between them than passion, something more than desire—something as precious and endless as the gold circle that gleamed on her wrist. Leaning toward him, she reached up to stroke his leathery cheek. Ruy raised his head. His gaze locked with hers. His breath, his life and her life, blended as their mouths gently met in a kiss of optimism and faith, a kiss of total fulfillment. And then Elaine's beeper sounded, signaling another new beginning.

JOIN THE CELEBRATION!
THE FIFTH ANNIVERSARY
OF HARLEQUIN
AMERICAN ROMANCE

1988 is a banner year for Harlequin American Romance—it marks our fifth anniversary.

For five successful years we've been bringing you heartwarming, exciting romances, but we're not stopping there. In August, 1988, we've got an extraspecial treat for you. Join us next month when we feature four of American Romance's best—and four favorite—authors.

Judith Arnold, Rebecca Flanders, Beverly Sommers and Anne Stuart will enchant you with the stories of four women friends who lived in the same New York apartment building and whose lives, one by one, take an unexpected turn. Meet Abbie, Jaime, Suzanne and Marielle—the women of YORKTOWN TOWERS.

Four believable American Romance heroines...four contemporary American women just like you...by four of your favorite American Romance authors.

Don't miss these special stories. Enjoy the fifth-anniversary celebration of Harlequin American Romance!

Harlequin Superromance

COMING NEXT MONTH

ATTRACTIVE, SPACE SAVING BOOK RACK

Display your most prized novels on this handsome and sturdy book rack. The hand-rubbed walnut finish will blend into your library décor with quiet elegance, providing a practical organizer for your favorite hard-or soft-covered books.

Only $9.95

**Approximately
16" x 8"
when assembled**

Assembles in seconds!

To order, rush your name, address and zip code, along with a check or money order for $10.70* ($9.95 plus 75¢ postage and handling) payable to *Harlequin Reader Service*:

Harlequin Reader Service
Book Rack Offer
901 Fuhrmann Blvd.
P.O. Box 1396
Buffalo, NY 14269-1396

Offer not available in Canada.

BKR-1A

*New York and Iowa residents add appropriate sales tax.

Lynda Ward's

LEAP THE MOON

... the continuing saga of *The Welles Family*

You've already met Elaine Welles, the oldest daughter of powerful tycoon Burton Welles, in Superromance #317, *Race the Sun*. You cheered her on as she threw off the shackles of her heritage and won the love of her life, Ruy de Areias.

Now it's her sister's turn. Jennie Welles is the drop-dead-gorgeous, most rebellious Welles sister, and she's determined to live life her way—and flaunt it in her father's face.

When she meets Griffin Stark, however, she learns there's more to life than glamour and independence. She learns about kindness, compassion and sharing. One nagging question remains: is she good enough for a man like Griffin? Her father certainly doesn't think so....

Leap the Moon ... a Harlequin Superromance coming to you in August. Don't miss it!